Knead You Now

A SHORT FAKE RELATIONSHIP, OPPOSITES
ATTRACT, VIRIGIN FMC, SLOW BURN ROMANCE

CORAL COVE
BOOK FOUR

JAX WILDER

RAINBOW QUARTZ PUBLISHING

Published by Rainbow Quartz Publishing

Edmonds WA, 98026

First Edition: 2024

Cover design by Miranda Townsend

Interior design by Miranda Townsend

Library of Congress Cataloging-in-Publication Data has been applied for.

For permissions or inquiries, please contact:

Rainbow Quartz Publishing

rainbowquartzpublishing@gmail.com

For Kaytie,

Magic happens in the most unexpected of places.

Jax Wilder

Foreword

Welcome back to Coral Cove, where love is sweet, magic has opinions, and everyone's happily-ever-after comes with a little chaos.

This book is part of the **Coral Cove** series, but Coral Cove also shares a world with my **Tarot Fantasies** series. Every story stands on its own, so you can read them in any order, but you may notice familiar faces, places, and a few magical overlaps along the way.

Dorothea's story continues in **The Devil's Temptation**, a Tarot Fantasies novel featuring her visit to **The Arcane Room**. Her appearance there connects directly to Chapter 8 of this book, so if you'd like to see what happens when Dorothea gets pulled into a little tarot-fueled temptation of her own, I hope you'll check out **The Devil's Temptation** too.

With love,

Jax Wilder

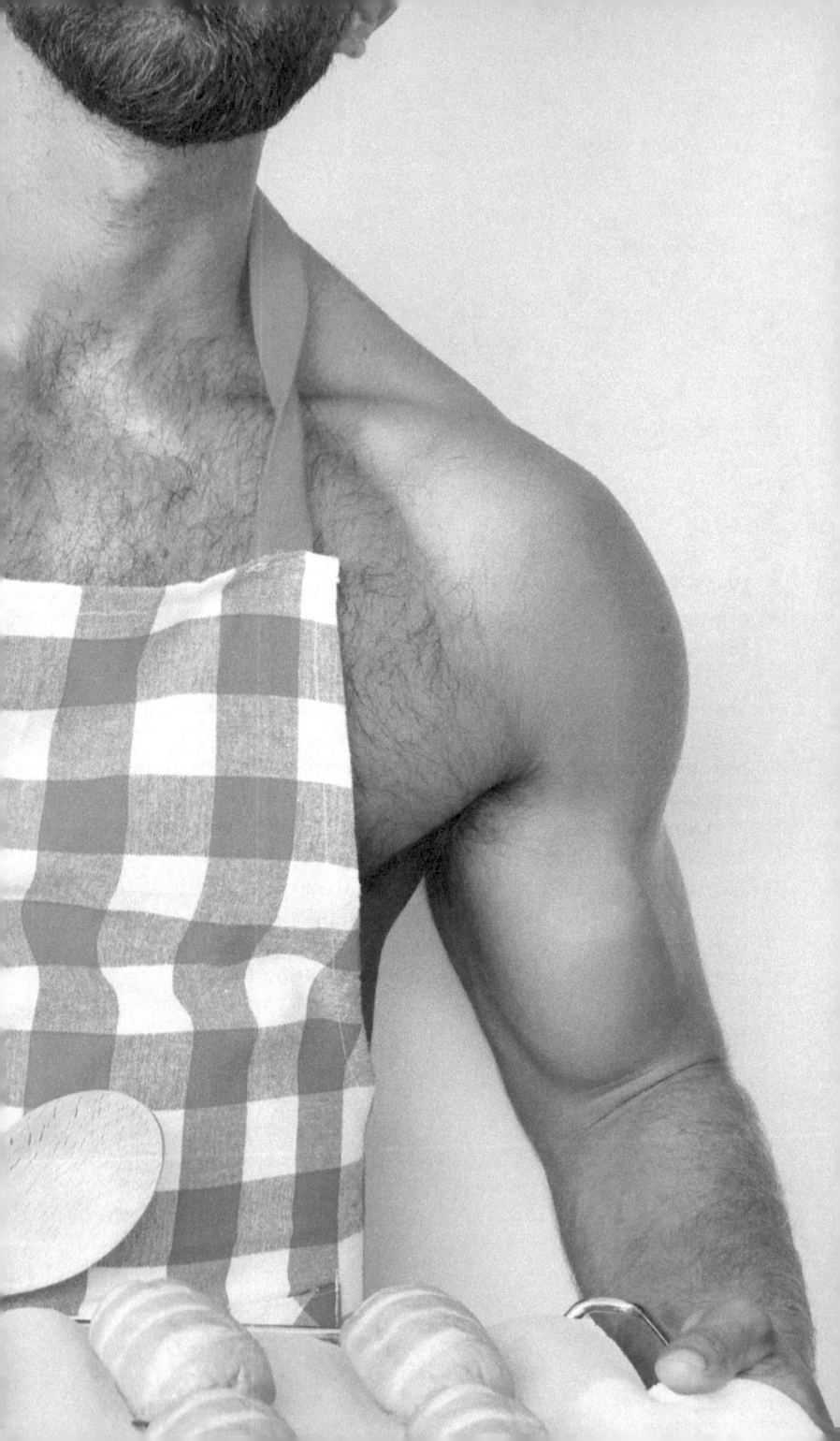

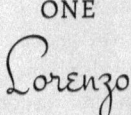

ONE

There are three kinds of people who come into my office.

The first kind wants me to save them.

The second kind wants me to punish someone.

The third kind wants both and has already decided I'm the kind of man who enjoys that.

Alison Davis sits across from me in a cream silk blouse, perfect makeup, and the brittle posture of a woman who has rehearsed her crisis in the mirror but still expects applause for surviving it. Her diamond bracelet catches the light every time she twists her wrist. The nervous gesture is not new. She did the same thing two years ago when she hired me to untangle a contract dispute with her family's real estate company.

Back then, I was her lawyer.

Six months after that case closed, I was a mistake she made in a hotel bar after too much champagne.

I don't sleep with clients.

I do, unfortunately, have a history of sleeping with women who later decide my competence should remain available to them in every capacity.

Alison's file rests between us. Divorce. Property. A husband with expensive lawyers. A prenup that is either iron-clad or full of hairline cracks, depending on how generous the judge feels and how much money she wants to burn proving a point.

She has gone over the same concern three times.

"What if he freezes the accounts before I can move anything?" she asks again. Her voice wavers at the edges, but her eyes are sharp. Alison has never been helpless. She only plays fragile when she thinks it will make a man move faster.

I lean back in my chair and lace my fingers over my stomach.

My suit is charcoal. My tie is black. My expression is calm, because calm is what people pay for when their lives catch fire. The office around me helps sell it. Polished walnut desk. Neatly stacked files. Floor-to-ceiling shelves full of legal texts I actually read. Framed degrees hung with military precision. A view of Coral Cove's main street through the window, pretty enough to soften the room without making me look soft.

Everything about this office says I'm in control.

That's the point.

"Alison," I say, keeping my voice low. "If your husband attempts to freeze marital funds without cause, the court won't look kindly on it."

Her fingers tighten around the strap of her purse. "But he could still do it."

"He could try."

"And if he does?"

"Then Diana Kerr will file an emergency motion and make him regret the impulse."

Alison blinks. "Diana?"

"Yes."

"You're referring me out?"

"I am."

Her mouth parts. Not shock exactly. More offense. Alison has always been better at receiving attention than boundaries.

"But you're the best attorney in town," she says.

I smile.

Not the full one. The full one has caused enough damage in my life. This is the professional version, warm enough to reassure, sharp enough to warn.

"I'm very good," I say. "Diana is better for this."

Alison studies me for a moment. "Because of us?"

Because I remember your mouth on my neck, and I don't need that memory sitting beside a billing agreement. Because my father may think I'm careless, but I have never been sloppy with the law. If I take your case, you will try to turn fear into intimacy, and I have been used as a weapon by enough lonely people to know better.

"Yes," I say.

Her face softens in a way that might be genuine if she did not know exactly how to use it. "Lorenzo."

"No."

She exhales through her nose, then looks toward the window. "You used to be more fun."

"I used to make worse decisions."

"That night was not a bad decision."

No, it was a predictable one.

A hotel bar. A woman with a laugh like expensive glass. A version of myself still trying to prove that if I could make someone want me, I could outrun the fact that I did not know what to do with being needed.

"It was a private decision," I say. "This is a professional one."

She holds my gaze for a few seconds longer, before she breaks eye contact.

I stand and pick up the referral sheet from my desk. "Diana's office is expecting your call. I already sent her assistant the basic conflict-free summary you authorized. Nothing privileged. Nothing beyond what you agreed to share."

Alison takes the paper, her fingers brushing mine.

The gesture is deliberate.

I don't react.

"You really have changed," she says.

That almost makes me laugh.

No, I have not changed nearly enough.

"I learned to document things," I say.

A reluctant smile touches her mouth. "Still arrogant."

"Accurate."

She rises from the chair, smoothing the front of her blouse. "Thank you."

"You're welcome."

"And Lorenzo?"

I open the office door for her.

She pauses on the threshold.

"If Diana is half as good as you say, I'll forgive you for rejecting me."

"I'll alert the court."

This time, she laughs for real.

Then she leaves.

The second the door closes, the smile falls from my face.

I stand there for a moment with my hand still on the knob, listening to the muffled sounds of my office beyond the door. Molly answering the phone at the front desk. A printer humming. A car passing outside. Normal things. Steady things.

My office is excellent at pretending I'm fine.

I return to my desk and sit.

The coffee near my elbow is cold. Again. I have reheated it twice already, which means it now tastes like punishment and ambition. I drink it anyway.

It's terrible.

I keep drinking.

The day is not even half over, and I'm already tired of people wanting something from me. Reassurance. Strategy. Teeth. Charm. A version of me polished enough to reflect back whatever they need to see.

I'm good at it.

That's the problem.

The degrees on the wall gleam under the office lights. University of Washington School of Law. Stanford for undergrad. Awards. Bar admissions. A newspaper clipping from a case I won three years ago, framed because Molly said clients liked proof. My father would call the whole room tasteful. Then he would find something to criticize before removing his coat.

The plant near the window is dying.

I bought it because the office looked too sterile. I have watered it exactly twice and overwatered it both times. There is probably a metaphor there, but I have no interest in being emotionally harassed by a fern.

My phone buzzes.

The sound cuts through the room.

I glance at the screen.

Papá.

My stomach turns cold.

There are some names that don't need to be spoken to change the temperature of a room.

I let it ring once.

Twice.

I could ignore him.

I have ignored him before. It only postpones the performance. José Moretti doesn't disappear when denied. He collects the insult, sharpens it, and brings it to the next conversation like evidence.

I answer.

"Hola, Papá."

"Lorenzo."

His voice comes through cold and precise.

He has never wasted warmth on greetings. Warmth, to my father, is a resource to be invested only when it will produce loyalty or fear.

"I've been hearing things," he says. "Things I don't like."

I look out the window.

Across the street, a woman walks a small white dog wearing a raincoat. The dog looks offended by the entire concept of weather.

"What things?" I ask.

"You know exactly what things."

"No, Papá. I don't."

A pause.

He dislikes making his accusations plain. He prefers people to bleed from implication first.

"I hear people talking about you," he says. "I hear whispers. My son, running around that little storybook town like the damn village bicycle. Everyone has had a ride, and you're still acting like this is a life."

My jaw tightens.

Sex, shame, legacy. He stacks them together like legal exhibits and pretends the case is already won.

"I run a successful practice," I say. "I have clients. I have a good reputation."

"You have notoriety. Do not confuse the two."

I close my eyes for one second.

A younger version of me would have argued immediately. Raised my voice. Told him to go to hell in two languages. The older version knows better.

The older version has learned that my father enjoys volume because it lets him pretend he is the rational one.

"My clients respect me," I say.

"They want to fuck you."

"Some of them want both."

"Do not be cute with me."

I lean back in my chair and stare at the ceiling.

The ceiling offers no legal advice.

"You should be in the city," he says. "You should be building something worthy of the name I gave you. You should be making partner at my firm, not playing small-town hero for people who pay you in gratitude and baked goods."

I think, unwillingly, of Knead the Dough down the street.

Of a pink storefront, yellow-striped walls, and the smell of pear pastry Molly brings back when she decides I'm too busy to feed myself.

Of Dorothea Thompson behind the counter, flour on her apron, eyes down until she realizes someone is watching.

I push the thought away.

My father doesn't get that.

"This is where I want to be," I say. "I built something here."

"With what?" he snaps. "Your charm? Your mother's memory? My money?"

The room goes still. There it's, the real knife.

I set my cold coffee down before I break the mug. "I pay my own office lease."

"You drive a car I bought."

"I told you I didn't want it."

"You drive it."

I do. Damn him.

"You still use the family account when it suits you," he continues. "You still come to my properties when you want the ocean view without the bill. You still benefit from the name and then pretend you're self-made because you opened an office in a town with one bakery and too many people who believe in crystals."

"Leave Coral Cove out of this."

"Listen to yourself. Defending a town that would forget you the moment a shinier scandal came along."

The anger rises.

I welcome it.

Anger is cleaner than guilt. "I'm happy here."

He laughs. It's a small, cutting sound.

"You're hiding there."

"I'm working."

"You're wasting your life!"

"It's my life!"

"And my name."

I grip the arm of my chair. The leather creaks under my hand.

"If your mother could see you now," he says, softer.

Every muscle in my body locks.

There are words people use because they don't know better. And there are words people use because they do.

My father knows.

"Stop, please" I say through gritted teeth.

"One of us should say it."

"I said stop."

"She would be ashamed."

The words hit exactly where he aims them.

They always do.

For a moment, I'm not in my office. I'm back in the rain. Back in the dark. Back with my phone pressed to my ear while my mother says my name over the sound of the storm, her voice strained but trying to be gentle because she was always gentle when I least deserved it.

Then metal.

Then silence.

Then my father's face at the hospital, pale and ruined, looking at me as if grief needed a body to live in and he had chosen mine.

I swallow. "Leave Mamá out of this," I nearly growl.

"You're the reason she was on that road," he says. "Do not speak to me as if I invented the truth."

My chest tightens until breathing feels like a legal argument I'm losing.

"She was coming because you called her," he continues. "Because you and I fought, and you needed her to clean up the mess. She went out in that storm for you. Now you honor her by disgracing everything she believed this family could be."

The office blurs at the edges.

I reach for anger again, but guilt gets there first.

Guilt is faster.

It's had years of practice.

"I know why she was there," I say. "I don't need you to remind me."

"No. You need someone to remind you what you owe."

"I owe her a life that means something."

"You owe her excellence."

"I'm excellent."

"You are small."

The word lands harder than it should.

Small.

That's what he sees when he looks at Coral Cove. My office. My practice. My clients. The life I chose after the funeral, after the city became unbearable, after every street corner reminded me of who I used to be and what I could not undo.

Small.

"I'm coming to Coral Cove for Ophelia and Lillian's wedding," he says.

I sit forward.

Ophelia had mentioned sending invitations, but I let myself believe my father would be too busy, too proud, too uninterested in a wedding that was not useful to him.

Hope, historically, is a fool.

"When?" I ask.

"Two weeks."

"That's short notice."

"It's not my problem if your calendar is provincial."

I close my eyes.

Ophelia and Lillian's wedding is going to be beautiful. Ocean views. Lighthouse Point. Flowers. Half the town crying into champagne. My father walking into that softness like a blade in a silk pocket.

"What do you want?" I ask.

"I want to see whether there is any man left in my son."

I almost laugh.

It would not sound sane.

"And how do you intend to measure that?"

"Your work. Your home. Your life. Whether you have anything stable, or if the rumors are true and you're still chasing any woman willing to call you charming."

"If you embarrass me," he says, "I will be done. No more financial support. No inheritance. No access to my properties. No favors. No soft place to land when this small-town fantasy collapses."

"I don't need your money."

"But you like knowing it's there."

The silence after that is brutal because he is not entirely wrong.

I hate his money. I hate the way it moves through rooms before he does. I hate the way it turns love into leverage and family into contract law.

I also know exactly what my life costs.

And what my pride has allowed me to keep because the safety net existed.

My father hears the silence and smiles through the phone. I can feel it.

"I'll be there Thursday," he says. "Have something to show me, Lorenzo. Or be ready to live with the consequences of becoming exactly as insignificant as you pretend to admire."

The line goes dead.

I keep the phone pressed to my ear.

For a moment, I don't move.

Then I lower it to the desk carefully.

Very carefully.

The kind of carefully a man uses when he is trying not to throw something expensive through glass.

My office is silent except for the faint hum of the building and Molly's muffled voice beyond the wall.

I stand.

The chair rolls back and hits the credenza behind me.

I want to break something.

The urge is physical. Hot in my hands. A flash of violence with nowhere useful to go. My father has always had that gift. He can make me feel sixteen again in under five minutes, all rage, shame, and helplessness dressed in a better suit.

I cross to the window.

Coral Cove looks painfully normal.

A couple strolls past the law office carrying paper cups from the coffee shop. A florist sets buckets of tulips outside her door. The bookstore sign swings gently in the wind. Farther down, Knead the Dough's pink facade catches a thin strip of sunlight breaking through the clouds.

Small town.

Godforsaken, he said.

I think of clients who bring me jars of jam after I win a case. Of Molly's ridiculous desk calendar. Of Ophelia and Lillian building a life here after the city tried to devour them. Of the way people in Coral Cove know everyone's business and still show up with casseroles when tragedy hits.

This place is not small.

It's specific.

My father has never known the difference.

I turn away from the window and open the top drawer of my desk.

The photo is beneath a stack of unused thank-you cards.

I should have framed it.

I have never been able to.

My mother stands in a kitchen I can barely remember, wearing a yellow dress and laughing at something outside the frame. Her dark hair is tied back. Flour dusts one cheek. She is holding a wooden spoon like a weapon and smiling as if joy is something ordinary people are allowed to keep.

I touch the edge of the photo.

"Mamá," I whisper.

The office doesn't answer. I set the photo on the desk and pick up my phone again.

Her contact is still there.

Mamá.

No number attached anymore. I kept deleting it and restoring it until the ritual became pathetic enough that even I had to admit it was a wound, not a habit. Now the contact holds only one saved voicemail.

I open it.

My thumb hovers over play.

I know every word.

I also cannot bear the first second.

Her voice is worse than silence because it proves she was here. A body. A laugh. A woman who sang while cooking and called me mijo even when I was being a self-important ass in law school.

A woman who got in a car during a storm because I called.

I lock the phone and set it facedown.

Not today.

Maybe not ever.

My chest hurts.

I press my palm flat to the desk and force myself to breathe.

Therapy says guilt is not a monument.

Therapy says grief is not proof of love if all it does is keep you kneeling.

Therapy says a lot of things that sound excellent in a room with neutral furniture and a water feature.

Therapy has never met José Moretti.

There is a knock at my door.

I straighten instantly.

Mask on.

"Yes."

Molly opens the door halfway, then stops.

She sees too much.

Damn her.

Molly has been my secretary for only a year, but she has the unnerving instincts of a woman who grew up in a family where moods entered rooms before people did.

"You okay, boss?" she asks.

"Fine."

She doesn't believe me.

Smart girl.

"Your eleven-thirty is rescheduled," she says. "Also, Ophelia's assistant called about the wedding RSVP. They need your plus-one name by Friday."

"Of course they do."

"And your father's assistant called."

My jaw tightens.

Molly lifts a hand. "Already handled. I told her your calendar is full Thursday afternoon and asked for his flight details so I can arrange a car."

I stare at her.

"You did?"

"You told me last month that if your father ever tried to make you pick him up from the airport, I should prevent it for your emotional health and my workplace safety."

I don't remember saying that.

It sounds like me.

"Good work."

"I'm adding it to my resume."

"You should."

Her gaze drops to the photo on my desk but she says nothing about it. "Do you need lunch?"

"No."

"That means yes."

"I have files."

"You also have a body, despite what law school taught you."

"Molly."

"I'm ordering from Knead the Dough."

The name hits me with unexpected force.

Pink storefront.

Warm pastry.

Dorothea Thompson.

I have seen her a hundred times, maybe more. Always behind the counter. Always working. Always polite in that careful way people get when they are used to making themselves easy to overlook. Most people call her Dottie.

I never have.

I don't know why.

No, that is a lie.

Dottie feels too small for her.

Too familiar in everyone else's mouth. Dorothea suits her better. Old-fashioned. Strong. A name with flour on its hands and a spine under the softness.

Molly is watching me.

"What?" I ask.

"Nothing."

"That was not a nothing face."

"It was a secretary face."

"Dangerous."

"Very."

I sit back down.

The photo of my mother remains on the desk between us.

"Order whatever," I say.

"Pear pastry?"

I look at the window again.

Knead the Dough's sign swings faintly in the wind.

"Black coffee," I say. "And whatever Dorothea recommends."

Molly's eyebrows rise.

I point at the door. "Do not."

"I said nothing."

"You thought loudly."

"I'll work on that."

She starts to leave.

"Molly."

She turns.

"RSVP for two," I say.

Her expression softens with curiosity, but she doesn't ask.

"Name?"

"I don't know yet."

"Living dangerously."

"Professionally."

"Sure, boss."

She closes the door.

I sit alone again.

The office is exactly as it was before the phone call. Same degrees. Same desk. Same dying fern. Same files. Same window looking out at the town my father believes is beneath me.

But the room feels different now.

Or maybe I do.

I pick up my mother's photo and slide it back into the drawer, but not all the way beneath the thank-you cards. I leave it on top.

Small act.

Ridiculous.

Still something.

Then I pull the next file toward me.

Applegate v. Thompson.

My hand stills.

Thompson.

I open the folder.

Property dispute. Commercial building. Bakery storefront. Complaint filed. Demand to vacate.

Knead the Dough.

Dorothea.

A chill moves through me.

The first page is sparse, just a preliminary notice forwarded through a records alert I set up for local property litigation. I do that sometimes. Watch filings. Track trends. Coral Cove is small enough that legal trouble tends to ripple before it breaks.

I read the plaintiff's name.

Applegate Holdings.

The knot in my stomach changes shape.

Not my father now.

Something cleaner.

Something I can fight.

I scan the complaint summary. They are claiming irregularity in a prior transfer. Seeking possession. Aggressive timeline. Pressure tactic, probably. Ugly, but not impossible.

Dorothea may not even know yet.

My phone buzzes with a text from Molly.

Knead the Dough has fresh lemon pastries. Also, Dottie says the pear ones need another twenty minutes. Also, she blushed when I said your name. Do with that what you will.

I stare at the message.

Then at the file.

Then out the window, toward the pink storefront down the street.

Two weeks until my father arrives.

A wedding RSVP that requires a name.

A property case aimed at a woman who has no idea a storm is already moving toward her.

I lean back in my chair and let out a slow breath.

My father thinks I have nothing to show for myself.

He is wrong.

I have this town.

I have my practice.

I have enough anger to burn through any man who thinks he can take a woman's home because he found a crack in old paperwork.

And apparently, I have a growing problem with a baker who has never once tried to make me feel like a Moretti.

Only Lorenzo.

That might be the most dangerous thing of all.

I pick up the file.

For the first time all morning, my hands are steady.

TWO

Dorothea

The bakery wakes before the town does.

That's one of the reasons I love it.

Before Coral Cove gets chatty and bright and determined to know everyone's business by nine in the morning, Knead the Dough belongs to ovens, timers, yeast, and me. The world outside is still gray-blue and damp, the storefront windows along Main Street reflecting the first thin gold of morning. Inside, the bakery is all heat and breath.

Butter melts into sugar.

Yeast blooms in warm water.

Coffee sputters through the machine with the exhausted rage of something that has been asked to perform too early.

The oven fans hum. The display case clicks and purrs. Somewhere in the back, Baylin slides another tray of bread from the deck oven, and the whole building seems to inhale around the smell. Wheat. Salt. Crust. Steam. A little char at the edge where she likes to push things close to burnt and then call it rustic, as if the French invented overconfidence.

Derek drops a pair of tongs near the pastry case.

The clang shoots through the front of the shop.

"Sorry," he calls.

"You're personally aging me," I call back.

"I said sorry."

"That doesn't give me my youth back."

"Do you want me to apologize to your joints?"

"Yes. Start with my knees."

He laughs, and I smile despite myself.

This is my favorite part of the day. Before customers. Before questions. Before the polite performance of being a functional local business owner with clean aprons, correct change, and no inner weather.

The bakery is quieter now, but not silent. It's never silent. A bakery is alive if you know how to hear it. Dough expanding in bowls under cloth. The low groan of the walk-in. The soft tick of cooling racks. The hiss of the espresso machine. The shuffle of Baylin's boots. Derek muttering to himself while he straightens napkins with the concentration of a man performing surgery on paper products.

Upstairs is technically my home.

Down here is the place that knows me.

Every shelf, every nick in the counter, every tile I keep meaning to replace but cannot quite afford yet. The pink exterior with the white trim, cheerful enough to look like a dollhouse and stubborn enough to survive coastal rain. The yellow-and-white striped interior Kaytie insisted was "sunny" and I privately thought was "aggressively custard" until the town loved it so much I stopped having opinions.

Four display cases curve along the front, each one polished until they reflect pastry and streetlight. Croissants in the first case. Cookies and brownies in the second. Cakes in the third, whole and sliced. The fourth is for the morning chaos: pear pastries, lemon twists, fruit danishes, cream horns, and whatever mistake turned out beautiful enough to sell.

The bread wall stands behind me, still half-empty while Baylin builds the morning. Sourdough. Country white. Rye. Rosemary focaccia. A row of baguettes that will be gone before lunch if the bread baddies behave as predictably as they always do.

Bread baddies are loyal.

Cookie people are chatty.

Cake people want to be left alone, which makes them my spiritual relatives.

Pastry people are on a schedule and don't care who they have to elbow to get a lemon twist before work.

Donut fiends are chaos in human form.

I know every species because I have spent years watching people reveal themselves through sugar.

A man who buys one black coffee and a plain croissant every Tuesday is not the same as a woman who asks for six macarons, then eats one in the car before she pulls away. A person who says "whatever you recommend" is either adventurous or trying very hard to be flirted with. A person who orders a slice of red velvet cake at eight in the morning deserves no judgment from me because red velvet is never wrong.

Knead the Dough is my sanctuary.

It's also my shield.

There is nearly always a display case between me and everyone else.

I used to think that was coincidence.

After last night, I'm less sure.

My palm tingles.

I freeze with a tray of croissants halfway between the cooling rack and the case.

Flour dusts the base of my thumb. There is a tiny burn near my wrist from yesterday .

The bell on the oven chirps.

I blink back into the bakery.

"Dottie?" Baylin calls from the back. "You good?"

"Fine."

The word leaves my mouth out of habit.

I grimace.

Fine is the most suspicious word in the English language. It's a storage closet with a lock on it.

"I'm thinking," I correct.

Baylin appears in the doorway with a tray of seed rolls balanced on one hand. Her silver hair is tied in a scarf printed with tiny moons, and her black eyeliner looks perfect despite the fact that she works a bread shift starting at two in the morning. I have never understood how she does that. I look haunted before coffee. Baylin looks like a retired rock star who knows where the body is buried and still has time to shape brioche.

"Thinking before seven is dangerous," she says.

"So is letting you operate an oven while sleep-deprived, yet here we are."

"I operate better sleep-deprived. It lets the ancestors steer."

"Please don't tell the health inspector that."

She grins and disappears back into the kitchen.

I set the croissants in the case.

They are beautiful. Golden. Flaky. Slightly curved like they are keeping secrets. I made them because repetition calms me. Butter block. Dough. Fold. Rest. Turn. Fold again. Lamination is not patience so much as negotiated restraint. If you rush, the butter breaks. If you overwork, the layers smear. If you let the dough rest, it rises into itself.

I'm not going to make that a metaphor.

Absolutely not.

The bakery already has enough emotional responsibility.

I slide the case door shut.

That's when I see it.

A line under the lower shelf near the corner of the bread wall.

Not a crack. Not exactly. A seam.

I frown.

That shelf has been there since before I owned the place. Kaytie used to keep extra cake boxes below it. I keep emergency napkins, seasonal signage, and a box of mismatched ribbon I pretend I will someday organize by color. I have scrubbed that corner a hundred times. Maybe a thousand.

I have never noticed the seam.

The morning light catches it again.

A little dark line.

A little invitation.

"No," I tell it.

The seam remains.

Rude.

I glance toward the kitchen. Baylin is singing something under her breath while sliding pans. Derek is up front refilling sugar packets with the gravity of a monk illuminating manuscripts. No customers yet. The sign still says Closed.

I crouch.

My knees pop.

"Uncalled for," I whisper.

I pull the ribbon box forward, then the napkin box, then a sad stack of Valentine's Day heart doilies I bought on clearance and immediately regretted. Behind them, the seam is clearer. There is a small notch in the wood, just big enough for a finger.

My heartbeat changes.

This building is old.

Old buildings have weird compartments sometimes. People hide cash. Love letters. Receipts. Dead mice, which is less romantic but more common. Kaytie once found a box of costume jewelry behind the upstairs closet wall and wore a fake emerald ring for a month because she said found glamour should not be wasted.

Still.

Something about this feels intentional.

I slide my fingertip into the notch and pull.

The panel sticks.

I pull harder.

It opens with a soft wooden groan, revealing a dark compartment tucked under the shelf.

For one second, I don't move.

Then the smell reaches me.

Dust first.

Old wood.

Dried herbs.

Then something stranger. Rain on hot stone. Orange peel. Clove. The sharp green snap of mint crushed between fingers. A sweetness like sugar left too close to fire.

My palm tingles again.

"No," I say, quieter this time.

Inside the compartment sits a wooden box.

It's old, but not fragile. Dark wood, metal corners, a carved rolling pin across the lid with little vines twisting around it. Beneath the rolling pin, in tiny letters, someone carved:

For the baker who listens.

I sit back on my heels.

"Well, that feels accusatory."

No one answers.

If the box had answered, I would have walked directly into the ocean.

I reach in and slide it out.

It's heavier than it looks.

Dust coats the top, but not as much as it should. That bothers me. The compartment should have been sealed for years. Decades, maybe. Kaytie ran this place before me, and Mabel ran it before Kaytie, and before that the building was something else entirely. A tea room, I think. Or a boarding-house. Coral Cove changes names but keeps ghosts in the walls.

I carry the box to the prep table.

Derek looks over.

"What's that?"

"Hopefully not paperwork."

"Do we need a shovel?"

"Why would we need a shovel?"

"I don't know. Secret boxes feel like shovel-adjacent situations."

"Go make sure the coffee station is stocked."

He salutes with a sugar packet and turns away.

I wait until he's busy before opening the box. The hinges don't squeak. That would be too normal.

Inside, jars nest in fitted compartments. Small glass jars with cork stoppers, each labeled in handwriting I don't recognize. Not English, French or Italian. Something looping and strange, with little symbols that remind me of steam, stars, and flower petals if I let my eyes unfocus.

Beside the jars rests a leather-bound book.

My breath catches.

The cover is dark brown, almost black, softened at the edges by handling. A brass clasp holds it closed, but the clasp is unlatched. Pressed into the leather is the same rolling pin and vine design as the box. Beneath it, written in gold that has not faded at all:

The Hearth Book of Knead the Dough.

My heart thumps once, hard.

This should feel ridiculous.

A magic recipe book hidden under the bread wall in a pink bakery with custard stripes. I should laugh. I should assume Kaytie had a theatrical phase. I should put the box back and make a dentist appointment or something equally grounded.

Instead, I touch the cover with two fingers.

The leather warms beneath them.

Not a lot.

"Oh," I whisper.

The book opens.

On its own.

Absolutely not ideal.

I don't scream, which feels worth noting. I do step back and bump the cooling rack. Croissants shudder dangerously.

"Dottie?" Derek calls.

"Still fine."

I close my eyes briefly.

Not fine.

Never fine again, apparently.

The book lies open on the prep table. The handwriting inside is English, though not modern in places. Recipes fill the pages, each one written in a mix of precise measurements and deeply unhelpful phrases like until the dough forgives you and when the sugar begins to remember summer.

I understand immediately that I'm going to hate and love this book.

The first page is not a recipe.

It's a note.

> To the baker who listens,
>
> Magic doesn't make a thing true. It reveals what has been mixed in. A sweet can warm a

heart, but it cannot create one. A bitter can sharpen courage, but it cannot invent it. A loaf can feed memory, but it cannot change what happened.

Don't bake what you would not eat.
Don't serve what you would fear receiving.
Don't mistake influence for consent.
The ovens know.

I read the last line three times.
The ovens know.
I look at the ovens.
They look like ovens.
Mostly.
"Okay," I whisper. "Good boundaries, terrifying delivery."
My palm tingles.
I press it flat against my apron.
The book turns a page.
I flinch.
It stops on a recipe headed:

Cinnamon Rolls for Warm Regard.

Below it, in smaller writing:

Often mistaken by fools for love potion. Doesn't create love. Encourages warmth, generosity, attraction already present, and courage to notice what one has been denying.

Well.
That's specific.

I lean closer.

The recipe looks ordinary at first. Flour, milk, yeast, butter, brown sugar, cinnamon. Then the ingredient list shifts. Not visually. My eyes simply understand more than they should.

Heart-cinnamon: one pinch.

Rose sugar: three teaspoons.

Salt of honest appetite: less than you think.

I glance at the jars.

One of the labels has changed.

Or maybe I can read it now.

Heart-cinnamon.

A laugh slips out of me.

Not because it's funny.

Because if I don't laugh, I might sit on the floor.

Magic. Actual magic. In my bakery.

Hidden by Kaytie or someone before her. Maybe waiting for me. Maybe waiting for any baker who listened hard enough. Maybe all buildings in Coral Cove have secret recipe books and no one told me because I look too practical to invite to occult potlucks.

I close the book halfway, then stop.

"Is this real?" I whisper.

The book gives no answer.

The ovens hum.

Unhelpful.

I should not use it.

That's the first clear thought.

I should absolutely not use a magical ingredient designed to influence emotions and sell it to customers who did not sign a consent form. I have recently become very invested in consent forms. Also safe words. Also hydration. But primarily consent.

The recipe says it doesn't create love.

That doesn't erase the problem.

A pastry that makes people cheerful is still doing something to them. Coffee does something to people too, yes, but caffeine at least has the decency to appear on nutrition labels and in jokes about addiction. Magical heart-cinnamon is not exactly FDA-approved.

I imagine Baylin seeing the book and saying, The ancestors have finally subscribed to our newsletter.

I imagine Derek asking if we can charge extra.

I imagine Lea leaning over the counter with the expression she gets when she is about to say something that sounds supportive and lands like a thrown brick.

I groan. "Not now, imaginary Lea."

The book remains open.

The recipe waits.

I read the note again.

Don't bake what you would not eat.

Don't serve what you would fear receiving.

Would I fear receiving warmth?

Yes.

Obviously.

That's not the same as saying no. My palm warms.

I'm not making a love potion.

Absolutely not.

But maybe, after the morning rush, I could test the base recipe with myself. One roll. Or a batch with no magical ingredient first. Or a tiny pinch, less than the recipe calls for, intention set toward comfort, not desire. Warmth, not manipulation. A pastry that says you're allowed to feel a little softer today, if you choose.

That still sounds ethically questionable.

It also sounds like exactly the kind of thing Coral Cove would buy by the dozen.

I close the book.

The cover is warm under my hand.

"I'm putting you away for now," I say.

The box doesn't object.

I slide the book and jars back into the compartment beneath the shelf, then cover the panel with napkins, ribbon, and my own rising suspicion. I stand just as Derek flips the sign to Open.

The bell over the door rings two seconds later.

Mrs. Talbot walks in first, as she does most mornings, wearing a yellow raincoat and the cheerful determination of a woman who believes gossip is a community service.

"Morning, Dottie," she calls. "Morning, Derek. Morning, Baylin, wherever you're hiding."

Baylin's voice floats from the kitchen. "I'm not hiding. I'm communing with rye."

Mrs. Talbot beams. "Good for you, dear."

"The usual?" Derek asks.

"Yes, darling. And one of those croissants. I could smell them halfway down the street."

"You say that every time," I tell her.

"And every time it's true."

Cookie people chatter. Bread people nod. Pastry people move like they are late for a train they technically could have caught if they had not needed a lemon twist first.

The rush hits fast.

For ninety minutes, I don't think about magic, hidden compartments, or the fact that my hand knows words my skin doesn't show. I think about orders. Change. Coffee. Boxes. Glaze. Fresh trays. Derek's tendency to hand people napkins like he is awarding medals. Baylin coming out with flour in her hair and selling three loaves of rosemary focaccia by simply describing them as "emotionally reliable."

The line shrinks.

The display cases empty.

The bakery grows louder, then quieter.

By nine-thirty, the first storm has passed.

I'm wiping the counter when the bell over the door rings again.

I look up.

And forget what I'm doing.

Lorenzo Moretti steps inside.

The bakery seems to notice.

Or maybe that is me.

Either way, the room changes.

He wears a dark gray suit today, cut so precisely it makes every other item of clothing in the bakery look like it owes him an apology. His black hair is styled but not too styled, which is unfair. His beard is trimmed close. His eyes sweep the room once, quick and assessing, before landing on me.

My hand tightens around the cleaning cloth.

Lorenzo is a known problem in Coral Cove.

Not legal problem. Not exactly. More like a weather event with a law degree. Feared attorney. Sharp tongue. Expensive watch. Reputation large enough to enter rooms before him and flirt with half the occupants.

I have heard stories.

Everyone has heard stories.

Some from women who smile when they tell them.

Some from men who sound jealous.

Some from clients who speak his name like a prayer and a threat in the same breath.

Lorenzo Moretti can ruin a man in court, charm a room at dinner, and make a person feel interesting by asking one question like he actually cares about the answer.

That's dangerous.

I prefer danger labeled clearly.

"Good morning, Dorothea," he says.

My name in his mouth hits me like a hand at the center of my back.

Not Dottie.

Not sweetie.

Not Miss Thompson.

Dorothea.

Lorenzo's voice is real.

That's the problem.

It can be careless. It can forget. It can say the wrong thing tomorrow. It can say my name in front of half the town and leave me to stand there with my pulse in my throat and no mystical guide to interpret the weather.

"Good morning," I say, which is a perfectly normal answer and therefore suspiciously difficult.

Derek looks between us.

I can feel him looking.

"Derek," I say without taking my eyes off Lorenzo. "Can you restock the napkins please?"

"They're already stocked."

"Restock them emotionally."

He snorts but moves away.

Lorenzo comes to the counter.

He is close enough now that I can smell him beneath the bakery air. Coffee. Rain. Something clean and expensive.

Leather, maybe. The same note that haunted the black door in the Hallway of Secrets, though not exactly. That was memory and desire. This is wet wool, skin, and a man who has walked in from the real street.

"I'll take a black coffee," he says. "And whatever you recommend today."

That's a trap of a sentence.

Whatever you recommend means he is either adventurous or trying to be flirted with.

Or he sent Molly in so often that he has learned the code and is weaponizing it.

I narrow my eyes.

"Do you actually want my recommendation, or do you want plausible deniability if you dislike the pastry?"

His mouth curves.

Oh no.

That smile should require permits.

"I trust your professional judgment."

"My professional judgment says people who order black coffee are trying to prove something."

"What am I trying to prove?"

"That you can survive bitterness."

His smile widens.

There are dimples.

I should have known.

"Can I?"

"Probably," I say. "But I would still suggest the lemon pastry. It cuts the coffee without making you admit you wanted sugar."

Lorenzo places one hand over his heart.

"Consider me seen."

The cleaning cloth is still in my hand.

I put it down because gripping it like a weapon seems unprofessional.

"Black coffee and lemon pastry," I say.

"Please."

I turn to grab a cup.

My body is behaving strangely, and apparently I've interpreted that as "feel everything at maximum volume." Lorenzo watches me move behind the counter. Not rudely.

Not obviously. But I feel his attention like heat near the oven doors.

I set the cup under the coffee dispenser and reach for the pot.

The bakery hums.

The glass pot is hot in my hand. I have poured coffee thousands of times. Tens of thousands, probably. My hand knows this motion better than my brain knows most things.

But then Lorenzo says my name again.

"Dorothea."

I look up.

Mistake.

His expression is not flirtatious now.

Or not only.

He is looking at my hand.

The one with the faint red oven burn near my wrist.

"You burned yourself," he says.

"This?" I glance down. "That's nothing."

His eyes lift to mine.

"Nothing?" The tone hits strangely.

Not scolding. Not soft either. A quiet challenge.

I remember my own voice in the bakery last night, saying scared, embarrassed, hungry, because if no one else was going to ask, I had to start asking myself.

"It's a small burn," I correct.

Lorenzo's gaze holds mine. "Better."

Still, my pulse jumps.

I look away too fast.

The coffee misses the cup.

Hot liquid splashes across the back of my hand.

Pain flashes bright and immediate.

I gasp and jerk back.

The pot hits the edge of the counter, slips, and shatters on the floor.

The sound cracks through the bakery.

Derek swears.

Mrs. Talbot, who has returned for napkins she did not need, says, "Oh, honey."

Baylin appears in the kitchen doorway with a bread knife in hand.

"For the love of laminated dough," she says. "What happened?"

"I'm fine," I say automatically.

Pain burns across my hand.

I cradle it against my chest.

Lorenzo is already moving.

He rounds the counter with a speed that makes Derek step back. Not dramatic. Not panicked. Efficient. Focused. Lawyer in a crisis, maybe. Man used to taking control of a room.

That should irritate me.

It does.

It also steadies me.

"Let me see," he says.

"I said I'm fine."

His eyes meet mine. "Dorothea."

The word is almost a warning.

A gentle one.

But a warning.

I stop.

The bakery feels too quiet.

Lorenzo doesn't grab my hand. He holds out his.

An offer.

I place my hand in his.

His fingers close around mine carefully.

Don't compare.

Not fantasy. Not practiced from my own hidden wants. Lorenzo's hand is real. Warm, dry, a little callused where I don't expect a lawyer to have calluses. He turns my hand under the light and studies the burn with a frown that makes my stomach do something deeply inconvenient.

"Sink," he says.

"It's not that bad."

"You're saying that because you're embarrassed."

My mouth opens.

Closes.

Rude.

Accurate.

"I'm saying it because I have burned myself before," I say.

"And because you have decided familiar pain doesn't deserve attention."

The words land too hard.

Baylin goes still.

Derek suddenly finds the floor very interesting.

I hate Lorenzo for seeing that much in under five seconds. I hate more that part of me wants to hand him the rest and see what he does with it.

"Sink," he repeats, softer.

I let him guide me.

Not because I cannot walk to my own sink.

Because I choose to stop arguing.

He turns on the water, testing it with his fingers until it's cool but not icy. Then he places my hand beneath it.

Relief moves through me so fast my knees weaken.

I grip the edge of the sink with my free hand.

"There," Lorenzo says. "Keep it there."

"I know how burns work."

"Good. Then you know this matters."

I glance at him.

He is close. Too close for a man in my kitchen. Too close for a man with a reputation. Too close for a man who says my name like it's not something I have spent years allowing other people to shrink.

His attention stays on my hand.

Not my mouth. Not my chest. Not the fact that I'm turning pink in front of him like a sugar cookie overbaked at the edges.

My hand.

The hurt.

I swallow. "It does hurt," I say.

The admission feels stupidly large.

Lorenzo looks at me.

Something in his face softens. "I know."

Not I told you so.

Not poor thing.

I know.

I turn back to the water quickly.

The cool stream runs over my skin.

Derek begins sweeping the broken glass. Baylin takes charge of the front with the terrifying calm of a woman who can score baguettes without flinching. Mrs. Talbot announces to everyone who enters that there has been "a minor coffee incident but no casualties," which is not legally accurate because my pride is bleeding out on the floor.

Lorenzo stays beside me.

After several minutes, he reaches for paper towels.

"First aid kit?" he asks.

"Under the register."

He gives me a look.

"What?"

"You store the first aid kit under the register?"

"Where would you store it?"

"Somewhere closer to the kitchen."

"This is a bakery. Everything is close to the kitchen."

He almost smiles.

Then he goes to retrieve it.

I stand alone at the sink and breathe.

My hand hurts. Not terribly, but enough. The skin is red across the back, angry but not blistered. It will be fine, which is not the same as nothing. Apparently I'm learning distinctions today.

Lorenzo returns with the first aid kit.

He opens it on the prep counter.

"You don't have to bandage me," I say.

"I know."

"I can do it."

"I know."

"Then why are you doing it?"

He looks up. "Because you're letting me."

That shuts me up.

He dries my hand carefully.

Every touch is practical. Cotton pad. Burn gel. Gauze. Wrap. No lingering. No performance. Yet my body responds to the care as if he has put his mouth on my neck, which is unfair to everyone involved and possibly a sign I need breakfast.

"You should keep an eye on it," he says. "If it blisters badly, get it checked."

"It won't."

"Dorothea."

I sigh. "I will keep an eye on it."

"Good."

There it is.

A real good. Not safe because it cannot hurt me.

He's real.

I draw my hand back.

"Thank you."

"You're welcome."

We stand there, too close, surrounded by the smell of coffee, broken glass, bread, dish soap, and every word I'm not brave enough to say before noon.

"If you need anything," he says, "I'm here."

The sentence should be ordinary.

It's not.

Because I know what here means now.

Here in town.

Here in the real world.

Here with cases and rumors and fathers and flaws.

Here, where he can disappoint me.

Here, where I can ask.

I look at him.

"Do you say that to everyone?"

His mouth curves. "No."

"Just injured bakers?"

"Only my favorite one."

"I'm the only baker in town."

"The grocery store sells donuts and bread."

"Those are emergency carbohydrates. Not baking."

"I stand corrected."

"You should. Often."

He laughs.

Low. Warm. Real enough to be a problem.

I package the lemon pastry with my uninjured hand, slower than usual. He reaches for the coffee, but I stop him.

"I'll make you a fresh cup," I say.

"You don't have to."

"I know."

The words echo his.

His eyes warm.

I pour this time without incident, mostly because I refuse

to let coffee win twice. I slide the cup and pastry across the counter.

"On the house," I say.

"No."

"For the trouble."

"I did not help you so you would comp my breakfast."

"I burned myself because you distracted me. Legally, this is your pastry."

His smile flashes.

"Legally?"

"Morally, then."

He considers me.

"Fine. But I'm coming back later to pay for it."

"That defeats the purpose."

"Good."

He picks up the cup and bag.

Our fingers don't touch this time.

I notice.

He notices that I notice.

Terrible man.

"Take care of your hand," he says.

"Take care of your bitterness."

He lifts the coffee. "Working on it."

Then he leaves.

The bell rings behind him.

I watch through the window as he crosses the sidewalk. The gray suit moves through Coral Cove like it's a court date with destiny and dinner plans with temptation.

I don't like him.

That feels important to say internally.

I don't like him.

I'm attracted to him, which is worse and less dignified. But I'm curious about him.

Curiosity is how people open doors.

Baylin appears beside me.

I jump.

"Subtle," she says.

"How long have you been there?"

"Long enough to know you should eat something."

"Why is everyone suddenly invested in my blood sugar?"

"Because you become haunted when underfed."

Derek leans around the case. "That's true."

"Restock something," I tell him.

"I'm restocking emotionally."

Baylin looks at my bandaged hand. "Bad?"

"No."

She raises an eyebrow.

I sigh. "It hurts, but it's not bad."

Her expression softens, just slightly.

"Better."

I close my eyes. "Not you too."

"Me especially."

The morning continues.

It has the nerve to do that.

Customers come in. Coffee is poured by Derek under my supervision, because apparently I'm not allowed to hold the pot for a while. Baylin sells out of rye by ten. The pear pastries come out late but perfect. Mrs. Talbot returns once more, allegedly for her neighbor, actually for updates.

By noon, the rush has died.

Derek heads out for a break. Baylin goes upstairs to nap in the little room above the kitchen she claims has the best ghost energy. I don't ask.

For the first time all day, the bakery is quiet.

Not empty.

Quiet.

My hand throbs beneath the bandage.

The hidden compartment waits under the shelf.

I should ignore it.

I last fourteen seconds before I retrieve the wooden box and place it on the prep table again.

The Hearth Book opens more gently this time, as if it has decided I'm skittish and should be approached like a feral cat with access to flour.

It opens to the same recipe.

Cinnamon Rolls for Warm Regard.

I read every line.

Then I read the opening warning again.

Don't serve what you would fear receiving.

Would I fear a pastry that made me softer?

Maybe.

Would I resent it if I learned someone had given it to me without telling me?

Yes.

So I don't follow the recipe while being clear about my intent the whole time..

Comfort, courage, and the belief that anything is possible..

A reminder that pleasure doesn't need to be earned before it's received.

I stare at that last line for a long moment.

Then I write it in the margin of the Hearth Book, because if a magical recipe book is going to invade my bakery, it can accept peer review.

The ink sinks into the page.

I take that as consent from the terrifying cookbook and so I make a small batch.

Not enough to sell out the town. Not enough to accidentally start a matchmaking epidemic. Six rolls. Flour, yeast, milk, butter, brown sugar, cinnamon. Normal ingredients first, because magic should not get to skip technique. I knead with my uninjured hand doing less work, letting my left hand lead.

The dough comes together slowly.

Soft. Sticky. Warm from the milk.

Kneading dough is not force. Not really. It's conversation. Press, fold, turn. Press, fold, turn. Too much pressure tears. Too little does nothing. The right touch develops structure.

I'm absolutely not making that a metaphor either.

The jar of heart-cinnamon sits beside the bowl.

I open it.

The scent rises.

Cinnamon, yes, but brighter. A little floral. A little smoky. Like spice held under sunlight until it remembers being bark on a living tree.

Intention matters.

"This is for warmth," I say quietly. "Just a little softness. If they choose it."

The ovens hum.

No objection.

I mix the cinnamon into the filling.

The dough tingles under my fingers when I roll it out.

I freeze.

Then keep going.

The sensation is strange, but not unpleasant. Like bubbles beneath the skin. Like kneading seltzer. The brown sugar darkens slightly when it hits the dough, glowing for one impossible second before becoming normal again.

I cut the rolls and place them in the pan.

Not hearts.

Absolutely not hearts.

I consider normal spirals.

Then, because I'm apparently still myself, I shape each one into a loose little knot.

Not a chain.

A knot.

Something that can be untied.

When they bake, the whole bakery fills with scent.

Cinnamon.

Butter.

Sugar.

Warm milk.

Orange peel, though I did not add orange peel.

The smell goes deeper than appetite. It settles in the chest. It makes the front windows glow softer. It makes the old wood under the counter seem warmer. It makes me think of blankets, rain, second chances, and sitting down before you fall apart.

I breathe it in and feel dangerously close to crying.

"Rude pastry," I whisper.

The bell over the door rings.

May walks in with a folded umbrella and her usual bright scarf, already smiling before she fully enters.

She stops.

Her eyes widen.

"What," she says, "is that?"

I look at the pan on the cooling rack.

"A new recipe."

"Cinnamon rolls?"

"Yes."

"Dottie Thompson, I have never smelled anything so good in my life."

My hand tightens around the spatula.

Here is the ethical moment.

Tiny, maybe.

Not tiny.

"Before I sell you one," I say, "I should tell you I'm experimenting with something a little unusual."

May's eyebrows lift. "Unusual how?"

I think of saying magical heart-cinnamon from a secret book hidden in my wall.

No.

Not yet.

Not because I want to deceive her.

Because I don't know what I have.

Because Coral Cove may be strange, but even here, that is a lot to put on a Tuesday afternoon.

"It's meant to be a comfort pastry," I say carefully. "Not just sweet. More like... a mood-lifter. I'm testing whether ingredients and intention can make something feel warmer."

May smiles softly.

"Oh, honey. That sounds lovely."

"You don't have to try it."

"I want two."

"May."

"One for me and one for Harold."

"You cannot blame me if Harold becomes emotionally available."

She laughs. "If that happens, I'll order a dozen."

I package two.

My stomach twists as I hand them over.

Not bad.

Aware.

A person can sell ordinary food and still affect someone's mood. A croissant can save a morning. A cake can make a birthday survivable. Bread can make a kitchen smell like home. Food has always been magic-adjacent. Maybe this is only more honest about it.

Maybe.

May pays and takes the box.

She eats one at the little table by the window before leaving, because she has never in her life successfully waited to eat pastry.

Her first bite makes her close her eyes.

"Oh," she says.

I hold my breath.

She opens her eyes.

They are wet.

Not glowing. Thank God. No heart pupils. No sudden declaration of love for the ficus plant.

Just wet.

"This tastes like my mother's kitchen," she says softly.

My chest tightens.

"Is that okay?"

May nods. "It's wonderful."

She buys four more before she goes.

The cinnamon rolls sell out within an hour.

Only six, I remind myself.

Still.

May must tell someone, because Mrs. Talbot appears, then Cora from the florist, then two tourists who say they smelled cinnamon from the sidewalk and "felt invited," which is not concerning at all. Each person who eats one reacts a little differently. A sigh. A smile. One man calls his sister from the corner table. A teenager stops scrolling long enough to tell her mother the roll is "actually kind of elite," which seems to make the mother happier than the pastry.

No one seems drugged or proposes to the espresso machine.

Everyone leaves a little softer than they came in.

When the last roll is gone, I stand behind the counter with an empty tray and a strange ache in my chest.

There is truth to the magic.

Not all of it.

I don't know how much.

But enough.

The hidden book waits beneath the shelf.

Lorenzo's voice waits in my memory.

Dorothea.

My palm tingles.

The bakery hums around me, warm and ordinary and not ordinary at all.

I look at the empty tray.

Then at the door Lorenzo walked through.

Then at my bandaged hand.

Accepting help doesn't mean surrendering myself.

The thought arrives quietly.

It doesn't feel like mine yet.

But maybe it could be.

I take the notebook and write beneath my altered recipe:

Test Batch One: Sold out. No obvious coercive effects. Emotional warmth observed. May cried, but in a good way. Further testing needed. Consent language pending.

Then, after a pause, I add:

Magic doesn't make love. It makes people notice what's already rising.

The words sit on the page.

My heart beats once, hard.

Outside, Coral Cove continues.

Inside, the bakery breathes.

And beneath the bread wall, something old and hidden waits for me to listen.

THREE

Lorenzo

The lemon pastry is still warm when Molly sets it on my desk.

That should not matter.

It does.

The paper bag carries the scent of butter, sugar, lemon, and something soft underneath that I cannot name. Yeast, maybe. Vanilla. The bakery itself. Knead the Dough has a smell that clings. Not in the cheap way, not like grease or over-sweet frosting, but like proof that someone made something with their hands before the rest of the world finished waking up.

Molly places the coffee beside it and gives me a look.

I don't like that look.

Molly has several categories of look. There is the please sign this before I commit workplace violence look. There is the client in reception is wearing perfume strong enough to qualify as a chemical weapon look. There is the your father called and I deserve hazard pay look.

"What?" I ask.

"Nothing."

"No."

"No?"

"You're not a subtle woman."

"I'm very subtle. You're simply suspicious."

"I'm a lawyer."

"Exactly."

I reach for the coffee and take a sip.

Black. Strong. Fresh. Better than the burnt punishment I made myself earlier. Dorothea must have poured it after Molly arrived, which means she made it for me, not for the abstract concept of a customer.

Molly's mouth twitches.

"Don't," I say.

"I haven't said anything."

"You're thinking loudly again."

"I'm thinking you should eat that while it's still warm."

"That's all?"

"Mostly."

"Molly."

She folds her hands in front of her, all professional inno-cence. "Dottie asked if your coffee should be topped off before I left."

I look down at the cup.

"She did?"

"She did."

I take another sip because my hands need something to do.

Dorothea Thompson has probably topped off thousands of cups of coffee in that bakery. The question means nothing. It's customer service. It's habit. It's what good business owners do when a secretary comes in for a standing order.

Still.

My mind provides the image of her behind the counter, gray bakery shirt, flour on her apron, careful hands wrapped around the coffeepot. The way she had looked at me before the coffee spilled. Not coy. Not practiced. Not like women in hotel bars who know the rhythm of attraction and dance it beautifully.

Dorothea had looked startled by herself.

That's what keeps bothering me.

Not her blush. Not her mouth. Not the curve of her body under that apron, although I'm still a man with eyes and a pulse, and her body is not something a man forgets because he has a legal degree.

No.

It's the way she had tried to dismiss the burn before she even knew how badly it hurt.

I'm fine.

Two words. Polite. Automatic. A locked door with a welcome mat.

Then, after I pushed, she corrected herself.

It does hurt.

That had done something to me.

Something sharper than attraction.

Something more dangerous than lust.

Molly clears her throat.

I look up.

"Yes?"

"Ophelia's assistant called again."

I close my eyes.

"Of course she did."

"They need your plus-one name by Friday."

"I heard you the first time."

"And your father's assistant sent his flight information. I forwarded it to the car service."

"Good."

"She also asked if you would be hosting him for dinner on Thursday."

I laugh once.

It doesn't sound like humor.

"Absolutely not."

"I wrote, Mr. Moretti's schedule won't permit that."

"You're worth every dollar I pay you."

"I know."

I reach for the pastry bag and open it.

Lemon and butter rise into the air.

The pastry is perfectly shaped, golden layers folded around a glossy pale filling. A little sugar dusts the top. Not too much. Dorothea has restraint with sugar. That's rare in a baker and almost unheard of in people generally.

I take a bite.

The pastry shatters delicately, flakes falling onto my desk.

"Damn," I say.

Molly smiles. "That good?"

"It's inconveniently good."

"Should I put that in the review?"

"No."

"You could say, 'Five stars. Pastry caused professional inconvenience.'"

"Get out."

She laughs and turns toward the door.

"Molly."

She stops.

"Clear my next hour."

Her eyebrows rise. "Already?"

"Already what?"

"Nothing."

"That was not nothing."

"I'm assuming this is about the Applegate file."

It should be.

It's, partly.

The Applegate v. Thompson notice is still open on my desk, the preliminary filing ugly in its aggression. I have spent the last half hour reading it between bites of lemon pastry, which is not my strangest work habit, but may be the most thematically unsubtle.

Applegate Holdings claims irregularity in the transfer that gave Dorothea ownership of the building. That could mean anything. A clerical error. A missing signature. A deliberately manufactured pressure tactic. They are asking for possession, expedited hearing, and costs. Which means they don't only want money.

They want her out.

The pink storefront. The yellow striped walls. The ovens. The upstairs apartment.

Her home.

My fingers tighten around the edge of the file.

"Yes," I say. "I want to step out."

Molly's expression changes, amusement softening into understanding. "To the bakery?"

"I need to check on her hand."

"Very legal."

"And possibly warn her that there may be a filing coming her way."

"Also legal."

"And get another coffee."

"Deeply legal."

I give her a look.

She gives me one back.

"You have a meeting with Cormac at one," she says. "I can push it to one-thirty."

"Do that."

"And Lorenzo?"

I pause.

She rarely uses my first name in that tone.

"What?"

"Try not to walk in there like you're about to litigate her pain."

I stare at her.

"That's not something I do."

Her silence is insulting.

"I don't litigate pain."

"You cross-examine discomfort until it confesses."

"That's a useful skill."

"In court."

I reach for my coat.

Molly steps aside.

"Noted," I say.

"That means ignored."

"It means noted."

"Do you want me to order a normal human lunch for when you return?"

"No."

"I'll order one."

"Fine."

She smiles. "Good talk."

I leave before she can say anything worse.

Coral Cove is the kind of town that looks like it was designed by a committee of people who believed charm could solve infrastructure. Flower boxes under windows. Painted signs. Old brick. Little shops with names that would be unbearable if they did not mostly mean them. Spellbound Stories. The Salty Gull. Golden Chopsticks. Knead the Dough.

The sky has cleared since morning, leaving the sidewalks damp and bright. Sunlight catches in puddles along the curb.

Somewhere near the harbor, gulls scream like they have been wrongfully accused.

People nod as I pass.

Some smile.

Some don't.

A man coming out of the pharmacy sees me, pauses, then crosses the street with his paper bag tucked under his arm.

I almost laugh.

I ruined his brother-in-law in a boundary dispute last year. Not personally. Legally. The brother-in-law had built a shed eighteen inches over the property line and decided bluster would substitute for compliance. It did not.

My reputation in Coral Cove is useful.

It's also ridiculous.

I'm either the town's legal attack dog, the charming bastard with too many exes, or the man people call when they want something handled quietly and aggressively. I have spent years cultivating parts of that image because image is easier than vulnerability and bills better than grief.

Then Dorothea looks at me like she cannot decide whether I'm a person or a weather system, and the whole performance feels suddenly cheap around the edges.

That's the part I don't like.

Dorothea makes me aware of the performance.

Not because she sees through it. She doesn't even seem interested in it.

Women usually want something from the act. Confidence. Heat. Danger without actual risk. The lawyer with the sharp suit and sharper tongue. The man who knows exactly when to smile, when to lower his voice, when to let silence do the work.

Dorothea looks at me and forgets how to pour coffee.

Then tells me black coffee means I'm trying to prove I can survive bitterness.

That's not seduction.

That's assault with insight.

I reach the bakery and stop outside.

Knead the Dough is painted pink, which should be absurd and somehow is not. White trim. Gold lettering. A little rolling pin painted under the sign. The front window displays tiered stands of pastries, a chalkboard menu, and a vase of yellow flowers. The place looks cheerful enough to be harmless.

It's not harmless.

No place that smells that good can be harmless.

Through the window, I see Dorothea behind the counter. Her hair is pinned back, but several strands have escaped around her face. Her apron is dusted with flour. Her injured hand is wrapped in white gauze.

She moves differently than she did this morning, compensating with her other hand, turning her body slightly when she reaches. Not helpless. Never that. Efficient. Adjusting around pain like she has done it a thousand times and resents anyone noticing.

Something tightens in my chest.

I don't get to be angry about that.

I don't know her well enough.

I enter anyway.

The bell over the door rings.

Dorothea looks up.

Her eyes widen.

Just a little.

She covers it quickly, but I see it.

I have always been good at seeing things people want hidden.

"Back so soon, Lorenzo?" she asks.

Her voice is soft, but there is a dry edge under it. A small defense, thin as sugar crust. "Should I be worried that you've developed a lemon pastry dependency?"

"Yes," I say. "It escalated quickly."

Her mouth twitches.

Victory.

A small one, but I will take it.

"I came to check on your hand."

Her cheeks color.

Not the full blush from earlier. This is something more complicated. Embarrassment, irritation, maybe a little pleasure she doesn't want to admit.

She lifts the bandaged hand. "Still attached."

"That's a low standard."

"It's a useful one."

"How does it feel?"

"Fine."

I tilt my head.

Her lips press together.

"It hurts," she says. "But not terribly. I rinsed it like you said, used the burn gel, and wrapped it. Happy?"

"Yes."

She blinks, as if she expected me to argue.

"I'm not unreasonable," I say.

"That feels like a claim requiring evidence."

I smile.

There it's again.

That little flash of wit, offered carefully, as if she expects humor to be taken as apology if it lands wrong. With other women, I'm usually the one setting the pace. With Dorothea, I find myself listening for the exact moment she decides not to hide.

It's addictive in a way I did not authorize.

Derek is behind the counter, restocking boxes. He sees me and immediately finds something to do in the back. Smart man.

An older woman at one of the bistro tables looks up from her coffee and brightens.

"Well, hello, Lorenzo."

"Mrs. Talbot."

Her eyes dart between Dorothea and me.

I can see the story forming in her head.

Coral Cove gossip moves faster than court filings and with fewer evidentiary standards.

"I didn't expect to see you again today," she says.

"Coffee emergency."

"Mmm."

That mmm is legally defamatory.

Dorothea turns to Mrs. Talbot with a paper bag. "Two comfort rolls for Harold and one oat cookie for you."

"One oat cookie for Harold," Mrs. Talbot corrects. "Two comfort rolls for me."

Dorothea gives her a look.

Mrs. Talbot smiles. "I'm an old woman, Dottie. I've earned my lies."

Dorothea laughs.

The sound changes her whole face.

That's the thing I notice.

Not the beauty, though she is beautiful in a way that sneaks up and then refuses to leave. Not polished. Not designed. Not like Alison in silk and jewelry. Dorothea's beauty is in movement. The way she tucks a loose strand of hair behind her ear with the back of her wrist because her fingers are dusted with flour. The way her mouth twists when she is trying not to smile. The way she brightens for customers and then retreats behind the counter the moment the attention might stay on her too long.

She is not innocent.

That's the wrong word.

She is guarded.

There is a difference.

Innocence is ignorance.

Dorothea looks like a woman who knows too much about being careful.

And I'm suddenly furious with every person who taught her that.

Mrs. Talbot takes her bag and heads for the door, still smiling too widely.

"Have a nice afternoon, you two."

Dorothea groans softly after the bell rings.

"She is going to tell everyone you came back."

"Probably."

"You sound calm about that."

"I have survived worse rumors."

"I have not."

I glance at her.

She looks away first, busying herself with the register.

There.

The small truth beneath the joke.

My reputation is armor because I can wear it. Hers is exposure because she cannot control the story once someone else picks it up.

I step closer to the counter, but not too close.

"Then I apologize."

Her eyes flick back to mine.

"For what?"

"For giving Mrs. Talbot material."

She studies me as if the apology is a pastry she is not sure she ordered.

"It's okay," she says. "She would have found material in a napkin if she had to."

"Still."

Her shoulders loosen a fraction.

The bakery around us smells different now than it did this morning. Cinnamon hangs in the air, warm and deep, threaded with butter and something else. Something that makes me want to sit down and call someone I have been avoiding.

That's a strangely specific reaction.

"What is that smell?" I ask.

Dorothea's face shifts.

Not guilt.

Not exactly.

Alertness.

"Cinnamon rolls."

"I don't see cinnamon rolls."

"They sold out."

"Already?"

"It was a test batch."

"Successful test."

"Possibly too successful."

She says it under her breath, almost to herself.

Interesting.

I glance at the empty tray near the side counter. A little glaze clings to the parchment. There are crumbs shaped like knots, not spirals.

"What made them different?"

Her hand moves to her apron pocket.

Then stops.

"Experimenting," she says.

With Dorothea, the word feels larger than baking.

"I respect that."

"You don't strike me as a man who experiments."

"I experiment constantly."

"With what?"

"Strategy."

"That's not the same thing."

"No?"

"No. Strategy is deciding how to get what you want. Experimenting is admitting you don't know what will happen."

The answer hits clean.

I stare at her.

She seems to realize what she said a second after she says it. Pink moves up her throat.

"Sorry," she says. "That sounded rude."

"It sounded accurate."

Her eyes widen.

I mean it.

That unsettles me too.

Most people either flatter me or fight me. Dorothea names things and then apologizes for the precision.

Molly's warning echoes.

Don't walk in there like you're about to litigate her pain.

I clear my throat. "Can I get another coffee?"

"Black?"

"Yes."

"And no lemon pastries."

"Tragic."

"You could try a cherry danish."

"Could I?"

"You asked for my recommendation."

"I did."

She reaches into the case with a piece of parchment and lifts a glossy cherry danish into a bag. Her hands are careful. Competent. The bandaged one does less but still helps. I watch the way she adapts, not making a show of pain, not asking for help, not expecting any.

My attraction to her shifts again.

It's not less physical.

God, no.

The curve of her wrist, the slope of her neck, the softness

beneath the apron, the quick flash of teeth when she bites her lower lip in concentration. I notice all of it.

But wanting her body is becoming tangled with wanting to see what would happen if she stopped bracing.

That's dangerous.

Not for her.

For me.

Dorothea is not the kind of woman I can use to prove I still have a pulse.

She makes my usual games feel cheap.

I don't like that.

I also don't want to leave.

She pours the coffee without incident this time, chin lifted as if daring the pot to try something. I take the cup when she slides it across.

"How much?"

She waves me off. "Tomorrow you can go back to being a paying customer."

"No."

"Lorenzo."

My name in her mouth is quieter than mine in hers.

It still moves through me.

"I'm not letting you comp me twice in one day because you burned your hand."

"I'm not comping you because of the burn. I'm comping you because the cherry danish is slightly less pretty than the others."

I look into the bag.

The danish is flawless.

"Dorothea."

"It has a personality problem."

"It does not."

"It does. Very subtle. You wouldn't understand."

"I charge by the hour to understand subtle personality problems."

"That sounds exhausting."

"It is."

She smiles.

Small.

Private.

The kind of smile a man could become stupid over if he had not spent years practicing control.

I set a twenty on the counter.

She looks at it.

"That's too much."

"Then apply the remainder to my future pastry debt."

"I don't run tabs."

"You do now."

"I absolutely do not."

"Consider it a retainer."

"For pastries?"

"For future emergencies."

Her eyes narrow. "Your legal metaphors are getting away from you."

"Occupational hazard."

She slides the twenty back toward me.

I slide it back.

She places her uninjured hand over it before I can push again.

The motion brings our hands close, but not touching.

A line of heat moves through the space between us.

She notices.

So do I.

For once, I don't use it.

I lift my hand away first.

"All right," I say. "You win."

Her surprise is almost insulting.

"You give up that easily?"

"No. I choose my battles."

"Convenient phrasing."

"Accurate phrasing."

"I'll charge you tomorrow."

"I look forward to it."

The words come out warmer than intended.

Her blush deepens.

I should leave.

I don't.

The question forms before I approve it.

"Have lunch with me."

Dorothea goes still.

Not dramatically.

A small freeze. Hands. Shoulders. Breath.

I feel it like a mistake.

I soften my voice. "Not right this second if you're busy. Another day."

Her eyes drop to the counter. "I can't close during lunch."

"Derek is here."

"Derek has a break."

"Baylin?"

"She sleeps during the day. Bread people are nocturnal."

I almost smile. "Dinner, then."

Her fingers touch the edge of her apron.

The silence is longer this time.

And I, idiot that I am, realize something.

I expected yes.

Not because I'm entitled to it.

Not because she owes me anything.

But because women usually say yes to me, especially when I ask like this, direct enough to flatter, casual enough to give them room to pretend they are not flattered.

I know the rhythm.

Ask.

Smile.

Lower my voice.

Let them feel chosen.

Dorothea doesn't follow the rhythm.

"I'm sorry," she says. "I already have plans tonight."

The answer is polite.

Clear.

No.

A complete sentence wearing an apology it doesn't need.

For half a second, I'm embarrassed.

Truly embarrassed.

It hits hot beneath my collar, unexpected and sharp. I'm standing in a pink bakery with a cherry danish in one hand, being gently turned down by a woman with flour on her apron and a bandage on her hand, and I have no script for it that doesn't make me an ass.

I probably needed that.

I nod once. "No worries."

Her eyes lift, searching my face as if waiting for irritation.

I give her none.

Because no is a complete sentence even when it bruises my ego. Because the last thing I want is for Dorothea to learn that my attention becomes punishment when it's not rewarded.

"I'll see you tomorrow for that coffee," I say.

Relief flickers across her face.

Then something else.

Regret?

Maybe.

Maybe I'm flattering myself.

"Tomorrow," she says.

I lift the coffee in farewell and leave before I make the moment heavier than it needs to be.

The bell rings behind me.

The air outside is cooler.

I stand on the sidewalk for one second, coffee in one hand, pastry in the other, pride in a small pile somewhere near my shoes.

Then I laugh under my breath.

"Pathetic," I mutter.

I'm not angry.

That's the strange part.

I'm unsettled.

There is a difference, though my father would never admit it. Anger moves outward. It wants a target. A filing. A fight. A person to pin down and defeat.

Unsettled moves inward.

It asks questions.

Why did I expect yes?

Why did her no feel less like rejection and more like a door I had approached too quickly?

Why did I admire her more for saying it?

I start walking back toward the office.

The cherry danish is warm through the bag.

Halfway down the block, I glance back.

Through the bakery window, Dorothea stands behind the counter, looking down at her bandaged hand. Then she looks toward the door.

For a moment, our eyes almost meet through the glass.

Almost.

Then a customer steps between us.

The view breaks.

I keep walking.

By the time I reach the office, Molly is at the front desk with a takeout container and the expression of a woman prepared to know too much.

"How's the hand?" she asks.

"Bandaged."

"And the baker?"

"Busy."

Molly's eyebrows lift.

"Don't," I say.

"I said nothing."

"You radiate commentary."

"It's a gift."

I toss the cherry danish bag onto her desk.

"For you."

She peers inside. "You're giving me pastry?"

"I lost a negotiation."

"With Dottie?"

"With myself."

"Oh, this is better than I hoped."

"Molly."

She holds up both hands. "I will enjoy my danish silently."

"That would be new."

She takes a bite.

Her eyes close.

"Oh my God."

"Yes."

"I understand why you're making bad choices."

"I have not made any bad choices."

"You cleared an hour to check on a woman who burned her hand."

"And discuss potential legal exposure."

"Did you discuss potential legal exposure?"

I pause.

Molly smiles.

"Get back to work," I say.

"Yes, boss."

I go into my office and close the door.

The Applegate file waits on my desk.

So does the lemon pastry wrapper.

So does my father's shadow, though I refuse to give it a chair.

I sit and open the file again.

Dorothea turned me down. She is not a game. She is not a distraction from my father. She is not a plus-one-shaped solution to a family problem. She is not a sweet, shy baker I can flirt into softening my own edges for a few hours.

She is a woman whose home may be under legal attack.

A woman who calls her pain nothing.

A woman who can look at me and say strategy is not the same as experimenting, then apologize for being right.

A woman who said no.

I respect that.

I want her more because of it.

That's inconvenient.

I take out a notepad and write three names.

Applegate Holdings.

Dorothea Thompson.

José Moretti.

Three problems.

Only one of them is allowed to touch the bakery.

I underline Applegate Holdings.

Then I circle Dorothea's name, immediately regret the intimacy of the gesture, and tear the page off.

Ridiculous.

I'm a grown man.

A successful attorney.

A grown successful attorney who was turned down once and is apparently now behaving like a teenager with a court license.

I start over.

I write: Applegate v. Thompson, preliminary review.

Better.

Professional.

Clean.

I can work with clean.

But as I begin listing records to request, my mind keeps returning to the moment outside the bakery window.

Dorothea looking at the door after I left.

Not chasing.

Not inviting.

Just noticing.

I have built a life out of making people react.

I don't know what to do with a woman who makes me want to be worthy of her response.

My phone buzzes.

A text from Molly.

> Molly: Ophelia still needs your plus-one name.

I stare at it.

Then at the Applegate file.

Then at the window, where Main Street continues in all its specific, stubborn smallness.

My father arrives Thursday.

And for the first time in a long time, the problem in front of me is not whether I can win.

FOUR

Dorothea

By seven o'clock, the bakery is closed, the ovens are cooling, and my body has begun the slow, suspicious process of believing the day might actually be over.

It never trusts that easily.

Neither do I.

Downstairs, Knead the Dough rests in the kind of quiet that only comes after a long day of being wanted. The display cases are empty except for crumbs and one lonely oat cookie Derek forgot to move to the discount tray. The bread shelves have been wiped down. The coffee machine is off. The floors are mopped. The air still holds the ghosts of butter, cinnamon, lemon glaze, coffee, dish soap, and old wood.

Upstairs, my apartment is small, warm, and aggressively mine.

Not impressive. Not magazine-worthy. No coastal cottage aesthetic with driftwood shelves and tasteful bowls of shells. Just mine.

The living room has a faded blue couch I bought second-hand from a woman who swore it came from a smoke-free home and then looked me dead in the eye like we were both agreeing to lie. The coffee table has a scratch down one side from when I tried to move it myself because asking for help felt more humiliating than dragging furniture up a narrow staircase. The rug is soft in the middle and curling at one corner. I keep meaning to tape it down. I don't.

There is one bookshelf packed too tightly, mostly romances from Lea, cookbooks, and books I bought because I wanted to become the kind of woman who reads essays before bed. Spoiler, I remain mostly a woman who falls asleep with a romance novel on her chest and butter under her fingernails.

The kitchen upstairs is barely worth the name. A tiny stove. A narrow counter. A sink that complains when the weather changes. It doesn't matter. My real kitchen is downstairs. My real kitchen has ovens large enough to climb into, if one were dramatic and not concerned about safety. My real kitchen has marble counters, proofing racks, flour bins, and a mixer older than Derek but twice as reliable.

I set the kettle on the stove.

Chamomile.

I'm lost in thoughts about curiosity and open doors, which I have recently learned is both the problem and the point.

The kettle begins to hum.

I take my mug from the cabinet. It's chipped on one side, yellow with little white flowers. Kaytie gave it to me my first Christmas after I bought the bakery.

Not my first Christmas working there.

My first Christmas owning it.

There is a difference.

Back then, the papers were signed, the keys were mine, and I had stood downstairs in the kitchen after midnight, alone with a box of ornaments I did not have time to hang. Kaytie had left the mug on the prep table with a note.

For the woman who finally stopped asking permission.

I cried into a bucket of buttercream for ten minutes.

Not my proudest moment.

Buttercream is not meant to receive grief, but it handled itself well.

The kettle whistles.

I pour water over the tea bag and carry the mug into the living room. My book waits on the couch, facedown, which Lea would call abusive. I sit, tuck my feet beneath me, and open it.

For two paragraphs, I almost manage to read.

Then someone knocks.

Three hard raps against my apartment door.

I freeze.

The sound doesn't belong up here.

Downstairs, knocks mean delivery people, Derek forgetting his keys, Baylin coming in too early with bread opinions. Upstairs, knocks mean someone has climbed the exterior stairs after closing and found my private door.

My apartment door.

My home door.

The tea warms my hand.

I set the mug down carefully.

Another knock.

I glance at the clock.

Seven.

For most people, early evening.

For a baker, practically midnight.

I stand, already annoyed because annoyance is easier than worry. I cross to the door, pausing long enough to look through the peephole.

A man stands outside.

Not Lorenzo.

Not anyone I recognize.

He wears slacks, a white button-up shirt, suspenders, and the emotionally vacant expression of a person paid to ruin evenings. He holds a stack of papers in one hand.

My stomach drops.

I open the door only halfway.

"Can I help you?"

"Dorothea Thompson?"

I hate the way my full name sounds in his mouth.

Flat.

Administrative.

"Yes."

He checks the top page.

Then he hands me the stack.

"You've been served."

For one second, I don't take the papers.

I stare at them.

Served.

Like a meal.

Like something prepared and delivered.

Like disaster with a cover sheet.

"What's this?" I ask.

He is already stepping back. "Have a good evening."

A strange thing to say after handing a woman something that makes her hands go cold.

"Wait. What's this?"

But he is walking down the stairs.

His shoes clang on the metal steps, one after another. Then he reaches the sidewalk, turns the corner, and disappears.

I stand in the doorway with the papers in my hand and the evening air brushing cold against my bare feet.

You've been served.

The words echo.

My first thought is absurd.

The cinnamon rolls.

What if I made someone sick? What if the magical ingredient did something after all? What if May cried in a bad way later? What if Harold became emotionally available and it caused structural damage to their marriage? What if I poisoned half of Coral Cove with enchanted cinnamon and now I'm going to prison, where I assume the ovens are terrible?

My second thought is worse.

What if this is about the bakery?

I close the door.

Lock it.

Then lock the deadbolt too, even though the papers are already inside with me.

Rain taps faintly against the window. My life, all still here, all unaware that a man in suspenders just handed me a stack of paper that may have teeth.

I sit on the couch.

No.

I stand again.

Then sit.

The papers slide in my hands because my fingers are shaking.

I read the first page.

I don't understand it.

Not because I cannot read. I can read. I read contracts when I bought the bakery. I read loan agreements. I read insurance forms. I read health department updates written by people who have never met joy. But legal documents do something to ordinary words. They take familiar language and make it stand in a dark hallway wearing someone else's coat.

Superior Court.

Complaint.

Applegate Holdings.

Plaintiff.

Dorothea Thompson.

Defendant.

My name is there.

Defendant.

I read faster.

Then slower.

Then realize none of it's entering me.

I start again.

Applegate Holdings claims irregularity in prior title transfer. Applegate Holdings claims superior right to possession. Applegate Holdings seeks declaratory relief. Applegate Holdings seeks immediate vacatur.

I stop.

Immediate vacatur.

My body understands before my mind does.

Leave.

They want me to leave.

My skin goes cold.

I flip to the next page.

There are dates. Parcel numbers. Addresses. My bakery address. The building description. Commercial space below, residential unit above.

My home written as legal description.

My kitchen reduced to square footage.

My bedroom reduced to residential unit.

My bakery reduced to premises.

I read the whole thing once.

By the end, I know nothing except that someone named Applegate believes the building was never Kaytie's to sell to me, or never transferred correctly, or was part of some old estate dispute that apparently decided to wake up now like a corpse with paperwork.

I read it again.

This time, the words land.

Hearing in less than two weeks.

Request for possession.

Demand to vacate.

Court costs.

Damages.

My chest tightens.

No.

No.

That's not a legal argument. I know that. Lorenzo would probably have something calm and cutting to say about it. No is not a strategy, Dorothea.

But it's the only word I have.

No.

This building is mine.

I bought it from Kaytie.

Fairly.

Legally.

I remember every signature because I had to grip the pen with both hands to keep from shaking. I remember Kaytie sitting beside me, crying a little, pretending not to cry by asking if I wanted peppermint tea. I remember the bank officer sliding papers across the table. I remember the number of years on the loan making my stomach flip. I remember thinking I had finally done it.

I had finally turned a key in a door no one could take back.

And now a stack of papers on my coffee table says maybe that was never true.

I stand so fast the papers slide to the floor.

"No."

The apartment doesn't answer.

Downstairs, the building creaks.

A normal sound.

Old wood. Cooling pipes. Rain.

But tonight, it sounds like something shifting under me.

I gather the papers and force myself to walk downstairs.

I don't know why.

Maybe because fear always sends me to the bakery. Maybe because the apartment feels too small for this much panic. Maybe because if someone is going to tell me my building is not mine, I need to stand in the place where I became myself and dare them to say it to my face.

The bakery is dark except for the security lights and the glow from the kitchen exit sign.

I switch on the prep lights.

The room brightens.

There.

Ovens. Counters. Display cases. Bread wall. Pink boxes stacked near the register. The little dent in the corner of the case from when Derek turned too fast with a sheet pan. The stool Baylin insists is haunted. The hidden compartment beneath the shelf.

My bakery.

Mine.

I walk to the bread wall and kneel.

My knees complain. I ignore them.

I pull away the napkin box, the ribbon box, the Valentine's doilies.

The secret panel waits.

I open it.

The wooden box is inside.

The Hearth Book.

The jars.

Magic hidden in the bones of my bakery.

My heart pounds.

Could someone know?

The thought enters clean and cold.

Could Applegate Holdings know about the book? About the ingredients? About whatever this place really is?

Maybe this has nothing to do with old title transfer. Maybe the building itself is the prize. Not the storefront. Not the apartment. Not the location on Main Street. This.

The Hearth Book of Knead the Dough.

For the baker who listens.

Did Kaytie know?

The note on the mug. For the woman who finally stopped asking permission. Did that mean the bakery? The book? Both?

The room tilts.

If I lose the building, I don't only lose income.

I lose the ovens.

The display cases.

The kitchen.

The upstairs apartment.

The recipe book.

The secret ingredients.

Derek's job.

Baylin's bread cave.

The regulars who come because the place smells like they remember being loved.

The loan I have spent years paying.

The one door I believed I could lock from the inside.

I sit on the floor.

Not gracefully.

I just sit.

The papers rest in my lap.

The prep lights buzz overhead.

For a moment, I'm not thirty. I'm seventeen again, standing in a caseworker's office with a black garbage bag full of clothes at my feet because no one had a spare suitcase and apparently children in transition are expected to rustle when they move.

The caseworker was kind. She had soft hands and a necklace with a tiny silver tree. She kept saying resilient.

You're so resilient, Dorothea.

People love that word when they have run out of shelter.

Resilient meant I slept on a stranger's floral couch for three weeks and thanked them for it.

Resilient meant I did not complain when a foster mother told me not to cook in her kitchen because she did not like "mess." I stood in the doorway and watched her burn pancakes while my hands ached to fix the batter, to lower the heat, to make something edible out of what we had.

Resilient meant leaving quietly.

Resilient meant not asking whether I could come back.

Resilient meant learning that any room could stop being yours if the adult with the clipboard said so.

I press my hand to my mouth.

"No," I whisper.

Not again.

I don't need pity.

I did not need it from foster families who called me a blessing until I became inconvenient.

I did not need it from the caseworker who cried once in the car because she could not find a placement and thought I was asleep.

I did not need it from Kaytie when she first hired me and realized I took home stale bread because it felt safer than asking for dinner.

I don't need it from Lorenzo Moretti because he saw me burn my hand and decided maybe I was a sad little baker who needed a pity date.

I don't need pity.

I need my building.

The papers blur.

My throat hurts.

The bakery is too quiet.

I reach for my phone.

Not Lorenzo.

Not yet.

I call Lea.

She answers on the second ring.

"Hey, you alive? Because if this is about the cinnamon roll text, I stand by what I said. Magical baked goods should come with a warning label and possibly a punch card."

I try to speak.

Nothing comes out.

The silence on the line changes her.

"Dottie?"

I swallow.

"I need you."

Three words.

Terrible words.

Small words.

A door opening.

Lea doesn't ask for explanation.

"Where are you?"

"Bakery."

"I'm coming."

The line clicks off.

She is there in eight minutes.

That should be impossible because Spellbound Stories is closed and she lives six blocks away, but Lea has always moved faster when someone's life is on fire. She lets herself in with the spare key I gave her for emergencies and book-related ambushes. Her hair is loose around her shoulders, her coat thrown over pajamas, boots unlaced.

She sees me on the floor by the bread wall.

Then she sees the papers.

Her face changes.

Not panic.

Lea is very good in crisis.

She gets angry instead.

"Give them to me."

I hand her the stack.

She sits cross-legged on the floor beside me and starts reading.

The bakery seems to hold its breath.

Lea reads fast. Faster than me. Her eyes move left to right, down the page, back up, then to the next page. Her mouth tightens. Once, she says, "Oh, fuck them," under her breath in a tone so cold it almost makes me smile.

Almost.

I pull the wooden box from the compartment and set it between us.

Her eyes flick to it.

"That the book?"

I nod.

She exhales slowly.

"Okay."

"Okay?"

"Not okay. But information."

"Do you think this is why?"

She looks at the box, then the papers.

"I don't know."

"I found it yesterday."

"I know."

"I made six cinnamon rolls with barely any magic."

"I also know. Half the town is texting about them."

"That's not comforting."

"I didn't intend it to be."

I wrap my arms around my knees.

"What if someone knows? What if Applegate knows? What if this building has always been something and Kaytie sold it to me because she knew and now someone is trying to take it?"

Lea sets the papers down.

"Look at me."

I don't want to.

"Dottie."

Her face is soft now, but not pitying.

Pity would make me mean, and I'm too tired to apologize later.

"This may be about magic," she says. "It may be about money. It may be about some legal technicality Applegate is exploiting because predatory people love old paperwork. We don't know yet."

"I can't lose it."

"I know."

"No, Lea. I can't. This is not just a shop."

"I know babe."

"It's downstairs and upstairs. It's my income. My apartment. My kitchen. Baylin works here. Derek works here. I have a loan. I have ingredients that hum, which is new and frankly rude, but apparently also mine. I have regulars. I have people who come here because May says my lemon bars make her feel like her husband is still alive for five minutes."

Lea's eyes shine.

I keep going because stopping will make me cry harder.

"This is the first place I didn't have to pack a bag because someone changed their mind about me."

Lea's face crumples for one second before she controls it. "Oh, Dottie."

"No pity."

"Not pity. Rage."

"That I'll accept."

She reaches for my hand.

I let her take it.

That should be its own miracle.

Her thumb brushes my bandaged burn, careful not to press.

"You know why I set up a visit for you at The Arcane Room?" she asks.

I let out a wet laugh. "Because you're a menace with excellent instincts?"

"Yes. But not only."

"Good to know."

"Because I could see you disappearing."

I go still.

Lea's grip tightens.

"You were working yourself into the floor. You were calling survival peace. You were treating every want like a bill you couldn't afford. And I knew if something big happened, something that asked you to depend on someone, you would either lock every door or drown quietly behind the counter."

The prep lights hum.

My chest aches.

"I didn't know this was coming," she says, glancing at the papers. "But I knew there was a chain. You just couldn't see it yet."

My palm warms. "I saw it," I whisper.

Her eyes flick to mine. "Did you?"

"Yes."

"And?"

"I don't know how to use that here."

Lea's mouth softens.

"Then we start small."

I laugh weakly. "Everyone keeps saying that. I'm beginning to resent small things."

"Small things keep people alive."

"Big things take buildings."

"Lawyers take buildings back."

My stomach drops.

"Lea."

"You know what I'm going to say."

"No."

"Yes."

"I cannot afford Lorenzo."

"You cannot afford not to talk to him."

"He asked me out yesterday."

Her eyebrows rise. "Did he?"

"I said no."

"Good."

I glare. "That's not supportive."

"It's extremely supportive. You said no when no was true. I'm proud of you."

"I think he was only asking because he felt bad about my hand."

Lea gives me a look so flat it could level cake layers.

"What?"

"Dottie."

"What?"

"Men like Lorenzo Moretti don't ask women out because of minor coffee burns."

"You don't know that."

"I know many things."

"You're a bookstore owner, not an oracle."

"I own a bookstore in Coral Cove. That's oracle-adjacent."

I sigh.

She picks up the papers again and taps the top page.

"This is not about him asking you out. This is about the building. This is about you needing a lawyer. He is the best in town."

"He is expensive."

"Yep."

"I have no money for a high-priced lawyer. I barely have money for a low-priced lawyer. I have money for ingredients, payroll, utilities, loan payments, insurance, and apparently future magical ethics consultations."

Lea's mouth twitches.

"Maybe he will work something out."

"I cannot ask him to do that."

"Yes, you can."

"No. I cannot walk into that man's office after turning him down and ask him to save my entire life."

"You're not asking him to save your entire life. You're asking a lawyer for legal advice."

"My entire life is legally described on page three."

"Fair."

I press the heels of my hands to my eyes.

"I hate that I need help."

Lea's voice softens. "That's the thing, isn't it?"

I lower my hands.

"What?"

"The chain."

I stare at her.

She nods toward the papers, the box, the bakery around us.

"This is not just Applegate trying to take your building. This is every room you ever got removed from. Every adult who made your safety temporary. Every time someone called you resilient and then left you to carry your life in a garbage bag."

My throat closes.

"And now," she says, "the universe has delivered the worst possible test with a court date attached."

"That's not comforting."

"No. But it's clear."

I look around the bakery.

The counters. The ovens. The hidden compartment. The display cases. The little tables where people sit and complain about the weather while eating cookies. The old wood. The floor I mop. The front door I lock every night.

Mine.

Or maybe not.

No.

Mine enough to fight for.

"What if he says no?" I ask.

"Then we find someone else."

"What if he says yes but makes me feel small?"

"Then I will ruin him socially and Baylin will probably curse his coffee."

"She can do that?"

"I assume."

I laugh.

It hurts, but it helps.

"What if he pities me?"

"Then you tell him you need legal help, not pity."

"I don't want him to see me like this," I say.

Lea looks at the papers. "Scared?"

"Yes."

"Dottie, everyone who loves you already knows you get scared."

"That's upsetting."

"It should not be."

"I prefer to be mysterious."

"You're a baker with a secret magic recipe book and a legal crisis. You have achieved plenty of mystery."

I laugh again.

This one lasts longer.

Then it dies.

"I can't lose this place."

Lea squeezes my hand.

"Then tomorrow, we go to Lorenzo."

"We?"

"I will walk you there."

"I can walk myself."

"I know."

I look at her.

She looks back.

And for once, I don't argue.

The next morning, I don't sleep because sleeping would require my body to believe the world is not actively trying to evict me.

I spend the night at the kitchen table upstairs with the papers spread out, reading them until every sentence loses meaning. I make notes. Bad notes. Notes like WHAT DOES THIS MEAN???? and APPLEGATE SOUNDS LIKE A MAN WHO WEARS BOAT SHOES. I gather the purchase agreement from my filing cabinet. The loan documents. The insurance policy. The deed copy Kaytie gave me. The folder of old building permits. Receipts. Tax statements. Anything that proves I did not imagine owning my life.

At four in the morning, I go downstairs and start the ovens.

Because the world can sue me, apparently, but it cannot stop bread from needing to proof.

* * *

Baylin arrives at two-thirty and says nothing when she sees my face. She only takes over bread and sets a mug of coffee beside my elbow.

Derek arrives at six, takes one look at me, and asks, "Should I be afraid?"

"Probably."

He nods. "Cool."

Good kid.

By nine, I have explained only the basics to them. Legal issue. Possible building dispute. Talking to lawyer. No panic.

Baylin laughs once at no panic.

Derek does panic, but quietly, and then asks if his job is gone.

That nearly breaks me.

"No," I say too fast. "No. We are not there. We are talking to a lawyer. We are not there."

He nods.

He doesn't look reassured.

Neither am I.

At ten, Lea arrives.

She wears black jeans, a dark green sweater, and the expression of a woman prepared to commit crimes in defense of independent businesses. She takes one look at me and holds out her hand.

"Papers?"

I hand her the folder.

"Coffee?"

I hand her a cup.

"Have you eaten?"

I glare.

"Dottie."

"I had half a croissant."

"Eat the other half."

"I don't know where it is."

"That's a troubling answer."

She finds it on a plate near the register, puts it in my hand, and watches until I take a bite.

"Bossy," I mutter.

"Alive," she returns.

At ten-thirty, I call Lorenzo's office.

My voice almost cracks on his name.

Molly answers.

"Moretti Law."

"Hi. Molly? It's Dorothea Thompson from Knead the Dough."

"Oh, hi, Dottie. Please tell me you're calling with mocha cream cookies."

"Not today. I need to make an appointment with Mr. Moretti. It's urgent."

Something in her voice changes at urgent.

Professional. Immediate.

"Are you safe?"

The question startles me.

"Yes."

"Good. What kind of urgent?"

"I was served papers last night. Property dispute. Hearing in less than two weeks. They're trying to take my building."

There is a pause.

Not long.

Long enough.

"Can you come at noon?"

I look at Lea.

She nods hard.

"Yes."

"Bring everything. Purchase documents, loan papers, the complaint, any notices, anything with the building address."

"I have a folder."

"Good. He'll see you at noon tomorrow."

"Thank you."

"Dottie?"

"Yes?"

"Eat something before you come."

I blink.

"Does everyone in this town think I don't eat?"

"Yes," Molly says. "See you at noon."

She hangs up.

I stare at the phone.

Lea smiles.

"What?"

"Nothing."

"That was a face."

"You're going to Lorenzo's office."

"I know."

"And?"

"And I feel like I'm going to throw up."

"Normal."

"Or pass out."

"Also normal."

"Or set fire to Applegate Holdings."

"Understandable, but save that for plan C."

"What's plan B?"

"Baylin curses them."

I look toward the kitchen.

Baylin calls, "I heard that and I'm willing."

* * *

The walk to Lorenzo's office the next day should take four minutes.

It takes twelve because I stop once to breathe, once to turn around, and once because Mrs. Talbot asks if I'm unwell and Lea lies directly to her face with the smoothness of a criminal.

"She has a meeting," Lea says.

"With whom?" Mrs. Talbot asks.

"Destiny."

Then Lea pulls me forward.

Spellbound Stories glows warmly across the street. The Arcane Room is farther down, its sign dark in the daytime. I don't look at it too long.

I'm not going to fantasy.

I'm going to a lawyer.

A real man.

A real office.

A real chance to be told no.

Lorenzo's office is in a restored brick building with black

trim, tall windows, and a brass plaque that says MORETTI LAW in clean, expensive letters. Everything about it looks calm, polished, and slightly intimidating. Like the building itself knows how to argue.

Lea stops beside me at the door.

"I can go in with you."

I almost say yes. "I need to do the first part alone," I say.

Lea's expression softens.

"Okay."

"But stay close."

"I'll be at Spellbound. Text me if you need me to come back with a shovel."

"I thought we were avoiding shovels."

"Plan D."

I laugh, and then I open the door before I lose my nerve.

The office smells like coffee, paper, leather, and something lemony from a cleaning product trying very hard not to smell like fear. Molly sits at the front desk, red hair clipped up, glasses perched on her nose. She looks up and smiles.

"Dottie," she says. "Come in."

"I brought the folder."

"I see that."

"I did not bring cookies."

"Tragic, but understandable under the circumstances."

That helps.

A little.

She gestures to the chairs. "He's finishing a call. It should only be a minute."

I sit.

The chair is too comfortable.

I clutch the folder in my lap and try not to rehearse every possible version of the conversation. He could say the case is impossible. He could say I waited too long. He could say his retainer is more than my monthly rent and then look at me with lawyer sympathy, which might kill me. He could bring up the dinner I turned down. He could not bring it up.

Molly watches me for a second.

Then she stands, walks to a little side table, and pours me water.

"Drink."

I almost laugh.

Hydration again.

Apparently every person adjacent to my life has joined a conspiracy of basic bodily maintenance.

I drink.

Molly returns to her desk.

"Lorenzo is good at this," she says.

I look up.

"At property disputes?"

"At people trying to take things that aren't theirs."

My throat tightens.

Before I can answer, the door to Lorenzo's office opens.

He steps out.

Dark gray suit. White shirt. No tie today, which somehow makes him look more dangerous, not less. His sleeves are rolled once at the wrist, revealing forearms I have no business noticing during a legal emergency.

His eyes find me.

The office narrows.

"Dorothea."

My name again.

Not fantasy.

Not safe.

Real.

I stand too quickly.

The folder nearly slips.

His gaze drops to it, then back to my face. Something in his expression shifts.

Softens.

Sharpens.

Both.

"Come in," he says.

I walk toward him, fear and hope moving side by side in my chest.

This is it.

My last chance to save my bakery.

My home.

The first place I ever stopped asking permission to stay.

I step into Lorenzo's office.

And for once, I don't apologize for needing help.

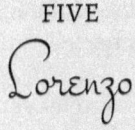

FIVE

Lorenzo

Dorothea steps into my office like a woman walking into court already certain the verdict has been decided against her.

That's the first thing I notice.

Not her hair, though it's impossible not to notice. Strawberry blond, pulled back beneath a pink bandana, with a few loose pieces curling around her face as if the bakery itself refuses to let her look too polished. Not the flour dusted across her forehead, although the sight of it does something to me I have no business examining while she clutches a folder like it's the only thing keeping the floor beneath her intact.

No.

The first thing I notice is how carefully she holds herself.

Shoulders set. Spine straight. Chin lifted just enough to look brave but not enough to convince me she feels it.

She is terrified.

And she is furious at herself for being terrified.

That combination is familiar enough to make my chest tighten.

"Please," I say, gesturing to the chair across from my desk. "Sit."

She does.

Not heavily. Not collapsing. She lowers herself into the

chair with control, as if even fear has to be managed neatly before it's allowed to take up space.

Her fingers grip the edge of the folder in her lap.

I close the door behind her.

Not all the way.

Then I think better of it and leave it cracked.

Dorothea notices more than she wants people to know.

"Molly is right outside," I say. "Door can stay open or closed. Your call."

Her eyes flick to mine.

For one second, something passes through them. Surprise, maybe. Or relief. Or suspicion about the fact that I anticipated a need she had not voiced.

"Open is fine," she says.

"Open it is."

I return to my chair.

My office feels different with her in it.

Usually, this room does exactly what I built it to do. It performs certainty. The polished walnut desk, the framed degrees, the shelves, the expensive chairs, the clean lines. Clients come in frightened, angry, desperate, or arrogant, and the office tells them I know what I'm doing before I say a word.

Dorothea sits across from me and somehow makes the whole room feel too polished.

Like a suit worn over a bruise.

I fold my hands on the desk.

"What happened?"

She takes a breath.

It catches.

Only a little.

Then she pulls a stack of papers from the folder and slides them toward me.

"I was served last night."

All the heat in my body cools.

I take the papers.

Complaint. Summons. Notice of hearing. Applegate Holdings.

I already know the top-level shape from the filing alert,

but holding the documents she was handed at her own door makes the case feel more personal. More invasive.

I force that thought aside.

Anger is useful only after facts.

I scan the first page.

Dorothea sits perfectly still.

That's the second thing I notice.

Not fidgeting. Not talking too much. Not trying to fill the silence. Her hands are folded in her lap now, fingers pressed together so tightly the knuckles have gone pale.

"How much have you read?" I ask.

"All of it."

"Did you understand it?"

"No."

The word comes quick. Bare.

Then she presses her lips together, as if embarrassed by honesty.

I find her eyes. "There is no reason you should understand this."

"It has my name on it."

"That doesn't mean it was written for you."

Her brow furrows.

"Legal documents are often written to intimidate as much as inform," I say. "This one does both."

Her throat moves when she swallows.

"So it's bad."

"It's serious."

"That sounds like lawyer bad."

"It's lawyer bad," I admit. "Not hopeless bad."

The smallest breath leaves her.

I return to the papers.

Applegate Holdings is claiming superior title through an old transfer irregularity. They allege that Kaytie Ann Heart lacked clear authority to sell the property, or that the title was defective when she acquired it. They are seeking declaratory relief, possession, costs, and an expedited hearing.

Aggressive.

Too aggressive.

The timeline is the point. They want pressure. They want

panic. They want Dorothea to look at the legal language, imagine losing everything, and make some desperate agreement before anyone competent reads the file.

Predatory.

I turn the page.

Then the next.

"Did Applegate contact you before serving this?"

"No."

"No demand letter? No inquiry? No title question? No offer?"

She shakes her head.

"Nothing."

"Have you ever heard of them?"

"No. I looked them up at three in the morning because apparently panic gives me research skills. It's a holding company. I couldn't find much."

"Who sold you the building?"

"Kaytie Ann Heart."

"How long ago?"

"Five years."

"And you worked for her before that?"

Dorothea nods. "Since I was eighteen. Apprentice baker at first. Then more. She taught me almost everything I know. She owned the building and the business. When I started talking about wanting my own bakery someday, she said she was ready for a change." Her mouth tightens slightly. "She sold it to me. The business. The equipment. The building. I used my savings for the deposit and got a loan for the rest."

"Do you have the purchase agreement?"

"Yes."

"Deed?"

"Yes."

"Loan documents?"

"Yes."

"Title insurance policy?"

She hesitates.

"I think so."

"Closing papers?"

"Yes."

"Prior tax statements? Payment history? Insurance?"

She lifts the folder in her lap.

"I brought everything I could find."

Good girl, I almost say.

The thought arrives so abruptly I have to look back at the papers.

Not the time.

Not the place.

Not mine to say.

"Excellent," I say instead.

Her cheeks color faintly anyway.

Interesting.

No.

Irrelevant.

Focus.

I take the folder when she hands it over. It's meticulously organized. Labeled tabs. Deed. Loan. Insurance. Taxes. Closing. Correspondence. Permits. Receipts.

I glance up.

"This is very good."

"I like paperwork when it proves things belong where they belong."

The sentence is quiet.

There is flour on her forehead. A bandage on her hand from the coffee burn. Shadows beneath her eyes from a night without sleep. She looks like someone who has been carrying the building on her back since the moment those papers hit her hands.

"If I lose," she says, "I lose the bakery."

The words come evenly, almost too evenly.

"Yes."

"And the apartment."

"I'm afraid so."

Her eyes shine, but she blinks hard before tears can form.

"If I can't open or I have to leave, I lose everything. The ovens, the kitchen, the upstairs, the loan, my employees." Her fingers twist in the fabric of her apron. "Baylin works nights. Derek is still learning, but he needs the hours. I have regulars who come in every morning like the place is part of their routine. Kaytie trusted me with it. I thought it was mine."

"It's yours."

Her eyes snap to mine.

I should not have said it that way. Too absolute. Too emotional. The law is a machine that punishes certainty when it gets ahead of evidence.

But I mean it.

At least enough to fight like hell.

"It's yours unless a court decides otherwise," I correct. "And from what I can see, Applegate has a lot to prove."

Her face folds for half a second.

Not crying.

Trying not to.

"They're trying to take the first place I ever got to keep," she whispers.

The sentence hits beneath the ribs.

I sit back slowly.

The office goes quiet.

Molly's phone rings outside, muffled through the cracked door. A car passes on the street below. Somewhere down the block, a gull screams.

Dorothea looks away quickly.

"I'm sorry," she says. "That was dramatic."

"No."

Her mouth twists. "It was."

"No," I repeat, firmer.

She looks back.

I keep my voice even. "That was relevant."

Her breath catches.

Relevant.

Not dramatic. Not pitiable. Not too much.

Relevant.

I can almost see the word enter her and look for a place to sit.

"I need to ask you some practical questions," I say.

She nods quickly. "Okay."

"Has anyone approached you about buying the building?"

"No."

"Any recent complaints from the landlord?"

"I don't have a landlord."

"Right. From neighbors, city, zoning, anyone?"

"No."

"Any repairs or permits outstanding?"

"Nothing major. The vent hood inspection passed. I have some old permit copies in the folder."

"Any reason someone would think the building is worth more than the purchase price now?"

She laughs once.

It's not humor.

"It's Coral Cove. Everything is worth more than it was five years ago."

True.

"Any unusual visitors? Anyone asking about the building history? Kaytie? Old recipes? Storage spaces?"

That last one is a risk.

I don't know why I add it.

Maybe because Dorothea's hand shifts toward her apron pocket before she stops it.

Maybe because Molly mentioned the cinnamon rolls and half the town suddenly behaving like they had been hugged by their grandmothers.

Maybe because Coral Cove has taught me that some legal disputes wear practical clothes over stranger bodies.

Dorothea's eyes flick away.

There.

Something.

"Dorothea."

"It's probably nothing."

"Probably nothing tends to become something at the worst possible time."

She presses her lips together.

"Someone came in a few weeks ago asking whether Kaytie left anything in the building."

I go still.

"Who?"

"I don't know. A man. Mid-fifties maybe. Gray hair. Expensive raincoat. He said he used to know Kaytie and wondered if she left any old boxes or records. I told him if he was looking for something, he needed to contact her directly."

"Did he give a name?"

"No."

"Did he buy anything?"

"A black coffee. He didn't drink it."

"Can you describe him?"

"Yes."

"I'll need that."

Her fingers tighten. "Do you think it's connected?"

"I don't know yet."

"But maybe."

"Maybe."

Her face pales slightly.

I hate that she is sitting in my office with her life translated into a file, and I hate that the first instinct in me is not merely professional. It's personal. Primitive. The kind of anger that wants to become a weapon before it becomes a strategy.

If someone is trying to take her home, I will end them.

Not physically.

Probably.

Legally, yes. Financially if necessary. Publicly if they invite it.

I will make them regret choosing her.

The thought arrives clean, immediate, and dangerous.

Not because I should not protect a client.

Because she is already more than that in my mind, and that is exactly where danger begins.

I set the papers down and take one breath.

Then another.

"Here is what I can do immediately," I say.

Dorothea leans forward.

"I will review every document you brought. I will pull the full chain of title. I will review county records, tax records, and prior transfers. I will look into Applegate Holdings, its owners, and any connected entities. If there is a defect, I will find out whether it's real, technical, curable, or manufactured."

"Manufactured?"

"Yes."

"People can manufacture legal claims?"

"People can manufacture almost anything if they assume the other side is too scared or too broke to fight."

She flinches.

"This hearing date is aggressive," I continue. "That doesn't mean they win. It means they are trying to force urgency."

"Can you stop it?"

"I can likely ask for a continuance if needed. Depending on the facts, I may also challenge the request for immediate possession."

Her hands open in her lap, then close again.

"How much will this cost?"

This is question I have been dreading. Not because I cannot answer. Because there is no answer that doesn't shift the ground between us.

"My standard hourly rate is five hundred dollars."

Her face empties.

Not shock.

Confirmation of dread.

"Okay," she says.

"I require retainers for litigation."

"How much?"

"Usually ten thousand to start."

She inhales. It's a tiny sound. Barely there.

But I hear it.

Then she nods once, as if someone has handed her a box too heavy to lift and she is calculating how to break it into pieces.

"I can't," she says. "Not right now."

"I know."

Her eyes lift to mine.

The shame in them infuriates me.

Not at her.

Never at her.

"I can recommend someone more affordable," I say.

The words taste wrong, but I say them because they are necessary. "There are competent property attorneys in Port Townsend and Seattle with lower rates. I can give you names."

She nods slowly. "Okay."

"I can also offer a reduced rate."

Her brow furrows. "A payment plan?" Her fingers tighten again.

"Or," I say carefully, "I can take this pro bono."

Her eyes widen. "No."

The speed of her refusal surprises me. "No?" I ask.

"No. I can't let you do that."

"Why?"

"Because it's too much."

"That's not a legal objection."

"It's a person objection."

I almost smile.

Then I see her face.

She means it.

"I don't take charity," she says.

"It's not charity."

"What is it then?"

I pause.

Professional responsibility? Community care? Attraction dressed as generosity? The satisfaction of using my skills against a predatory company? A chance to prove my father wrong? A chance to be the kind of man my mother believed I could become?

Too many answers.

"It would be my decision," I say.

"And then I would owe you."

"No."

"Yes," she says, sharper now. "I would. Maybe not legally. Maybe not because you'd say it that way. But I would feel it. Every time I saw you. Every time your name came up. Every time something went wrong. I would feel like I had accepted something too big to repay."

My mouth closes. Accepting help as a door someone can lock later.

I sit back.

Molly's warning echoes again.

Don't litigate her pain.

I want to argue. To say that is not how I work. To insist I

don't hold debts over people. To promise I would never make her feel trapped.

But this is not about my intent.

It's about the shape of help in her body.

I choose my words carefully.

"I hear you."

She looks startled.

"I won't force pro bono representation on you," I say. "That would defeat the purpose of helping."

Her shoulders loosen a fraction.

"But I need you to understand something. If you leave here today with only names, Applegate keeps moving. You need someone who can act quickly."

"I know."

"And I'm good at this."

"I know."

"And expensive."

"I also know that."

A small smile flickers at the corner of her mouth.

"Reduced rate," I say. "Payment plan. Referral. Pro bono. Those are real options. You can take time to think, but not too much time."

She looks down at the papers.

"What would you recommend if I were anyone else?"

That question has teeth.

"If you were anyone else," I say, "I would tell you to hire the best litigator you can afford immediately."

"And if I can't afford one?"

"I would tell you to ask anyway."

She looks at me.

I hold her gaze.

Silence stretches between us.

This is where a better man might stop. This is where an ethical man should be very careful.

I'm ethical.

I'm not always better.

The fake girlfriend proposition sits behind my teeth like a bad idea wearing a tuxedo.

I hate that part of me thought of it before she even arrived.

Father in two weeks. Wedding plus-one. His threats. His obsession with appearances. Dorothea's honesty. Her softness that is not weakness. Her ability to make my usual charm feel like a cheap suit.

A mutual arrangement.

Legal services for a favor.

Dangerous.

Too easy to make coercive.

Too easy to dress my desire as practicality.

Too easy to use her desperation as leverage, even if I don't mean to.

I stand and walk to the window, needing the space.

Dorothea watches me, silent.

I deserve the discomfort.

Outside, Main Street moves in its usual small-town rhythm. A tourist couple looks into the window of Spell-bound Stories. Mrs. Talbot talks to a woman outside the florist. Across the street, Knead the Dough sits bright and vulnerable, pink paint under gray sky.

Her building.

Her home.

Her first kept place.

I turn back.

"I have a proposition," I say.

Dorothea goes very still.

I lift one hand before she can speak.

"And before I say it, I want to be very clear. Your legal options don't depend on agreeing. I will still give you a referral. I will still spend an hour today reviewing enough to tell you what danger you're in. If you want a payment plan, we can discuss one. If you want me to take it pro bono, that remains on the table, even if you say no to what I'm about to ask."

Her eyes narrow.

"You're making me nervous."

"It was not meant to." I return to my chair but don't sit. "My father is coming to Coral Cove in two weeks."

"Okay."

"He is difficult."

"That sounds like a polite word."

"It's the polite word."

"What's the accurate word?"

"Cruel."

Her face softens before she can hide it.

I don't want the softness.

I do.

I continue before I make that complicated.

"He believes I have wasted my life here. He wants me back in the city, at his firm, under his control. He has threatened to cut financial ties if I cannot prove I'm building something respectable."

Dorothea's mouth tightens.

"I'm sorry."

"I'm not looking for sympathy."

"I didn't think you were."

The quiet answer lands.

I sit.

"There is a wedding coming up. Ophelia and Lillian's. My father will be there. There will also be at least one dinner with him and possibly several town events where he will attempt to assess my life as if it's a poorly organized deposition."

"That sounds awful."

"It will be."

"And you need a date."

"I need a buffer," I say. "A witness. Someone he cannot easily dismiss."

"Why me?"

Because you say no.

Because you look at me like you don't care who my father thinks I am. Because you're the only person in town who makes me feel like I might have to tell the truth if you asked the right question. Because when you called the bakery the first place you got to keep, I wanted to burn the world down and build you a better one.

I say none of that.

"Because you're honest," I say. "Because you're kind without being weak. Because you're respected here. Because my father expects flash and performance, and you're neither."

Her eyebrows lift. "That was almost a compliment."

"It was entirely a compliment."

"Needs work."

"I'm told that often."

Her lips twitch.

The room eases by one degree.

"I'm asking," I say carefully, "if you would be willing to pretend to be my girlfriend while he is in town."

She blinks.

Once.

Twice.

"Your fake girlfriend."

"Yes."

"To impress your father."

"To survive him, if we are being precise."

"And in exchange…"

"In exchange, I handle your case at no cost to you."

Her shoulders tense.

I hate myself a little.

"But only if that feels better to you than the other options. This is not your only path. If it feels like I'm using your crisis to get what I want, say no."

Her eyes search my face.

"Are you?"

The directness of it almost makes me smile.

Almost.

"I'm trying not to."

"That's an interesting answer."

"It's the honest one."

She sits back slowly.

I let the silence work.

Not as pressure.

As room.

She looks at the papers. Then at me. Then down at her bandaged hand.

"What exactly would being your fake girlfriend involve?"

"Public appearances. Dinner with my father. Ophelia's wedding. Possibly a few casual sightings around town to make it believable."

"Sightings," she repeats.

"Coral Cove does most of the surveillance for free."

"That's true."

"No one can know the arrangement is fake."

"Lea?"

I pause.

"Would you need to tell her?"

Dorothea gives me a look.

"I tell Lea when I find weird mushrooms at the farmers market."

"Then Lea."

"And Molly?"

I glance toward the cracked door.

Molly is absolutely listening.

"Molly," I say.

From the front desk, a faint cough.

Dorothea's mouth twitches.

I close my eyes for one second.

"Anyone else?"

"No," she says. "Not unless necessary."

"Agreed."

She chews her lower lip.

I notice.

I wish I did not.

"Stop that," I say before I can think better of it.

Her eyes widen.

I immediately regret the tone.

"Sorry," I say. "That sounded like a command."

"It was."

"Yes."

A flush creeps up her neck.

Interesting again.

Still irrelevant.

Mostly.

"You bite your lip when you're thinking," I say. "I thought you were going to hurt yourself."

Her gaze drops.

"Oh."

I clear my throat.

"We should write this down."

Her eyes snap back up.

"The fake relationship?"

"The terms."

Relief moves through her face so quickly I almost miss it.

Then something else.

Recognition.

Like I have said a word in a language she has only recently learned.

"Yes," she says. "Terms."

I pull a legal pad from my drawer and set it between us.

"Not a formal contract," I say.

"Why not?"

"Because I don't want a paper trail titled fake girlfriend agreement."

"Fair."

"And because I'm not making this feel like a binding exchange you cannot leave."

She watches me carefully.

I write at the top of the page:

Fake Relationship Terms

"That sounds terrible."

"It sounds accurate," she says.

"Accuracy is not always branding."

"Add tentative."

I glance at her.

She lifts her chin.

"Everything should be revisable."

Fake Relationship Terms, Tentative and Revisable

She nods once, satisfied.

Something in my chest loosens "First," I say. "You can end this arrangement at any time."

She leans forward.

"Any time?"

"Yes."

"Even if your father is at dinner?"

"Yes."

"Even if we are at the wedding?"

"Yes."

"Even if it makes you look bad?"

I look at her. "Yes."

She studies me. Then nods. "Write that."

I do.

Dorothea may end the arrangement at any time, for any reason.

I push the pad toward her.

She reads it.

"Lorenzo may also end the arrangement," she says. "at any time, for any reason."

I lift an eyebrow.

"I'm not trapping you either," she says.

Something warm moves through me.

Lorenzo may end the arrangement at any time, for any reason.

"Legal services?" she asks.

"Yes."

I think carefully.

"If either of us ends the fake relationship, I continue representing you unless you choose otherwise."

Her lips part slightly.

"You would?"

"Yes."

"Even if I embarrass you in front of your father?"

"Yes."

"Even if I end it because I just don't want to do it anymore?"

"Yes."

"That seems unfair to you."

"It's necessary."

"Why?"

"Because otherwise your consent to the arrangement is contaminated by fear of losing your lawyer."

Dorothea looks at me in a way I cannot read.

Not easily.

That bothers me.

It also makes me want to earn the answer.

She nods slowly.

"Write that."

I do.

Legal representation continues regardless of relationship arrangement, unless Dorothea chooses to end representation.

She looks at the line for a long moment.

Then she says, softer, "Thank you."

"You're welcome."

"Events," she says, shifting like she needs to move before the feeling gets too large.

"Advanced notice."

"Yes. I wake up at four most mornings. Sometimes earlier. I need time to schedule coverage. Derek is still training, Baylin works nights, and if I'm out too late, the bakery suffers."

"What's reasonable notice?"

"For planned events? At least forty-eight hours."

"For emergencies?"

"Define emergency."

"My father appearing without warning."

She grimaces. "Twenty-four if possible. If not, I reserve the right to say no."

"Good."

Her eyes flick up.

Planned events require at least forty-eight hours' notice. Emergency events require as much notice as possible. Dorothea may decline any event.

She watches the pen move.

"What about duration?" she asks.

"Until my father leaves town or until Applegate is resolved, whichever comes first?"

"That ties it to the case too much."

She is right.

I pause.

"Until after Ophelia and Lillian's wedding, with option to extend by mutual agreement."

"Yes."

I write it.

Arrangement lasts through Ophelia and Lillian's wedding, with extension only by mutual agreement.

Dorothea exhales.

"Public behavior."

I set the pen down for a second.

"We should discuss what you're comfortable with."

She nods, but pink rises in her cheeks.

"Hand-holding?" I ask.

"Yes."

The answer is quiet, but clear.

Hand-holding: yes.

"Arm around your waist?"

She thinks.

"Yes, in public."

"Not private?"

Her eyes lift to mine.

The room warms.

"Maybe private," she says.

Arm around waist: yes in public, maybe in private.

She looks at the page.

"Maybe," she repeats, almost to herself.

"Is maybe useful?"

Her mouth curves faintly. "Very."

"What else?"

"Hugging," she says.

"Yes?"

"Yes, but not surprise hugs from behind."

"Absolutely not."

Hugging: yes. No surprise touch from behind.

She stares at the line.

"Thank you."

"Dorothea."

"What?"

"That should not require thanks."

"Maybe not."

"But it does?"

Her gaze slips away.

"Sometimes."

I want to ask who taught her that touch arrives without warning.

I do not. Not yet anyway.

"Kissing," I say.

Her blush deepens.

My body reacts with immediate, inconvenient interest.

I ignore it, because I'm a professional and not a boy who has never seen a woman's mouth.

Mostly.

"Kissing," she repeats.

"It would be natural in a fake relationship."

"Yes."

"We can limit it."

"To what?"

"Cheek. Forehead. Mouth. Public only. Private only. No kissing unless discussed in the moment."

She frowns in thought.

The fact that she takes the question seriously nearly does me in.

So many people treat boundaries as mood killers. Dorothea looks at them like ingredients. The difference between collapse and structure.

"Cheeks are fine," she says.

I write it.

"Forehead is..." She pauses. "Maybe. It feels more intimate than cheek."

"It is."

Her eyes flick to mine.

Forehead: maybe.

"Mouth?" I ask.

Her throat moves.

"Public mouth kissing is yes if needed."

My hand stills.

If needed.

God help me.

"And private?"

She looks at me for one long second.

My office disappears at the edges.

"Maybe," she says.

The word lands low.

Mouth kissing: yes in public if needed, maybe in private.

"No surprise kisses," she adds quickly.

"Agreed."

"No copping a feel."

A laugh breaks out of me before I can stop it.

Her eyes narrow.

"I'm serious."

"I know."

"I mean it. No hand drifting where hands should not drift for theatrical effect."

"I agree."

"No goosing my ass."

"I have never goosed anyone's ass in my life."

"That cannot possibly be true."

I grin. "Fine. Not since law school."

Her mouth opens.

I laugh again. "I'm joking."

"I don't believe you."

"Good. Skepticism will serve you well in this world."

She crosses her arms making the apron pull tighter over her chest.

I look at the legal pad because I'm not an idiot.

No sexual touching. No "accidental" touching. No goosing.

She leans over the pad. "Put ass after goosing, so there's no ambiguity." Her cheeks are bright pink, but her chin is lifted.

I make the correction

She nods solemnly.

"This is the least formal legal document I have ever drafted," I say.

"Then it can have ass in it."

I press the back of my hand against my mouth.

She smiles.

Small.

Victorious.

I'm in trouble.

"What about signals?" I ask.

Her smile fades into concentration.

"Signals?"

"If you're uncomfortable and don't want to say so in front of people."

She sits back. "That's smart."

"I have moments."

"Rarely?"

"More often than you think," I wink. "Choose a phrase."

"For stop?"

"For pause, check in, get me out of here, or I need a second."

She thinks.

"Could we have more than one?"

"Absolutely."

She looks down at her palm. "Green means okay," she says.

I find her eyes again. "Green."

"Yes. Yellow means slow down, check in, or change something. Red means stop."

My chest tightens.

Those are not random.

I don't ask.

Not yet.

"Good system," I say.

Her eyes soften in a way that suggests the words matter.

Signals: green means okay. Yellow means pause/check in/adjust. Red means stop immediately.

I underline red.

She watches. "Immediately," she says.

"Immediately."

"Even if it's inconvenient."

"Especially then."

The room shifts around us.

Something fragile settles.

"Privacy," she says.

"What about it?"

"No talking about my personal history with your father unless I offer it. No making me sound like a charity project."

"I would never."

She holds my gaze.

I write it anyway.

No charity language. No pity narrative. Dorothea controls her personal history.

Her shoulders lower.

"My father will pry," I say.

"Does he know how not to?"

"Nope."

"Fantastic."

"You can deflect. You can tell the truth. You can tell him it's not his business. I will back you, always."

"Will you?"

The question is soft. It's not about my father. Not entirely. "Yes," I say.

Her gaze holds mine.

For the first time since she walked in, she looks like she might believe me.

"Your turn," she says.

"My terms?"

"Yes."

I glance at the pad. Then at her. "No lying about the case to me."

She blinks. "I would never."

"Panic lies count."

Her mouth closes.

"Minimizing counts."

Her expression shifts.

"Fine," she says.

"Good."

Dorothea won't minimize case facts, financial facts, or relevant fear.

She leans over.

"Relevant fear?"

"Yes."

"Is all fear relevant?"

"Not all. Most."

"That seems broad."

"It is."

She sighs. "Fine."

Lorenzo won't use fear against Dorothea.

She reads that line twice.

"Good," she whispers.

I continue.

"No accepting contact from Applegate or anyone connected to them without telling me."

"Agreed."

"No signing anything."

"Obviously."

"You would be surprised."

"I would not."

"No direct negotiation without counsel."

"That means you."

"Yes."

Her mouth curves. "Counsel sounds fancy."

"I'm fancy."

"You're wearing a suit in a town where half the businesses have pun names."

"I contain multitudes."

She laughs softly.

I write the terms.

Then pause.

"There is another issue."

Her smile fades.

"What?"

"I have to say this plainly. If I'm your lawyer and we are pretending to date, there are ethical complications."

Her face goes still.

"Okay."

"The fake relationship is public performance, not real intimacy. But perception matters. Power dynamics matter. Your ability to fire me matters. Your ability to end the arrangement matters. If at any point this feels like pressure, we stop."

"Okay."

"If this becomes real…" I pause.

The word hangs there between us.

Real.

Her cheeks color.

Mine probably do too, though I have more practice hiding it.

"If anything changes," I say, correcting course, "we revisit representation. I won't let my personal interest compromise your case."

Her eyes sharpen.

"Personal interest?"

I should have known she would catch that. "Yes."

Dorothea locks eyes. "What kind of personal interest?"

"The kind that makes me want to be very careful."

Her lips part.

Only the truth, set on the desk between us like a glass of water.

She swallows. "Careful is good."

"Yes," I say. "It is."

I write:

> *If personal circumstances change, both parties revisit legal representation and arrangement boundaries.*

She watches the pen move.

Then she says, "Add right to renegotiate."

I do.

> *Right to renegotiate at any time.*

She reaches for the pen.

I hand it to her.

Her fingers brush mine.

A small touch.

She writes at the bottom:

> *No, is a complete sentence.*

Her handwriting is rounder than mine. Less aggressive. More careful.

She looks at the line. "Okay?"

I nod. "More than okay."

She sets down the pen.

I read the whole page aloud. Because I want both of us to hear the structure.

By the time I finish, Dorothea's posture has changed. Not relaxed exactly. But steadier. Less like a woman waiting to be trapped by someone else's generosity.

More like a woman standing inside her own yes.

"What do you think?" I ask.

"I think this is ridiculous."

I smile.

"And weirdly helpful," she adds.

"Both can be true."

"Unfortunately, yes."

"Do you want time to decide?"

She looks at the papers. The folder. The legal pad. Then at me. "Yes." Her brow furrows.

"But not too much time," I say. "For the legal case. The fake relationship can wait."

"My building cannot."

"No."

"I can say no to the fake girlfriend part and you'll still review the case?"

"Yes."

"And if I say yes, I can change my mind?"

"Yes."

"And if I say yes, you're not allowed to act like you own me."

The words are sharper than before.

Not playful.

I meet them directly.

"I will never own you."

Her eyes widen slightly.

I continue, because this matters to her and that means it matters to me too. "Not publicly. Not privately. Not as your lawyer. Not as your fake boyfriend. Not if something else ever happens."

"Okay," she says, softer. She looks at the legal pad again. "I'll do it."

I keep still.

"Dorothea."

"I'll pretend to be your girlfriend. Through the wedding. With the terms. And with the understanding that legal representation continues even if I stop."

"Yes."

"And you won't call me a charity project."

"Never."

"And you won't flirt your way around my boundaries."

A smile tugs at my mouth. She narrows her eyes. "Lorenzo."

"I won't flirt my way around your boundaries," I say. "I may flirt within the boundaries if that is acceptable."

Her blush returns with force.

"Maybe," she says.

Flirting: maybe.

She stares. "You did not have to write that."

"Everything is revisable."

"Oh my God." The laugh leaves her unexpectedly. It's small, startled, and beautiful.

My chest tightens.

I want to make her laugh again.

I also want to win her case, ruin Applegate, survive my father, and find out what Dorothea Thompson looks like when she lets someone else carry one corner of what she has been hauling alone.

That's too much wanting for one office.

I tear the page carefully from the legal pad and make a copy. One for her. One for me. Not a formal contract. Not filed. Not billed. But real enough to matter.

When I return from the copier, Molly is staring very hard at her computer screen.

Too hard.

I place a copy in front of Dorothea.

"For you."

She folds it and tucks it into her folder.

Then she reaches into her apron pocket and pulls out a small notebook.

"What's this?"

"My own notes."

"About the case?"

"Partly."

She opens it and writes something.
I don't mean to read it. I catch it anyway.

Legal help doesn't mean surrendering myself.

My throat tightens.
She snaps the notebook shut.
I pretend I saw nothing.
"Next steps," I say.
"Yes. Please."
"I will copy your documents, review the title chain today, and contact Applegate's attorney by close of business. I will also prepare an initial response and assess whether we need to move to continue the hearing."
"Okay."
"You won't panic if I call with questions?"
She gives me a look.
"Please try not to panic," I amend. "You will eat something?"
"I own a bakery."
"That doesn't answer the question."
Her mouth twists. "Fine."
"And you will call me if anyone contacts you about the property."
"Of course. Thank you."
I slide my card across the desk. "My cell is written on the back."
She picks it up.
Her thumb brushes over the ink.
"Thank you."
"You said that already."
"I mean it more now."
That does something to me.
I stand because I need the desk between us to stop feeling like a suggestion.
She stands too.
For a moment, neither of us moves.
The fake girlfriend agreement sits between us in duplicate.
My father arrives in less than two weeks.

Applegate thinks Dorothea will fold.

Dorothea stands across from me with flour on her forehead and a legal storm in her hands, and I realize I have entered a case I cannot afford to lose for reasons that have nothing to do with my record.

I hold out my hand.

Not to shake.

Then realize that is exactly what it looks like.

Professional. Safe. Expected.

She looks at my hand.

Then at me.

Her palm slides into mine.

Her hand is warm. Smaller than mine. Stronger than it looks. A simple handshake should not feel like a first touch.

It does.

Her fingers tighten once.

"Green," she says softly.

The word is barely audible.

I understand enough.

I close my hand around hers with careful pressure.

"Green," I echo.

Her eyes lift to mine.

For one breath, the office disappears around us.

Then Molly drops something outside. "Shit."

Dorothea jerks back, laughing.

I release her hand immediately.

The door swings open.

Molly appears, cheeks pink, holding a file folder she absolutely dropped on purpose.

"Everything okay in here?"

I look at her.

She widens her eyes innocently.

Dorothea tucks hair behind her ear, flustered but smiling.

"Yes," she says. "I think so."

Molly's gaze flicks between us, then to the legal pad, then back to me.

"Great."

"Molly," I say.

"Yes?"

"Please copy Ms. Thompson's documents and open a file."

"Of course."

"And order lunch."

Dorothea starts to protest.

I point at her. "You agreed to eat."

"I agreed to eat generally."

"Now is general."

Molly grins.

Dorothea looks between us, then sighs. "Fine. But I'm paying for my own food."

I almost argue but remind myself not to litigate her pain. "Fine," I say.

Her eyes narrow. "That was too easy."

"I'm evolving."

"Suspicious."

"Reasonable."

Molly coughs into the file folder.

Dorothea gathers her things. At the door, she pauses. "When do we start?" she asks.

"The case?"

"The pretending."

My pulse shifts. "Not today."

Her brows lift. "Why?"

"Because today, you're my client with a legal emergency. That comes first."

Something in her face softens.

"And tomorrow?"

"Tomorrow, if you want, we can discuss public strategy."

"Public strategy," she repeats.

"Yes."

"Is that lawyer for fake dating practice?"

"Yes."

Her cheeks color.

"Okay."

"Okay?"

"Tomorrow."

She leaves my office with Molly, folder in hand, shoulders still tense but not collapsed.

I watch her go.

Then I close the door, return to my desk, and sit.

The office is quiet.

On the legal pad in front of me, my copy of the fake relationship terms waits.

I should be thinking about Applegate.

I am.

Mostly.

But my eyes keep going back to one line.

No is a complete sentence.

I tap the pen against the page once.

Then I write beneath it, small enough that only I will notice:

So is yes.

And then I open the Applegate file and go to war.

SIX

Dorothea

The bakery sounds different when a person's life is held together by one thin legal folder and a fake boyfriend agreement.

Not bad different.

Just sharper.

The oven fans hum like they know something. The walk-in groans in the back with the dramatic timing of a ghost who wants attention but lacks commitment. The espresso machine hisses like an irritated dragon every time Derek steams milk. Even the display case seems louder this morning, its soft mechanical purr turning into a reminder that refrigeration is expensive, electricity is expensive, flour is expensive, lawyers are expensive, and breathing is apparently free only because no one has figured out how to invoice me for it yet.

I wake before my alarm.

That's rude.

My alarm is set for four. I wake at three-twenty-seven, already thinking about Applegate Holdings, Lorenzo's legal pad, the fake relationship terms folded in my notebook, and the way he said green like he understood enough to be dangerous.

I lie in bed upstairs for exactly four minutes pretending I might go back to sleep.

Then I give up.

There are people who can rest while their entire life is under threat.

I'm not those people.

By four, I'm downstairs with my hair twisted into a messy knot, my gray bakery shirt half tucked into my jeans, and my apron tied too tightly around my waist. The bakery is dark except for the kitchen lights. The air is cool. Not yet bread-warm. Not yet sugar-warm. Just old wood, clean counters, and the faint lemon bite of the sanitizer I used too aggressively last night because scrubbing is what I do when panic tries to climb out of my skin.

The Hearth Book is still hidden beneath the bread wall.

I don't open it.

Not this morning.

This morning, I need regular magic.

Flour.

Water.

Yeast.

Salt.

Butter folded into dough and told, politely but firmly, to behave.

I start the croissants first because they demand timing and don't care about court dates. Then cinnamon rolls. Normal ones. No heart-cinnamon. No magical warmth. No emotional pastry experiments before sunrise. I'm a professional, and also, I don't have the bandwidth to accidentally make the town forgiving before seven in the morning.

Baylin arrives at four-thirty instead of two-thirty, which tells me she adjusted her sleep schedule on purpose.

That's suspiciously kind.

She comes through the back door with a canvas bag over one shoulder, a thermos in one hand, and a portable speaker tucked beneath her arm. Her dark hair is braided today, though half of it has already escaped. She wears a flour-dusted black T-shirt that reads DOUGH IS A LOVE LANGUAGE in cracked white letters.

"Morning," she says.

"Too early for that word to mean anything."

"True." She sets the thermos on the counter. "Coffee."

I narrow my eyes. "Why are you being nice?"

"Because your face looks like a Victorian child about to cough blood into a handkerchief."

"That's vivid."

"I have layers."

She presses play on the speaker.

A crackling guitar fills the kitchen.

Then a voice, rough and nasal and unmistakably old-soul strange, drifts through the air.

Bob Dylan.

I glance at her.

"It's a Dylan kind of morning?"

Baylin nods solemnly. "It's a truth-telling kind of morning."

"Oh no."

"What?"

"That sounds like something someone says before making me emotionally uncomfortable."

She grins and ties on her apron.

The morning finds its rhythm around us. Baylin starts bread at the far table, her hands moving through dough with a competence that looks almost violent until you understand bread. Press. Fold. Turn. Rest. She works like she is arguing with something ancient and expects to win through persistence.

The Dylan song scratches through the speaker.

Not pretty.

Real.

Baylin closes her eyes briefly as she kneads, like she is listening to scripture.

I pour coffee into the mug she brought me. It's strong enough to file taxes.

"Okay," I say. "Explain."

Her eyes open. "Explain what?"

"Why Dylan? Because I know you. You're about to make it mean something."

Baylin smiles. "His voice is not perfect."

"That feels generous."

"It's not pretty," she says. "Not polished. Not built to make anyone comfortable. But it's honest. That's why it works. He sings like the truth doesn't need to be attractive before it deserves to be heard."

I take a sip of coffee.

It's too hot, but I'm stubborn.

"Is this about Bob Dylan or me?"

"Yes."

"Baylin?"

"You asked."

"I asked about music. Not an unsolicited diagnosis."

"Music is an unsolicited diagnosis if you listen correctly."

I stare at her.

She keeps kneading.

The dough slaps the table.

"Also," she continues, "he reinvented himself over and over. Folk. Rock. Country. Gospel. Whatever annoyed people the most at the time, honestly. But even when he changed, he didn't become false. He kept changing toward himself."

I set my mug down.

Changing toward yourself.

That's exactly the kind of phrase that sounds beautiful until it looks directly at you.

The kitchen lights buzz softly overhead. The ovens warm. Butter softens on the counter. The world smells like yeast and coffee and all the things that happen before anything is ready to rise.

Baylin looks at me. "You went to Lorenzo yesterday?"

"Yes."

"And?"

"He is representing me."

"Good."

"There are terms."

"Legal terms?"

"Fake relationship terms."

Her hands pause in the dough. "Excuse me?" Slowly, she turns her head.

I close my eyes. "Not like that."

"That phrase means several things, and all of them require me to know more."

I tell her the condensed version.

Lorenzo's father. The wedding. The fake girlfriend

114

arrangement. His legal services continuing even if I end the fake relationship.

I leave out the way Lorenzo's hand felt when he shook mine and said green.

Baylin says nothing for a long moment.

Then she turns back to the dough.

"Well."

"That's all?"

"That's not all. That's me deciding which of my seven responses should come first."

"Start with the least alarming."

"You made a written agreement for fake dating."

"Yes."

"That's adorable."

"It's practical."

"It's both."

"It's legally adjacent."

"It's romantically doomed."

"Don't say doomed."

"I mean doomed in the way every good romance arrangement is doomed. Fake dating only works in fiction until the first emotionally loaded hand-hold."

"This is not fiction."

"No. It's Coral Cove. We are worse."

I pick up my coffee again.

"The arrangement is temporary."

"So is proofing," Baylin says. "Still changes the dough."

I point at her. "Don't weaponize bread craft against me."

"I learned it from you." She laughs and shapes the dough into a round. Then her expression softens. "Are you okay?"

The question is simple. They make lying too obvious. "No," I say.

Baylin nods. "Are you pretending to be okay?"

"Professionally."

"Mm."

"What does that mean?"

"It means Dylan voice."

I sigh. "Please translate from Baylin speak to my language please."

"It means maybe today you try sounding like yourself even if it isn't pretty."

My throat tightens. "I don't know how to do that with Lorenzo."

"Then start where you're."

"Scared and undercaffeinated?"

"Perfectly authentic."

"Terrible brand."

"Excellent song."

The front bell jingles faintly as Derek arrives through the front entrance, even though we are not open yet. He forgets his key half the time. I should stop letting him in early. I never do.

"Morning," he calls.

"Restock the napkins," I call back.

"They're already stocked."

"Emotionally."

He pauses. "Is this a trauma morning?"

"Yes," Baylin says.

"Cool. I'll make backup coffee."

Good kid.

* * *

The morning rush arrives fast.

It's easier to breathe when people need things. A woman wants twelve lemon twists for a staff meeting. A tourist asks if the sourdough is "authentic," and Baylin gives an answer so intense he buys two loaves out of fear. Mrs. Talbot comes in for one oat cookie, leaves with three cinnamon rolls and a promise to "keep an eye on things," which is the most terrifying phrase in Coral Cove.

I work.

I smile.

I hand over change.

I don't think about Applegate for almost six minutes at a time.

Progress.

At nine-thirty, the rush thins.

Derek wipes the tables. Baylin wraps bread. I stand

behind the counter and stare at the fake relationship terms tucked inside my notebook under the register.

Then I immediately tell myself not to wonder things like that because wondering is the yeast of bad decisions. Give it warmth, sugar, and a little time, and suddenly it's doubled in size and is trying to escape the bowl.

The bell over the door rings.

I look up.

Lorenzo walks in.

Because apparently thinking about him now summons him like a tailored demon with excellent posture.

He wears a navy suit today, no tie, white shirt open at the throat. It should look less formal. It doesn't. It looks like formality off duty. His hair is slightly wind-touched, and his eyes find mine before he looks anywhere else.

"Good morning, Dorothea."

There it's again.

My name.

My body reacts before I can remind it that we are at work, in public, with a trainee wiping tables and a bread witch watching from the kitchen door like she has paid for a ticket.

"Good morning," I say.

Derek drops a spoon.

Baylin makes a noise suspiciously close to a laugh.

I ignore both of them.

Lorenzo approaches the counter.

"Coffee?" I ask.

"Yes. And whatever you recommend."

"You keep saying that."

"I keep meaning it."

"That's reckless."

"I've been accused of worse."

"Cherry danish?"

"Do you recommend it?"

"No. I recommend the almond croissant. It has structural integrity."

His mouth curves.

"Then almond croissant."

I turn to get it.

My hand is better today. Still tender, still bandaged, but

not as angry. I feel Lorenzo's gaze drop to it and back up, though he doesn't comment immediately. I appreciate that more than I want to.

When I hand him the coffee and pastry, he pays without arguing.

"Do you have a few minutes?" he asks.

The words send a little jolt through me. "For the case?"

"Partly. For public strategy as well."

Public strategy.

Fake dating practice.

My cheeks heat.

I should not blush at the phrase public strategy. It sounds like a city council meeting.

"Derek can watch the counter for ten minutes."

Derek looks up too quickly. "I can?"

"You can."

"I can." He straightens like he has been promoted.

Baylin quips from the back, "Try not to flirt near the register. It confuses the card reader."

"Baylin."

"What? It gets temperamental."

Lorenzo's eyes warm with amusement.

I lead him to the small bistro table by the front window because it's visible, which is the point, and because if I sit in the back with him, my nervous system may mistake it for something intimate and throw itself into the sea.

He pulls out my chair.

I stare at it.

"What?" he asks quietly.

"Nothing."

"Dorothea."

I sit. "It's just a chair."

"Yes."

"You made it feel like a gesture."

"It was."

"On purpose?"

"Yes."

"Why?"

"Because if we are pretending to date, small public gestures matter."

Right.

Fake.

Practice.

Public strategy.

Nothing to panic about except everything.

He sits across from me. The coffee steams between us. Morning light comes through the window, turning his eyes greener than usual.

Green.

"What did you want to discuss?"

"First, the case." He opens a slim folder. "I reviewed your purchase documents. The deed was recorded. The sale appears legitimate on its face. Title insurance exists, which is good. I pulled initial county records this morning. There is an old trust document in the chain that Applegate may be trying to exploit, but I need more time."

My stomach twists. "Exploit how?"

"Possibly claiming Kaytie's predecessor never had clear authority to transfer the property out of the trust. That doesn't mean they are right."

"But it means something is there."

"It means they found something they think they can use."

"Do you think I'll lose?"

He doesn't answer fast. "I think you have a strong defense," he says. "I also think they are moving aggressively because they want you frightened."

"Well, good news. Very effective."

His expression softens. "Dorothea."

"I know. Don't panic."

"I was going to say panic is understandable."

I blink.

He looks at me over the folder. "Just don't act alone while panicking."

That's annoyingly reasonable. "Fine." My pulse does the stupid thing again.

He closes the folder. "Second, us."

The word us comes across the table and sits down with no invitation.

I glance toward the counter. Derek is wiping the same spot three times. Baylin is not even pretending not to watch.

"This feels public."

"It's meant to."

"Right."

Lorenzo lowers his voice. "We don't have to do anything today."

"I know."

"But people need to begin seeing us as familiar."

"Familiar how?"

He rests his hand on the table, palm up.

Offering.

My heart gives one hard, theatrical thump.

Ridiculous organ.

"Hand-holding is on the yes list," he says.

"It is."

"Still yes?"

I look at his hand.

Large. Warm-looking. Capable. Real.

But Lorenzo can misunderstand. Lorenzo can forget. Lorenzo can disappoint me.

Lorenzo can also ask.

He is asking.

My palm tingles. "Green," I say.

His eyes meet mine.

"Green."

I place my hand in his.

The touch is simple.

It's not simple at all.

His fingers close around mine with careful pressure. Not too tight. Not limp either. His thumb rests along the side of my hand, not moving. Just there. Public. Visible.

Derek drops the cloth.

Baylin says, "Hmm," like she is reviewing a chord progression.

I shoot her a look.

She smiles angelically.

Then the bell rings.

May walks in.

Not Mrs. Talbot, thank God, but May is not much better. She owns Golden Chopsticks and knows everyone's order, love life, food allergies, and emotional weaknesses. She stops just inside the door, raincoat folded over one arm, eyes landing on our joined hands like a fork hitting porcelain.

"Oh," she says.

My entire body tries to snatch my hand back.

Lorenzo's fingers don't tighten.

They don't trap.

They remain steady.

I can pull away if I choose.

That's the only reason I don't.

"Morning, May," I say, too brightly.

Her smile spreads. "Morning, Dottie. Lorenzo."

"May," he says, calm as a man who has not just accidentally turned my bakery into a rumor nursery.

"Well," she says. "Isn't this lovely?"

My mouth opens.

The truth rushes up.

No, no, it's not what it looks like. This is fake. Legal. Strategic. Please don't tell Mrs. Talbot, because she will make it a community project.

But I agreed.

No one can know.

The secret catches in my throat.

For one second, I hate the whole arrangement.

Not Lorenzo.

The performance.

The way public perception slides over my skin and claims it knows what is happening before I do.

Lorenzo's thumb moves once.

A question.

I glance at him.

His eyes are on me, not May.

Yellow? his face seems to ask.

I breathe.

Green, I decide.

Mostly.

"It's new," I say.

May's eyebrows shoot up.

"Oh, I bet it is."

My cheeks burn.

Baylin coughs into a towel.

Derek flees to the kitchen.

Coward.

May approaches the counter, still smiling. "I need six almond croissants and whatever cookie looks most forgiving."

"Forgiving?"

"I forgot Harold's sister's birthday."

"Oatmeal chocolate chip," I say. "It says I tried, but not too hard."

"Perfect."

I start to pull my hand from Lorenzo's.

He releases immediately.

No hesitation.

That should not matter so much.

It does.

While I box May's order, I can feel her looking between us. Lorenzo stays seated, drinking his coffee like a man who has never once been emotionally bullied by a restaurant owner with excellent dumplings.

When May leaves, she pauses at the door.

"Dinner tonight?" she asks, too casually.

I freeze.

Lorenzo glances at me. "We were considering Golden Chopsticks," he says.

Smooth.

Too smooth.

May's grin becomes wicked. "I'll save you a quiet table."

The bell rings behind her.

I stare at the door.

"Well," I say.

Lorenzo rises and comes to the counter.

"You okay?"

"No."

His expression sharpens.

"Yellow?"

A laugh escapes me before I can stop it.

The fact that he asks here, in my bakery, with Baylin absolutely listening from behind the bread racks, nearly undoes me.

"Not yellow," I say. "Just publicly perceived."

"That's a terrible feeling."

"Yes."

"Do you want to stop?"

I consider.

Truly consider.

Then I look at the folder on the table. The bakery around me. My bandaged hand. The line on our agreement.

"No," I say. "I want dinner. Golden Chopsticks is familiar. May already knows, apparently, and if I cancel now, she'll assume I'm pregnant or in witness protection."

Lorenzo laughs softly.

"Seven?"

"Seven."

He lifts his coffee. "I'll see you then."

He leaves, and the bakery exhales around me.

Baylin appears at my side immediately.

"Green?" she asks.

I glare. "You heard that?"

"The bread heard that."

"Wonderful."

She nudges my shoulder.

"Dottie."

"What?"

"You did good."

I close my eyes. "Don't make that word weird for me."

"I don't know what that means, and I suspect I should not ask."

"Correct."

* * *

After work, I spend twenty minutes standing in front of my closet like clothing has become a legal deposition.

Golden Chopsticks is not formal. It's a comfortable place with red lanterns, warm light, and the kind of booths that have held half of Coral Cove's emotional turning points. I have eaten takeout from there on the floor of my apartment. I have cried over dumplings there twice, both times discreetly. Once because Kaytie retired. Once because Lea gave me a romance novel that hit too close to home and I refused to discuss it.

A first fake date should not require wardrobe panic.

And yet.

I choose a summer dress in soft pink with tiny white flowers. Then I take it off because it feels too sweet. Then I put it back on because I like it and am trying to stop dressing only for emotional defense. I leave my hair down for exactly three minutes, panic, put it half up, then accept the compromise.

In the bathroom mirror, I look flushed and uncertain.

Not bad.

At seven, Lorenzo is already at the table May promised.

Corner booth. Low light. Two waters waiting. A pot of tea. He stands when I approach.

My stomach flips.

Not because of the fake relationship.

Because he looks at me.

Not quickly. Not with theatrical hunger. He simply sees me arrive, and his face changes before he has time to polish it.

"Dorothea," he says.

"You're very punctual."

"I was nervous."

I blink.

That was not the expected answer.

"You?"

"Yes."

"About fake dinner?"

"About real conversation."

Oh.

Well.

That's not fair.

"You look beautiful," he says.

I inhale.

Compliments are terrible because they require receiving, which is an entire skill no one taught me in foster care or baking school.

"Thank you," I say.

The words come out stiff but present.

Then I add, because truth apparently has a taste now and

I'm learning to swallow it, "I'm uncomfortable, but I like hearing it."

His eyes warm. "Noted."

May appears beside the table with a smile so bright it should come with a warning.

"Dorothea. Lorenzo. Well, well."

"May," I say. "Please behave."

"I own a restaurant. I behave for a living."

"That's not true."

"No, but it sounded nice." She sets menus down. "I put you somewhere quiet."

"Thank you," Lorenzo says.

May looks between us. "Drinks?"

"Tea is good," I say.

"Same," Lorenzo says.

May's eyes soften at me for half a second.

Not teasing.

Not pity.

Something like approval.

Then she leaves.

I slide into the booth. Lorenzo sits across from me rather than beside me, which I appreciate. We are public enough to be seen, private enough to talk, and separated by a table, which is sometimes the only thing keeping my nervous system from filing a complaint.

The restaurant is warm and golden. Red paper lanterns hang from the ceiling. The walls are lined with framed photos of Coral Cove through the years, fishing boats, festivals, school teams, old Main Street before half the storefronts discovered whimsical signage. The air smells like ginger, garlic, chili oil, soy sauce, fried scallions, and sugar caramelizing somewhere in the kitchen.

I already know what I want.

I always know what I want here.

That realization lands with uncomfortable force.

Sometimes wanting is not the problem.

Sometimes saying it is.

"So," Lorenzo says. "Should we practice?"

I look at him over the menu. "That sounds ominous."

"Getting to know each other."

"Still ominous."

"We need to answer questions if people ask."

"Right. Strategy."

He smiles faintly. "Yes. Strategy."

"Do you always make emotionally dangerous things sound like paperwork?"

"Only when I'm also afraid of them."

The answer is too honest.

I lower the menu slightly.

Lorenzo looks back at me, calm on the surface, but I see the tension near his mouth. He meant to say it. He also did not expect it to sit between us so heavily.

Maybe Baylin is right.

Maybe truth doesn't need to be pretty.

"Okay," I say. "Practice."

"What do you like to do when you're not baking?"

Easy question.

Terrible question.

My instinct is to deflect.

I could say, oh, not much.

I could make a joke about sleeping standing up.

I could say the bakery is my whole life and leave it at that, because people accept obsession when it produces pastries.

But Lorenzo is watching me like he will know the difference.

"The bakery is most of my life," I say. "But when I have a day off, I like to go to Chetzemoka Park. Usually with takeout from here. I like the swings if no children are using them, because I'm not a monster. Sometimes I bring a blanket and read in the gazebo."

Lorenzo smiles. Not teasing. "Why the gazebo?"

The easy answer is because it's pretty.

The true answer presses behind it.

I breathe.

"Because it feels like being outside without being completely exposed."

His expression shifts.

Softens.

I look at the table. "That sounded dramatic."

"It sounded specific."

I glance up.

He doesn't rescue me from the honesty. He also doesn't poke it until it bruises.

"What do you read?" he asks.

"A bit of everything."

"That was a dodge."

I glare. "We have known each other as fake partners for one day, and already you're difficult."

"I'm a fast learner."

"Romance," I say.

His eyebrows lift.

"Not exclusively. But often."

"What kind?"

"Depends on my mood."

"And your mood lately?"

I think of Lorenzo's hand around mine, the way my body keeps waking up to real danger and real desire at the same time.

"Stories where guarded people learn to ask for what they want," I say.

Lorenzo nods once. "Those sound useful."

"They are."

"What's your favorite?"

"Pride and Prejudice. Every year. It's predictable, but in a comforting way. The language slows me down. The world feels sharp, but polite about it. And everyone is constantly misunderstanding each other in excellent outfits."

His laugh is low and warm.

"I've never read it."

"You're saying that too calmly."

"I have other virtues."

"Name three."

He leans back. "I can cross-examine a hostile witness, repair drywall passably, and order well in restaurants."

"Two and a half virtues."

"Drywall counts."

"We'll see."

His smile widens.

May returns for our order. Lorenzo waits for me to go first. That shouldn't feel like a test.

It does.

"I'll have the sesame noodles, cucumber salad, and scallion pancakes," I say.

May nods. "Comfort order."

"Don't psychoanalyze my noodles."

"I would never."

She turns to Lorenzo.

"Mapo tofu, char siu, and bok choy," he says.

May smiles. "Good choices."

"I try."

When she leaves, I look at him. "Tofu?"

"You sound skeptical."

"I'm a texture person."

"Then you have not had the right tofu."

"Bold claim."

"I stand by it."

"Strategy or experiment?"

His smile turns slow. "Experiment."

That word lands between us with all the force of our earlier conversation. Strategy is deciding how to get what you want. Experimenting is admitting you don't know what will happen.

My cheeks warm.

He remembers too.

"Your turn," I say quickly. "What do you do when you're not lawyering people into submission?"

"Work on my house."

"That sounds surprisingly wholesome."

"I'm a deeply wholesome man." He laughs. "No?"

"I'm considering the evidence."

"I bought a fixer-upper out near North Beach when I moved here. The house was a disaster, but the bones were good and the view was better. Ocean on one side, trees on the other. I tore out the kitchen first."

That surprises me.

"The kitchen?"

"It was tiny. Closed off. Low ceiling. Bad cabinets. No light. Whoever designed it hated food, conversation, and joy."

"That's morally offensive."

"I thought so."

"What did you do?"

"Opened the wall into the dining room. Raised the ceiling where I could. Added windows. Redid the floors. I'm still working on it."

"You did that yourself?"

"Some of it."

"YouTube?"

His eyes brighten. "A lot of YouTube."

I laugh.

The image of Lorenzo Moretti, feared attorney and town heart hazard, standing in a half-demolished kitchen watching a man named Brad explain tile adhesive is almost too much.

"I respect that," I say.

"You should. I bled for that backsplash."

"What color?"

"Green."

"Of course it is."

"Of course?"

"Your favorite color is green."

He tilts his head. "I don't remember telling you that."

I freeze and clear my throat. "It's in your eyes." The sentence leaves my mouth before I can stop it.

Oh no.

Lorenzo's expression shifts into something warm.

The kind of warmth that makes every candlelit fantasy room in my memory roll its eyes and say, yes, that one is real.

"My eyes," he says.

"Don't make it weird."

"I would never."

"You absolutely would."

"Yes."

I drink water.

Too fast.

He has the mercy not to laugh.

May brings the food, saving me from my own mouth. Steam rises from the dishes. Sesame, chili, pork, scallions, soy. The table fills with color and heat.

Lorenzo picks up his chopsticks. "You should try this."

"What is it?"

"Mapo tofu."

"The texture crime."

"The alleged texture crime." He holds out a bite. "If you want," he says.

I look at the bite. Crisp-edged tofu, red sauce, scallions.

Then at him.

I could let him feed me. Publicly. Intimately. Very fake. Very not fake.

"On my plate," I say.

"Green?"

I smile despite myself.

"Green."

He places it on my plate.

I taste it.

Heat blooms over my tongue first. Chili. Peppercorn tingle. Garlic. Richness. Then the tofu, crisp outside, soft inside, carrying the sauce instead of collapsing under it.

"Oh," I say.

He smiles like he knew. "Good?"

"Don't look smug."

"Impossible."

"This is unfairly good."

"Tofu is misunderstood."

"So are many of us, apparently." The words slip out.

He looks at me. And I immediately glance at my noodles. Smooth, Dorothea.

Very subtle.

"Do you feel misunderstood?" he asks.

I almost make a joke, *only by tofu*. Instead, I breathe. "Sometimes," I say.

He waits.

I twist noodles around my fork because chopsticks and emotional honesty together seem overly ambitious.

"When people call me hardworking, they usually mean it kindly. But sometimes it feels like they're praising the fact that I don't need anything."

Lorenzo's gaze is steady.

I keep going before I lose the nerve. "And resilient. I hate that one."

"You hate resilient," he says.

"Yes."

"Why?"

"Because people said it when they didn't know how to help me."

The table quiets as the the restaurant continues around us. Low conversations. Plates. May laughing near the kitchen. Rain beginning again against the windows.

Lorenzo doesn't reach for me.

If he touched me right now, I might break.

"I was in foster care," I say. "From six until I aged out. Nineteen homes. My birth mother gave me up. My adoptive parents died in a car accident. After that, I was moved around a lot."

His jaw tightens. Anger, maybe? "I'm sorry," he says.

I nod.

The words are inadequate. They always are. But he says them like he knows that, which helps.

"I was called resilient constantly. Usually when someone was about to leave me in another place I didn't choose."

Lorenzo looks down at his hands. "That word is easy for the person saying it."

My throat tightens around his understanding. "Yes."

"What would you rather be called?" he asks.

The question catches me off guard.

No one has asked that before.

I think of Baylin. Dylan. Raw voices. Truth-seeking. Changing toward yourself.

"Stubborn," I say.

His mouth curves.

"Stubborn?"

"Yes. Stubborn means I chose to stay standing. Resilient sounds like I was made to bounce back for someone else's comfort."

Lorenzo nods slowly. "Stubborn, then." The word in his mouth settles somewhere warm.

"Thank you."

"You're welcome," He takes a moment eat another bite before responding."My mother used to call me stubborn." He takes a sip of tea, but I can see his hand tighten around the cup.

"Was she right?"

"Yes."

"What was she like?" The question comes gently.

Still, I see the door close halfway behind his eyes.

For a moment, I expect a deflection.

How about those sports ball teams?

That's what I would do.

Instead Lorenzo looks down at the table. "She was warm," he says. "Not soft. People confuse those. She could cut my father down with a look when she wanted to, but she mostly chose kindness. She liked cooking. Badly."

I smile. "Badly?"

"Terribly. She thought seasoning was a suggestion made by radicals."

I laugh softly.

His mouth curves, but grief sits behind it. "She died in a car accident," he says. "It was a storm. She hydroplaned. It was a few years ago."

"I'm sorry."

He nods once.

His throat moves. "She was coming to see me."

The admission is quiet.

Lorenzo finds my eyes like he expects me to say something gentle and useless.

I know gentle and useless. I have received it in casseroles, social worker offices, and funeral homes.

So I choose honest.

"That sounds like the kind of grief people try to turn into math."

His eyes sharpen. "What do you mean?"

"If I had not called, if it had not rained, if she had waited ten minutes, if I had done this instead of that." I look at my plate. "As if finding the right equation could make it your fault, and if it's your fault, at least the world makes sense."

Lorenzo doesn't move.

For a second, I worry I have gone too far.

Then he exhales. "Yes," he says.

One word.

A door opening.

We sit with it.

No fixing.

No performance.

No fake girlfriend strategy.

Just two people in a restaurant with legal papers, dead parents, and food cooling between them.

May passes our table, sees our faces, and keeps walking.

Bless her.

Eventually, Lorenzo reaches for the tea.

"More?"

I nod.

He refills my cup.

His hand is steady.

Mine is not, so I let him.

That feels like its own kind of practice.

After that, the conversation softens. Not less real. Just less raw. We talk about favorite festivals. I confess I have never seen a full film festival lineup because extra tourists mean extra pastry sales. He says the outdoor movie on hay bales is one of his favorite Coral Cove rituals, especially with popcorn and a blanket. I say that sounds like he is auditioning for small-town wholesomeness. He says he contains multitudes.

I ask about his house again because I want to see his face change when he talks about something he builds with his hands. He tells me about the kitchen, the green tile, the window seat he is planning, the shelf he built wrong three times before admitting defeat and calling a contractor.

He asks about the bakery, and I tell him about Kaytie. How she hired me. How she taught me pastry. How she sold me the place and made me promise never to cheap out on butter.

I don't tell him about the Hearth Book.

Not yet.

That truth feels too tender and too strange to place on the table beside scallion pancakes.

But I think about it.

By the time dinner ends, I'm tired in a different way.

Not depleted.

Opened.

May brings the check. Lorenzo reaches for it.

I reach faster.

He looks at my hand on the little black folder.

I look at him.

"I pay for my own food," I say.

"We are supposed to be dating."

"Fake dating."

"People are watching."

"Then they can watch us split the bill like modern adults."

His mouth twitches. "Do you need this?"

"Yes."

He releases the folder.

Just like that.

No argument.

No wounded pride.

No I'm the man nonsense.

Just release.

My chest aches. "Thank you," I say.

"You're welcome."

We split the bill.

May sees.

Her eyebrows lift.

I dare her silently to comment.

She doesn't.

Apparently mall miracles do exist.

Outside, the rain has slowed to mist. The street shines under lamplight, every puddle reflecting gold and red from restaurant signs. Coral Cove smells like wet pavement, salt air, fried garlic, and ocean. The kind of smell that makes the whole town feel half-real.

Lorenzo walks me to the edge of the sidewalk. Not to my apartment. Not without asking.

"I had a good time," he says.

I look at him.

The easy answer is me too.

The truer answer has more edges.

"I did too," I say. "And I was scared for parts of it."

His expression softens. "Thank you for telling me."

That should not feel romantic.

It does.

"I don't know how to do this," I say.

"Fake dating?"

"Any dating."

The mist gathers in his hair.

I almost take it back.

I don't.

"I'm not asking you to respond to that," I say quickly. "I just wanted to say something true instead of making a joke and running away."

His eyes hold mine.

"I'm glad you told me."

My heart is absurd.

"I should go."

Neither of us moves.

Then he asks, "Hand?"

I smile despite myself. "In public?"

"We are on Main Street."

I look down the street.

May is almost certainly watching from the window. Mrs. Talbot could materialize from a storm drain at any moment. Coral Cove has eyes in decorative planters.

"Green," I say.

Lorenzo offers his hand again and I take it.

We stand there for one breath, then two.

No kiss.

No performance.

Still, it feels intimate.

Maybe because he doesn't ask for more.

Maybe because I want him to.

That's a problem for future Dorothea.

Current Dorothea has had enough emotional development for one dinner.

"Goodnight, Lorenzo."

"Goodnight, Dorothea."

He releases my hand.

I walk back toward the bakery with rain on my cheeks and my pulse in my throat.

When I reach the door, I look back once.

He is still there.

Not following.

Not leaving.

Watching just long enough to know I get inside.

Then he turns and walks away.

I unlock the bakery door and step into the dark familiar smell of butter, yeast, sugar, and home.

My home.

Still mine.

For now.

I lock the door behind me and press my palm against the cool glass.

Tonight was not safe because nothing could go wrong.

Tonight was safe because I said true things and the world did not end.

I turn toward the kitchen.

The ovens wait for morning.

The hidden book waits beneath the shelf.

The legal storm waits in Lorenzo's office.

And somewhere under all of that, something in me has begun to rise.

SEVEN

Lorenzo

By six-thirty in the morning, Applegate Holdings has already made me want to commit several profession- ally inadvisable acts.

I do none of them and call it growth.

Instead, I sit at my desk with a cup of coffee gone cold beside my keyboard, three county property searches open on one monitor, the Secretary of State business registry open on the other, and Dorothea Thompson's file spread across my desk like a crime scene.

A very organized crime scene.

That part is Dorothea.

She brought me documents in labeled tabs. Deed. Purchase agreement. Loan documents. Insurance. Tax state- ments. Correspondence. Permits. Inspection reports. Receipts. I have seen corporate clients with legal departments bring me worse files than this woman assembled after being served at her apartment door and not sleeping.

She thought she was showing me she belonged here.

She did not have to.

The building is hers in every way that matters to a human being.

The law, unfortunately, has never been satisfied with what matters to human beings.

It wants signatures. Dates. Authority. Chains of title. Not

memories of flour on the counter or a mug from the woman who sold you the place. Not the fact that you turned a building into a home by working until your hands cracked. Not the fact that an entire town uses your bakery as a morning ritual, confession booth, and sugar-based emotional support system.

The law wants proof.

So I look for proof.

The online property record gives me the clean surface first.

Current owner: Dorothea Elaine Thompson.

Warranty deed recorded five years ago.

Grantor: Kaytie Ann Heart.

Consideration listed. Parcel number. Legal description. Recorder's stamp.

At first glance, clean.

Too clean for Applegate to have filed this aggressively unless they have something they think is sharper.

I open the historical chain.

Kaytie acquired the building from Mabel Whitcomb nineteen years ago. Before Mabel, the building belonged to the Whitcomb Family Trust. Before that, it belonged to Harbor Hearth Properties, which sounds like a charming local company but was actually a landholding entity created in the seventies by two families with money and poor naming instincts.

The gap appears there.

It's small.

Legal problems often are.

A missing trustee consent.

A reference to an exhibit that is not included in the digitized file.

A recorded memorandum that mentions a transfer condition but doesn't attach the original trust language.

One missing document in the middle of a chain of title can become a crowbar in the wrong hands.

Applegate Holdings has found the crowbar.

I lean back in my chair and rub both hands over my face.

"Damn it."

The office is quiet around me. Molly won't arrive for

another hour. Main Street outside my window is damp and gray, the storefronts still mostly asleep. Across the street and down the block, Knead the Dough glows with kitchen light.

Dorothea is already working.

She probably never stopped.

I picture her at the counter last night, saying she did not know how to do any dating. Saying she was scared for parts of dinner. Saying resilient was a word people used when they did not know how to help.

I'd wanted to reach across the table.

Wanting is not the problem.

Forgetting where the line is would be.

I'm her lawyer now. I'm also her fake boyfriend, by written agreement, tentative and revisable, with the word ass appearing in a document I still cannot believe exists in my office file. I'm attracted to her. I like her. I respect her. I want to protect her.

Each of those facts is manageable alone.

Together, they are a professional ethics seminar wearing perfume and flour.

My body has other opinions about the way Dorothea looked under the lantern light at Golden Chopsticks.

I turn back to Applegate.

The Secretary of State listing is boring in the way shell companies usually are. Applegate Holdings LLC. Registered in Washington six months ago. Registered agent: Seabright Corporate Services. Principal office in Seattle. No member names listed.

I search the address.

A suite in a tower downtown. Shared office. Mailbox with expensive rent.

I search connected entities.

Applegate Coastal Development.

Applegate Restoration Group.

Harborlight Mixed Use Partners.

And there, buried two companies deep, a name.

Grant Applegate.

I click.

His website loads with a glossy photograph of a man in

his late fifties standing in front of a renovated brick building. Silver hair. Expensive raincoat. Smile like a handshake that checks your pockets.

My body stills.

The man Dorothea described.

Mid-fifties. Gray hair. Expensive raincoat. Asked whether Kaytie left anything in the building. Bought a black coffee and did not drink it.

Grant Applegate.

Developer. Investor. Historic coastal revitalization specialist.

I read the phrase twice and hate it more each time.

His portfolio is exactly what I expect. Old waterfront buildings turned into luxury mixed-use spaces. Boutique condos over polished retail. "Preserving community character while creating profitable modern environments." A sentence designed to murder a town and sell souvenirs from the corpse.

He doesn't want one bakery.

He wants a corridor.

I pull up recent purchases.

Two buildings near the harbor. One old boardinghouse. A defunct antique shop. A former cannery office. All acquired through different LLCs with the same registered agent. All within a few blocks of Main Street.

Knead the Dough sits in the middle.

I sit back slowly.

This is not only legal opportunism.

It's development strategy.

If Applegate can force Dorothea out, he gets a prime corner building with residential space above, commercial kitchen infrastructure, and frontage on one of the town's most walkable blocks. He can call it restoration. He can tear the soul out carefully enough for the paint to remain charming.

He picked the wrong woman.

And the wrong lawyer.

My phone buzzes.

Molly: Running late by ten. Coffee?

I type back.

> Lorenzo: Yes. Large. Also find me everything public on Grant Applegate, Applegate Coastal Development, Harborlight Mixed Use Partners, and Seabright Corporate Services.

Then after a moment I add *please*.

Because Molly has started circling things in my emails when I forget basic courtesy, and I'm not in the mood for another workplace manners annotation.

Her reply comes seconds later.

> Molly: On it. Also, you sound murdery.

> Lorenzo: Only professionally.

> Molly: Hmm well that's defiantly worse for me.

I almost smile.

Then my office phone rings.

I answer without looking away from the property records. "Moretti."

"Lorenzo, you sound like you've been awake since the dead started confessing."

William Hunter.

I glance at the clock. "Good morning to you too."

"It's morning. Good is speculative. Molly texted me that you were about to make someone cry in a property dispute."

"Molly is supposed to support me."

"Molly supports the continued operation of the firm. That includes preventing you from calling opposing counsel before coffee."

I pinch the bridge of my nose. "I need your eyes."

"I assumed."

"Can you come in early?"

"I'm already here."

I look toward the closed door.

A moment later, there is a knock.

William enters without waiting.

He is in his early sixties, tall, lean, and permanently unimpressed. His silver hair is combed back. His suit is older than mine and somehow looks more expensive because he doesn't care whether anyone notices. William Hunter has been practicing law since before I learned to weaponize eye contact, and he has the calm of a man who has watched arrogant men explode in court and still made his lunch reservation.

He sits across from me and drops a yellow legal pad onto the chair beside him.

"Show me," he says.

I turn the monitor slightly and lay out the basics.

Dorothea's purchase. Kaytie's deed. The Whitcomb transfer. The Harbor Hearth document. The missing exhibit. Applegate's complaint. The hearing date.

William listens without interrupting.

It's one of the reasons I like him.

Most attorneys listen only long enough to reload.

When I finish, he leans forward and reads the complaint.

"Predatory filing," he says.

"Yep."

"Thin on detail."

"Intentionally."

"Fast hearing."

"Pressure tactic."

"Client has title insurance?"

"Yes."

"Good. Tender claim immediately. Copy insurer on everything."

"Already on my list."

He flips another page.

"What do they claim the defect is?"

"That Kaytie's predecessor lacked full authority due to a trust restriction. The complaint references an unrecorded schedule and a reversionary interest."

William's brows lift.

"Unrecorded."

"Yes."

"Convenient."

"Extremely."

"Who is Applegate?"

"Developer. Already acquired several nearby properties. Looks like he is assembling a corridor."

William's expression hardens.

"Ah."

"Dorothea also mentioned a man came into the bakery asking if Kaytie left old records or boxes behind. He matches Grant Applegate."

William looks up.

"Before she was served?"

"Weeks before."

"Then he went fishing."

"My thoughts exactly."

"And she didn't know what pond he was standing in."

My jaw tightens. "No."

William studies me for a second.

"What?"

"You look personally offended," he says.

"I am professionally offended."

"Lorenzo."

"What?"

He sets the complaint down. "You're representing her."

"Yes."

"You're also dating."

My silence answers too much.

William sits back.

"Molly?" I ask.

"Molly said nothing."

"Then?"

"Because you asked me to review a local property dispute before seven in the morning, you look like you have not slept, and there is a bag from Knead the Dough in your trash."

I glance at the trash can.

The pear pastry bag from yesterday sits on top.

Betrayal by pastry.

Well, let the lying begin. "Nothing's happened, she turned me down," I say. "But I'm hopeful."

William closes his eyes.

I wait.

He opens them. "I'm going to pretend I didn't hear any of that."

"Probably a wise decision."

Control is easy. I know control. I use it every day. Control is a pressed suit and a calm voice when my father tries to cut me open over the phone. Control is not touching Dorothea when she says something that makes my chest hurt. Control is writing ethics notes in a file because the alternative is admitting how badly I want to be allowed near her.

Careful is different.

Careful asks what she needs more than what I can withstand.

William nods, "Just be her lawyer first. If you cannot do that, transfer the case."

William is right to say it.

"I can do that."

"Can you lose?" he asks.

"What?"

"Can you lose and not make it about saving her?"

The office goes cold.

I glance out the window and down the block.

Knead the Dough's light is brighter now. Someone moves behind the counter. Dorothea, maybe. Or Derek. Or Baylin, if she has decided dawn needs bread and attitude.

"I'm not going to lose," I say.

William sighs. "That's not the question."

"It's the only acceptable answer."

William doesn't blink. "You're good," he says. "Better than good. But if you make this about proving something to your father, to yourself, or to her, you will miss something. Don't fight the case in front of you as if it's a ghost from another room."

My father's voice presses in at the edges.

Small.

Wasting your life.

Nothing stable.

Nothing respectable.

Then Dorothea's voice.

The first place I ever got to keep.

I exhale slowly.

"Applegate first," I say.

William nods.

"Good. Now, the case is defendable. If the deed to Kaytie was recorded, if taxes were paid, if there was title insurance, and if Dorothea bought in good faith, Applegate has a climb. The missing exhibit matters, but unrecorded restrictions are not magic words."

"Applegate may have acquired an alleged beneficial interest from a distant trust heir."

"Then we force them to prove standing."

"Yes."

"We demand the unrecorded schedule."

"Yes."

"We tender to title insurer."

"Yes."

"We pull the paper archives. Not only digital. Digital misses old exhibits all the time."

"I'll call the county."

"Call the title company too. Old closing files may have copies."

"I will."

"And contact Kaytie."

"I was going to ask Dorothea."

"Don't wait. If she is a witness, preserve her memory now."

Witness. Kaytie Ann Heart. Prior owner. Sale to Dorothea. Any pre-sale inquiries. Applegate contact.

William taps the complaint.

"And Grant Applegate coming into the bakery matters. If he was looking for documents before filing, he knew there was a weakness in his own record search. It suggests fishing, not certainty."

Fishing, not certainty.

Useful.

"Also," William says, "developer assemblage gives motive."

"Yes."

"Motive is not law."

"No. But it's leverage."

"Now you sound like yourself."

I look up. "Was that a compliment?"

"A warning."

"Same thing from you."

He stands and gathers the papers.

"Send me scans of everything. I'll review tonight."

"You have a full day."

"I'm old. I can read while ignoring people."

"Thank you."

He pauses at the door. "Lorenzo?"

"Yes?"

"Don't promise her certainty."

I think of yesterday, almost saying everything will be okay. The lie of comfort. The temptation to give Dorothea a world where the outcome is controlled because I want to be the kind of man who can give that.

"I won't."

"Promise work. Promise strategy. Promise you won't abandon the case. Don't promise the court will behave."

"Understood."

He leaves.

I sit alone.

The office feels heavier now.

Better.

Heavier means grounded.

I pick up the phone and call the county recorder.

The first transfer sends me to records.

The second to archives.

The third to a woman named Patricia who sounds like she has guarded old deeds for forty years and respects no attorney under the age of seventy.

"Parcel number?" she asks.

I give it.

Keys clack.

"Current owner Thompson."

"Yes. I need the historical file for the Harbor Hearth transfer, especially any exhibits attached to the trust memorandum recorded in 1978."

A pause.

"That's not digitized."

"I suspected."

"It's in the basement."

"Can I get a copy?"

Another pause.

"You can request one."

"I'm requesting one."

"In writing."

"I can email."

"Mail."

"Mail?"

"Or fax." Because the law can move a woman toward eviction in days, but the document that may save her lives in a basement and requires faxing.

"Fax number?" I ask.

She gives it to me and I jot it down.

"Can you tell me whether the file contains an Exhibit C?"

"I cannot give legal advice."

"I'm not asking for legal advice. I'm asking whether a piece of paper exists in a public record file."

More clacking.

Then a sigh. "You lawyers."

"Frequently."

"There is an Exhibit C listed in the index."

My pulse changes. "Is it attached?"

"I cannot see the image."

"But the paper file may have it."

"The paper file may have it."

I smile for the first time all morning.

"Patricia, you're a gift to public records."

"Don't flirt with me, counselor. Fax the request." She hangs up.

I laugh once.

Then I draft the fax.

Molly arrives while I'm sending it through the office machine, because yes, we have one, because older county records offices treat email like a moral failing.

She carries coffee, a breakfast sandwich, and the expression of a woman who already knows too much.

"You're using the fax machine," she says.

"Patricia demanded tribute."

"County archives?"

"Yes."

"Basement file?"

"Yes."

She sets the coffee on the credenza. "I love when a case gets dusty."

"You would."

"You have a meeting at nine-thirty, Mr. Patel at noon, and your father's assistant sent a second email about dinner."

"Delete it."

"I archived it. More professional."

"Fine."

She looks toward my desk, where Applegate's website remains open.

"Is that him?"

"Grant Applegate."

She leans closer.

"Ugh."

"Legal analysis?"

"Vibe analysis."

"Accepted."

"He looks like he says revitalization when he means rent increase."

"Accurate."

Molly sets a stack of printouts on my desk.

"Public articles. Press releases. Shell company connections. He bought the old cannery office last month through Harborlight. He bought the boardinghouse through Seabright, then transferred it to Applegate Restoration Group. Also, the antique shop owner gave an interview saying she sold after a 'misunderstanding' over property access."

I look at her.

"Find the interview."

"Already in the stack."

"You're terrifying."

"Efficient."

"Both."

She smiles.

"Also," she says, "Dottie called. She found another envelope from Kaytie in a filing cabinet upstairs. She wants to know if she should bring it."

"Yes."

"I told her eleven."

"Good."

"And I told her to bring coffee because you're unpleasant when undercaffeinated."

"Molly."

"What? She asked if you needed anything."

I don't know what to do with that.

Dorothea asked if I needed anything.

I should not be touched by coffee.

I am.

Molly sees it and wisely says nothing.

Mostly.

"You look like a man having feelings about a beverage," she says.

"Leave."

"Yes, boss."

The next several hours disappear into calls.

The title insurer.

A records request.

A message to Kaytie Ann Heart's listed number, which goes to voicemail.

An email to Applegate's counsel.

A search of litigation history showing Applegate entities have filed three similar actions in small towns over the last eight years. Two settled. One property owner defaulted. One case dismissed after the owner found title insurance coverage and a recorded correction affidavit.

A pattern.

Not enough to win by itself.

Enough to know the shape of the monster.

At ten-fifty-eight, I hear Molly greeting Dorothea in the outer office.

My body reacts before my brain approves.

That's becoming a problem.

I stand, then sit back down because standing at attention when a woman enters is not subtle.

Then I stand again because she is a client and standing to greet a client is normal.

Pathetic.

The door opens.

Dorothea steps in carrying a cardboard document box, two coffees, and a pastry bag tucked under one arm. She is still wearing her pink apron with the Knead the Dough logo. Her hair is pinned back, but one lock has escaped near her cheek. Flour dusts the side of her wrist. The bandage on her hand is smaller today.

She looks tired and incredibly stubborn.

Good.

No.

Not good like that.

Focus.

"Dorothea," I say.

"Lorenzo."

Molly appears behind her, takes the document box, and gives me a look that clearly says Don't let her carry everything, idiot.

"I had it," Dorothea says.

"I know," Molly and I say at the same time.

Dorothea looks between us.

"That was unsettling."

Molly grins. "Teamwork."

She sets the box on my desk and disappears.

Dorothea holds out the coffee and pastry bag.

"I brought these."

"You did not have to."

"I know."

Her eyes meet mine.

This time, I understand what the answer means.

Not obligation.

Choice.

I take the coffee.

"Thank you."

"And before you ask, I ate. Baylin watched me do it like I was a suspicious raccoon."

I smile. "Good."

She points at me. "Don't start."

"I said one word."

"It was a loaded word."

"It often is."

Her cheeks color.

The office warms.

I take a sip of coffee to keep myself from saying something unwise.

"What did you find?" I ask, gesturing to the box.

She sits across from me.

"Kaytie kept old building files in a cabinet upstairs. I thought I brought everything, but then I remembered she had a folder labeled Ancient Building Nonsense. I assumed it was permits and tax stuff from before my time. It was mostly that, but there were old letters too."

"Letters from whom?"

"Kaytie. Mabel Whitcomb. Someone named Harlan Pruitt. I don't know what matters."

"We will find out."

I open the box.

The first file is exactly what she said: Ancient Building Nonsense.

The label makes me like Kaytie.

Inside are old receipts, faded photocopies, handwritten notes, a floor plan, inspection reports, and several letters.

One envelope is thick, yellowed, and marked in blue ink.

For Kaytie, if anyone asks about the trust again.

My pulse slows.

I look up.

Dorothea watches my face.

"What?"

"This may matter."

Her fingers grip the edge of the chair.

I open the envelope carefully.

Inside is a letter from Mabel Whitcomb to Kaytie Ann Heart, dated nineteen years ago, shortly before the sale.

Kaytie,

If the Pruitt boy or anyone from that side of the family comes sniffing around again, don't let them frighten you. My mother settled the old Harbor Hearth trust before I took title, and I had full right to sell. The building was never theirs in the way they like to pretend. Harlan signed his release in 1981. He spent the money within a year and then spent the rest of his life regretting that he could not sell the same horse twice.

I'm enclosing copies of the release and the correction affidavit. Keep them with the building papers. People with old names and empty pockets love to discover principles when property values rise.

Mabel

I read the last line twice.

People with old names and empty pockets love to discover principles when property values rise.

Mabel Whitcomb, I could have used you in court.

Behind the letter are photocopies.

One labeled Release of Beneficial Interest, signed by Harlan Pruitt.

One labeled Trustee Correction Affidavit.

One copy is not recorded, but the affidavit has a recorder's stamp.

I turn it over.

The stamp number is faded but legible.

There you're.

Dorothea leans forward.

"Is that good?"

I keep my voice measured because William's warning is still in my ear.

"It's helpful."

"How helpful?"

"Potentially very."

Her eyes fill so quickly she looks down.

I want to reach across the desk. Instead, I slide the letter toward her.

She reads it.

Her mouth trembles on the last line.

"I like Mabel," she says.

"So do I."

"Does this mean Applegate is lying?"

"It means Applegate either did not find this, ignored it, or hopes you could not find it in time."

Her expression hardens.

There she is.

Stubborn.

Not resilient.

Stubborn.

"I hate him."

"Appropriate."

"Legally?"

"Morally."

"Good enough."

I smile.

Then my office phone rings.

Molly's line.

I answer. "Yes?"

"Applegate's counsel is on line one. Nathan Torrence."

"Put him through."

Dorothea's eyes widen.

I hold up one hand.

"You can stay," I say. "Or step out."

"Can I stay?"

"Yes."

"Then I want to."

I press line one.

"Lorenzo Moretti."

"Nathan Torrence," a smooth voice says. "I represent Applegate Holdings."

Men like this always sound recently polished.

"I received your email," he says. "I understand you're representing Ms. Thompson."

"You understand correctly."

"Good. I wanted to reach out before this becomes unnecessarily adversarial."

I look at Dorothea.

She looks like she wants to bite the phone.

A feeling I respect.

"You filed for possession of a woman's home and business without prior notice," I say. "We are already adversarial."

A pause.

Then a faint laugh.

"Fair enough. Grant is prepared to be reasonable."

"How generous."

"Your client is in a difficult position. If the trust issue is as we believe, she may not have valid title. Litigation will be costly. Applegate is willing to offer relocation assistance and a walk-away payment."

Dorothea goes still.

I keep my eyes on her.

"How much?"

"Thirty thousand dollars."

Her face empties.

Thirty thousand.

For a building worth many times that.

For her home.

For her bakery.

For the first place she ever got to keep.

I smile.

The dangerous one.

The one Nathan cannot see but can hear when I speak.

"No."

"You should discuss it with your client."

"My client is in the room."

Dorothea's eyes snap to mine.

Nathan pauses.

"Then I would encourage Ms. Thompson to consider the certainty of payment against the uncertainty of litigation."

Dorothea's fingers curl into fists in her lap.

"Mr. Torrence," I say, "tell Grant Applegate he can keep his insulting offer. We will be filing an appearance, tendering the claim to the title insurer, demanding a continuance, and requesting every document your client claims supports standing, including any alleged trust schedule, assignment, release, or reversionary interest."

Another pause.

This one colder.

"That may not be wise."

"No. Wise would have been picking a target who had no records."

Dorothea's eyes widen.

I continue.

"We have documents your complaint seems to have forgotten. A recorded correction affidavit. A release of beneficial interest from Harlan Pruitt. And a very interesting pattern of Applegate entities pressuring legacy property owners in small coastal towns."

Nathan says nothing.

"You have twenty-four hours to send the documents," I say. "After that, I will move to compel and ask for fees. I will also be looking closely at whether your client's pre-suit visit to my client's business was an attempt to locate or remove records before filing."

"That's a serious accusation."

"It's a serious question. I suggest your client prepare a serious answer."

I hang up.

The office goes silent.

Dorothea stares at me.

I set the phone down.

"That was perhaps less diplomatic than it could have been."

Her mouth opens.

Closes.

Then she says, "That was the hottest legal thing I have ever heard."

The words hit both of us at the same time.

Her face goes bright red.

My body reacts with the force of a verdict.

I look at the desk.

The file.

The coffee.

Anything that is not Dorothea blushing in my office after calling me hot.

"Noted," I say carefully.

She covers her face with both hands.

"I cannot believe I said that."

"I can pretend you didn't."

"Please."

"I will fail, but I can try."

A laugh breaks through her hands.

God help me.

I like her.

Not in the abstract. Not as a body. Not as a solution to my

father problem. Not as a client, which would be unethical and flat and wrong.

I like the way she fights embarrassment with humor. I also like that, when offered thirty thousand dollars to surrender her life, she looked ready to burn Applegate Holdings with a toaster.

I stand.

Distance.

Careful.

"I need to make copies of these immediately."

She lowers her hands.

"Okay."

"And I need your permission to contact Kaytie."

"Yes."

"And the title insurer."

"Yes."

"And to file an appearance today."

"Yes."

"Good."

This time, the word is not loaded with heat.

"Lorenzo," she says.

"Yes?"

"You didn't promise it would all be okay."

I still.

She looks down at Mabel's letter.

"I noticed."

"I cannot promise that."

"I know." Her fingers touch the page. "Thank you for not lying."

Something in my chest twists.

"You're welcome."

"But do you think we have a chance?"

I look at the documents. The complaint. The notes. The old release. The motive. The pattern. The woman across from me trying not to need too much and needing everything anyway.

"Yes," I say. "I think we have a real chance."

Her breath leaves her.

"Okay."

"I can promise you this. I will work the case. I will fight

hard. I will tell you the truth, even when it's uncomfortable. I won't let them scare you into surrendering what is yours."

Her eyes shine.

This time, she doesn't look away.

"Green," she whispers.

The word is small.

Not about touch.

Not exactly.

About trust.

About staying in the room.

I nod.

"Green."

Molly knocks once and steps in with a stack of copies.

Then she freezes.

Her eyes move from Dorothea to me to the documents.

"Did I interrupt a legal murder?"

"Possibly," Dorothea says.

Molly smiles.

"Excellent. I made extra copies."

The rest of the afternoon becomes motion.

Dorothea goes back to the bakery because she has a lunch rush and because fighting for a place apparently doesn't stop it from needing to sell sandwiches. Molly copies everything. I scan Mabel's letter and the affidavit. William reviews the stamp number and actually says, "Well, well," which from him is equivalent to a standing ovation.

By five, we have tendered the claim to the title insurer, filed my notice of appearance, drafted a demand letter to Applegate's counsel, faxed Patricia in county archives twice, left a second message for Kaytie, and prepared a motion outline in case Nathan Torrence decides to play games.

At six-thirty, Molly leaves a sandwich on my desk without asking.

At seven, the office is empty.

I sit alone, reading Mabel Whitcomb's letter again.

The case is more than defendable.

Not won.

But alive.

That should be enough to let me breathe.

It's not.

My father arrives in days. The wedding plus-one name is due. The fake relationship has already started to feel less fake in the places where I most need it to remain manageable. Dorothea is my client. She is also the woman whose hand fit in mine this morning across a bakery table while May watched like a woman seeing the first act of a play she already planned to review loudly.

Across the street, Knead the Dough's lights glow against the darkening evening. I can see movement inside. Dorothea behind the counter. Baylin near the bread wall.

The bakery is still standing.

Tomorrow, I will make sure it stays that way.

And tonight, I will do the harder thing.

I won't go over there just because I want to see her.

I will give her space.

I will work.

I will be careful.

My phone buzzes.

A text from Dorothea.

Thank you for today. Also, Baylin says if legal murder requires pastries, she recommends the espresso brownies.

I smile before I can stop myself.

Then another text appears.

I recommend the pear danish. But I'm biased because I saved you one.

My chest tightens.

Small things.

Real things.

> Lorenzo: I will accept expert recommendations. I will also send you copies of everything we filed tonight.

> Dorothea: That sounds very professional.

> Lorenzo: I'm trying.

Three dots appear.

Disappear.

Appear again.

Dorothea: Me too.

I set the phone facedown and close the Applegate file.

For a moment, I sit in the quiet of the office and let myself feel the truth without dressing it in strategy.

I'm not afraid of losing because I think Applegate has the stronger case.

I'm afraid because Dorothea has started to matter in ways no retainer agreement can contain.

That's the part I cannot litigate.

Not yet.

EIGHT

Dorothea

T he morning after a magical erotic reckoning should come with instructions.

Not dramatic instructions. I don't need a scroll sealed in red wax or a raven landing on my windowsill with a message in its beak. Honestly, if a raven showed up before coffee, I would throw a croissant at it and apologize later.

But something practical would be nice.

Drink water.

Don't panic-text anyone.

Avoid all emotionally complicated lawyers until after breakfast.

Don't touch your palm every four minutes like it's going to light up in public.

That last one would have been useful.

Because I keep doing it.

By five in the morning, I have already touched the center of my palm seven times.

Nothing appears.

No red letters. No glowing words. No magical proof that I did not hallucinate an entire night in The Arcane Room, complete with Lucian, doors, cuffs, hot springs, and the kind of self-knowledge a person should probably be eased into over several calendar years.

Still, my palm remembers.

Yes.

Maybe.

No.

Green.

Yellow.

Red.

The key is already in your hand.

The words are not visible, but they sit beneath my skin like heat held under cooling sugar.

I stand at the prep table downstairs, alone in the bakery, pressing butter into flour for scones while the ovens warm behind me. The kitchen lights are bright, too bright for this hour, but the bakery is kinder when it's awake before everyone else. The storefront is dark. The display cases are empty. The chairs are still upside down on the little tables. The air smells like old wood, yeast, coffee grounds, lemon cleaner, and the faint cinnamon ghost of yesterday's pastries.

Knead the Dough has always been my safe place.

That's both beautiful and a little damning.

A safe place can become a hiding place if you lock the door too many times.

I don't appreciate knowing that now.

It was more convenient when I could call myself hard-working and avoid looking too closely at the difference between devotion and disappearance.

I press my thumb into the dough.

Too hard.

The butter smears.

"Great," I mutter. "Now the scones are emotionally overworked."

The oven fan hums as if agreeing.

Rude appliance.

I scrape the dough together and try again. Lighter touch. Less force. Let the cold butter stay in little pockets, because scones need tenderness disguised as structure.

I'm absolutely not making that a metaphor.

No.

Not today.

My phone rings.

I jump so hard I nearly drop the pastry cutter.

The screen lights up with Lea's name.

I should have known she would sense emotional instability from two storefronts away. Bookstore owners are not legally witches, but that is mostly because no one has pushed the issue in court.

I answer with flour on my fingers.

"Spellbound Stories, how can I assist you?" Lea says.

I blink. "Did you call me from the store phone?"

"Yes."

"Why?"

"Ambience."

"It's five in the morning."

"Exactly. This is mysterious."

I close my eyes. "Lea."

"Dottie."

"What the hell was that?"

A beat of silence.

Then she laughs.

She laughs.

I stare at the phone as if I can glare through it.

"Why are you laughing?"

"Because you went."

"I did."

"And you came back."

"I did."

"And you sound like someone who found a key and is furious about the existence of doors."

I hate her.

I love her.

Both things can be true, apparently. The universe keeps insisting on that.

I lean my hip against the prep table. "I don't think I have words for it."

"You do. You just don't want to use them."

"That's not the same thing."

"It often is."

I look down at my palm.

Nothing visible.

Still, warmth gathers there.

"I saw things," I say.

"I figured."

"I did things."

"I very much don't need details unless you want to give them, and then I will need tea and possibly an emotional support chair."

A laugh slips out of me before I can stop it. It's nice to know that laughing still works.

"I'm serious," I say. "It was… I don't know. Illuminating."

"Ah. The Arcane Room special."

"You knew?"

"I knew it might help."

"That's not an answer."

"No, but it's the only one I have."

I press my palm flat to the table.

"Lea."

"Yeah?"

"Did you know it would be like that?"

"I knew it would show you something you were ready to see."

"That's a terrible sentence."

"It's also true."

"I hate when people say that."

"I know."

The bakery hums around me.

The scone dough waits in front of me, pale and unfinished.

"I thought I wanted safe experience," I say slowly. "Something contained. Something that would let me understand myself without having to risk anything real."

Lea says nothing so I keep going. "But the whole point was that fantasy is not the same as freedom. Safety matters. Boundaries matter. Asking matters. But staying somewhere because it can't reject you…" I swallow. "That's still a chain."

Lea's voice softens. "Did you come back with a key, or are you still standing outside your own door?"

My eyes sting.

Rude.

Powerful, but rude.

"I don't know."

"Yes, you do."

"I know I should."

"That's different."

I breathe.

The bakery is quiet enough that I can hear the old building creak around me. Pipes. Wood. The walk-in refrigerator starting its low rumble in the back. A place alive with practical noises.

"I came back with a key," I whisper.

"Good."

"But I don't know how to use it."

"Also good."

"How is that good?"

"Because if you thought you knew exactly how to use it, you would probably hit someone with it instead of unlocking anything."

"That sounds like me."

"It does."

I laugh again, but it comes out shakier this time.

Lea lets the silence sit for a second.

Then she says, "What did you promise?"

My throat tightens.

I knew she would ask something like that. Maybe not the exact words, but Lea has always been good at finding the hinge.

I look toward the front windows, dark with early morning. Main Street is empty beyond the glass, only rain on the sidewalk and the faint glow from the streetlamps.

"I promised I would stop pretending the fake part with Lorenzo is the only part."

Lea inhales softly.

"Dottie."

"I know."

"That's not small."

"It's supposed to be small. Everyone keeps telling me to do one small thing, and then the small thing turns out to be emotionally life-threatening."

"That sounds accurate."

"I promised I would ask him what he actually wants. From me. Not the bakery case. Not the fake girlfriend arrangement. Me."

"And?"

"And if he wants me, I promised I would tell him what I need."

"What do you need?"

I immediately want to hang up.

That's how I know the question matters.

"Slow," I say.

"Okay."

"Specific."

"Okay."

"Honest. No games unless we both know they're games. No making me feel breakable. No assuming I can be brave just because I can run a business and lift fifty-pound flour bags."

Lea is quiet.

Too quiet. "Are you crying?" I ask.

"No."

"Lea."

"Maybe."

"Oh my God."

"I'm allowed to have feelings. My best friend just articulated needs after years of treating wants like contraband."

I roll my eyes, but my face is wet too, so I have no moral high ground.

"I'm scared," I say.

"I know."

"What if I mess it up?"

"Then you revise."

That word hits harder than it should.

Revisible.

Everything should be revisable.

"Did Lorenzo make the fake dating terms feel like a trap?" she asks.

"No."

"Did he make legal help conditional on your performance?"

"No. He was careful about that."

"Did he listen when you said no?"

"Yes."

"Then maybe start there."

I stare at the dough.

Start there.

Not with forever. Not with love. Not with whether he could hurt me, leave me, want me, disappoint me, or become another room I lose.

Start with what he has already done.

He asked.

He listened.

He released my hand.

He did not promise the case would magically be fine.

He sent documents.

He said he was trying.

That's not everything.

It's not nothing.

"I hate this," I whisper.

"Of course you do. It involves vulnerability and a man with cheekbones."

"He does have cheekbones."

"Dangerous cheekbones."

"Legally dangerous cheekbones."

"Worse."

I laugh through the last of the tears.

Then I wipe my face with the back of my wrist and leave a streak of flour near my temple. Wonderful. Beautiful. Very romance heroine, if the heroine has lost several fights with dough before sunrise.

"May told me you two looked like sparks at Golden Chopsticks," Lea says.

I groan. "May needs hobbies."

"May owns a restaurant. Gossip is garnish."

"It was fake."

"Was it?"

I open my mouth.

Close it.

Lea makes a triumphant little sound.

"I hate you."

"No, you don't."

"No. I don't."

"But you want to hide behind fake because fake has rules."

"Yes."

"And real has consequences."

"Yes."

"And Lorenzo is real."

Too real.

That's the entire problem.

Lucian had been real enough to change me, not real enough to choose instead of me.

Lorenzo can choose or fail. He can say yes and mean something different than I mean. Lorenzo can say no.

My stomach twists.

The scone dough begins to look neglected.

"I need to work," I say.

"No, you need to process."

"I process through butter."

"Valid."

"Thank you."

"Dottie?"

"Yeah?"

"Don't be so scared of losing something that you refuse to find out whether it wants to stay."

My hand tightens around the phone.

"That was mean."

"That was love."

"Same thing from you."

"Sometimes."

I smile.

"I love you, Lea."

"I love you too. And remember, what happens in The Arcane Room stays in The Arcane Room, except for the key. Bring the key with you."

The call ends.

I stand there for a long moment with the silent phone in my hand.

Bring the key with you.

I touch my palm again.

Then I finish the scones.

By opening, my hair has been up and down three times.

Up is practical.

Down is vulnerable.

Half up is a cowardly compromise, and I'm comfortable with that.

I twist the top section back with a clip and let the rest fall over my shoulders. It feels ridiculous. Hair near food is a real concern, so I keep it controlled enough for health code and loose enough to prove something to myself I cannot explain to Derek without sounding haunted.

Derek arrives at six, looks at me, and immediately says, "Your hair is down."

"Observant."

"Is this a crisis or a good thing?"

"Yes."

He nods as if that answers everything. "Cool. I'll make coffee."

Baylin comes in twenty minutes later, carrying a crate of late-season apples and humming a Dylan song under her breath.

She sees my hair.

She sees my face.

She says nothing.

Then she sets the apples down and pats my shoulder once.

"Authentic," she says.

I point at her. "No."

She smiles. "Yes."

The morning rush arrives hard and fast.

There is mercy in work.

For a few hours, I'm not a woman trying to understand the emotional fallout of a magical room, a fake boyfriend, a property case, and a lawyer with green eyes. I'm a baker. I box pastries. I refill coffee. I tell a tourist that no, we don't have gluten-free croissants because some miracles remain beyond modern science. I remind Derek that chocolate chip cookies go in the second case, not the first, because cookie people are territorial and will revolt if confused.

Molly arrives at eight-thirty for Lorenzo's usual coffee and an order of cookies.

Not Lorenzo.

Molly.

My stomach does a humiliating little drop. I realize I already prepared his coffee before the bell even rang.

Molly sees it because Molly sees too much.

"That for him?" she asks, nodding toward the cup.

"No."

The lie is so bad the espresso machine hisses in judgment.

Molly's mouth curves.

"He's buried in filings this morning. County records and Applegate nonsense. He asked me to pick up his order so he wouldn't come in here and get distracted."

My hand stills on the pastry bag.

"He said that?"

"Not in those words."

"What words did he use?"

"He said, *Molly, please get my coffee and tell Dorothea I will send the filings before noon.*"

I glance off, stupidly disappointed.

"And then," Molly adds, "he stared at the wall for a while and said, also tell her good morning."

My eyes lift.

Molly smiles like a criminal.

"I'm relaying that last part with embellishment, but the spirit's accurate."

"You're dangerous."

"I work for Lorenzo. Occupational hazard."

I hand her the coffee and cookies.

"And these?" she asks.

"Espresso brownies for legal murder."

Her smile turns wicked. "Excellent."

After Molly leaves, Derek appears beside me with a tray of clean mugs.

"You're staring at the door."

"I'm looking at the door as an architectural feature."

"You do that a lot lately."

"I'm a fan of hinges."

"Is this about Lorenzo?"

"No."

"Because he called you beautiful yesterday in front of the old ladies from quilting group and May texted three people before he left the sidewalk."

I close my eyes. "Why do you know that?"

"Mrs. Talbot told me." He bumps my shoulder gently. "Get it, girl."

I glare at him.

He grins. "You're too young to say that to me."

"I'm twenty-two."

"Exactly. Go restock something."

"Emotionally?"

"Physically this time."

"On it."

The bell over the door rings at ten-oh-three.

I know before I look.

Which is unfortunate.

Knowing is dangerous. It means some part of me has already learned the shape of his arrival. The shift in the air. The pause of conversation. The way the bakery seems to square its shoulders and become aware of its flour on the counter.

Lorenzo steps inside.

Not Molly.

Him.

Dark suit. No tie. White shirt open at the throat. A navy coat damp from the rain. His hair is touched by mist, and there is a faint shadow under his eyes that tells me he has been working too early and sleeping too little.

He looks at me.

His expression changes.

Not the polished public smile.

Something quieter.

"Good morning, beautiful."

The word hits my body first.

Warmth. Softness. Panic. Pleasure.

Then Lucian's voice rises from memory, steady and infuriating.

Being desired is not the same as being inspected.

I breathe.

I let Lorenzo's compliment exist without turning it into a debt.

"Good morning," I say.

My voice is steadier than I feel.

His gaze moves once over my hair, my face, my apron, my

bandaged hand. Not consuming. Not cataloging for owner-ship. Seeing.

"Your hair is down."

"So everyone keeps telling me."

"It suits you."

My face warms.

Deflect. Dismiss. Roll my eyes. Say it's a mess.

Or receive.

Small things.

Real things.

"Thank you," I say. Then, because apparently honesty now comes in annoying little aftershocks, "That's uncomfort-able, but I like hearing it."

Lorenzo goes very still.

Not in a bad way.

In a way that tells me the sentence landed somewhere he was not expecting.

His voice lowers. "Noted."

My stomach flips.

Derek drops something in the back.

Not subtly.

I ignore him.

"Your usual?" I ask.

"Yes. Unless you recommend rebellion."

"Almond croissant. It's less rebellious than necessary, but more dependable than a muffin."

"Poor muffins."

"Muffins know what they did."

His mouth curves.

I prepare his coffee and pastry, grateful for the motion. Pour. Lid. Bag. Napkin. Ordinary movements to keep my hands from shaking.

When I slide them across, he places his card on the counter.

"Before you ask," he says, "yes, I'm paying."

"Growth."

"I'm proud of us."

"I'm proud of the almond croissant."

"As you should be."

I run his card.

The screen asks if he wants a receipt.

I look up.

He is still watching me.

Not with the public charm.

With nerves.

That should not be endearing.

It is.

"Do you need something case-related?" I ask.

"I sent the filings to your email. We tendered the title insurance claim, filed my appearance, and sent a demand to Applegate's counsel. William is reviewing the old documents. County archives may have the missing exhibit in the basement."

"The basement?"

"Apparently justice lives near old pipes."

"Comforting."

"We also found more on Grant Applegate. He has been acquiring properties near Main Street through shell companies. This appears bigger than your building."

My chest tightens.

"So I'm in the way."

His jaw shifts.

"Yes."

A clean answer.

No softening.

I appreciate it even as it scares me.

"But you're not alone in the way," he says.

My throat tightens.

Don't cry near the pastry case.

It startles the customers.

"Okay," I whisper.

He sets his hand on the counter, palm down, not reaching for mine. "I also came to ask about tonight."

"Tonight?"

"My father gets into town tomorrow. Friday is dinner with him. The wedding is Saturday. I thought maybe tonight could be quieter. No audience. No strategy meeting. Just..." He pauses, and that pause changes everything. "Dinner."

My pulse jumps.

"At a restaurant?"

"I was thinking my place."

Oh.

The bakery blurs at the edges.

Not literally.

Emotionally.

A restaurant is public.

A restaurant has exits and witnesses and May bringing dumplings while silently reading every shift of my face. A restaurant is performance, which I understand because performance has rules.

His house is private.

His house has no display case.

No counter between us.

No town watching to remind us we are pretending.

No easy way to say this is for appearances when there are no appearances to maintain.

A private dinner is not fake girlfriend strategy.

Or not only.

It's a door.

My palm tingles.

Yes.

Maybe.

No.

Lorenzo sees something change in my face.

"If you would prefer a restaurant, say so," he says immediately. "Or not tonight. Or we keep it case-only for today. I'm not asking as your lawyer."

That sentence matters.

I grab onto it.

"Then who is asking?"

He takes a breath.

The bakery quiets around us, or maybe I only stop hearing it.

"I am."

No charm.

No smoldering nonsense.

No beautiful lady, no sunshine morning, no blown kiss to make Derek whoop behind the espresso machine.

Just Lorenzo.

Real.

"I would like to cook for you," he says. "Badly, possibly. But earnestly."

A laugh catches in my throat.

"That's a dangerous combination."

"I have backup takeout options."

"Good. A man with contingency plans."

"I'm a lawyer."

"No, this is bigger than law. This is dinner."

His smile appears, softer now.

"I don't have people over often," he says.

Something about the admission changes the invitation again.

It's not only me entering his private space.

It's him opening one.

"Why not?" I ask before I can stop myself.

His eyes flicker.

"Because it's easier to be charming in public."

Oh.

Well.

That's honest enough to be annoying.

"I understand that," I say.

"I thought you might."

There is a silence.

Not empty.

Full of too many possible answers.

Derek is absolutely listening.

Baylin is probably listening from the kitchen and pretending the bread told her to.

A customer coughs near the cookie case.

Right. The world exists.

I look at Lorenzo.

"I need a second."

"Take it."

I turn away under the pretense of straightening the pastry bags, but really I'm asking myself questions.

Do I want to go?

Yes.

Am I afraid?

Yes.

Is fear a no?

Not always.

Is this fake?

No.

That answer arrives too quickly.

I close my eyes.

It's not entirely real either. Not defined. Not safe. Not promised. But it's not fake in the way dinner at his house cannot be fake.

Not for me.

When I turn back, Lorenzo is still waiting.

No pressure in his face.

Only attention.

"Green with a yellow border," I say.

He exhales softly.

"Thank you for telling me."

"I want to come," I say, and my cheeks immediately heat because words are terrible and that one has layers. "To dinner. I mean dinner."

His mouth twitches.

He fights the smile like a gentleman.

Mostly.

"I understood."

"Did you?"

"Yes."

"Good. Don't make that face."

"What face?"

"The one that knows exactly what I said."

This time, he smiles.

"Noted."

I point at him. "Dangerous."

"Yes."

"I need terms."

His expression sharpens, but not with irritation. With focus.

"Name them."

I grip the counter.

"No expectation that I stay late."

"Agreed."

"No alcohol for me tonight. I want a clear head."

"Agreed. I can skip it too."

"That's not necessary."

"I want to."

My chest tightens.

Fine.

"Okay," I say. "No touching unless discussed or clearly within our agreement."

"Of course."

"Dinner, only."

He nods. "Dinner only."

"Okay," I say.

"Okay?"

"Yes."

A customer steps closer to the register with a tray of cookies, eyes wide with the unmistakable expression of a person pretending not to overhear something worth telling at least three friends.

I smile at her.

It may be too bright.

"Hi. I can help you."

Lorenzo steps aside, coffee in hand, giving me room to work.

He waits while I ring up the customer. That feels intimate too, somehow. Him standing in my bakery while I do my job. Watching without interrupting. Not needing the moment to belong to him.

When the customer leaves, definitely with a story, he looks back at me.

"I'll text you my address," he says. "Six?"

"You said you were leaving work early for little old me?"

His eyes warm. "I'm leaving work early for stubborn, terrifying, flour-covered you."

My breath catches.

Stubborn.

Not resilient.

He remembered.

"Good answer," I say softly.

His expression shifts.

For a second, the word hangs there.

Good.

Mine, not his.

A little power moving back and forth between us.

Then he lifts the coffee in a small salute.

"I'll see you at six, Dorothea."

"Six."

He turns to leave.

At the door, he pauses.

No blown kiss this time.

No performance for Derek, Baylin, or the customers.

He only looks back once.

Then he leaves.

The bell rings behind him.

I stand very still.

Derek appears beside me approximately one second later.

"So," he says.

"No."

"I didn't even say anything."

"You were about to."

"I was only going to say get it, girl."

"Still no."

Baylin leans through the kitchen doorway with a tray of apple galettes.

"I like him," she says.

"You like everyone with dramatic cheekbones and unresolved grief."

"I'm consistent."

Derek looks toward the door. "Are you guys, like, real now?"

The question lands harder than it should.

Real.

Fake.

Maybe.

My palm warms.

I pick up a cloth and wipe a clean section of counter because my hands need something to do.

"We're figuring it out," I say.

Derek grins.

Baylin smiles, softer.

Neither of them teases me.

That's how I know they heard the tremor under the words.

The rest of the day moves strangely.

Every task feels both ordinary and charged. I glaze apple galettes. I answer questions about wedding cake tastings. I tell a tourist that no, Coral Cove doesn't have a formal ghost tour, but if they want gossip with supernatural implications, Mrs. Talbot is usually at the post office at eleven.

I check my phone too many times.

At noon, Lorenzo sends his address.

> Lorenzo: No pressure. Text me if you change your mind. I will still send case updates either way.

I stare at that second sentence for a long time.
Legal help separate from dinner.
Dinner separate from obligation.
Desire separate from debt.

> Dorothea: I'm still coming to dinner. No mushrooms please.

His reply comes back almost immediately.

> Lorenzo: Roger that. I suppose I'll be the only Fun-gi tonight. Emergency takeout on standby, I promise .

> Dorothea: I'm holding you to that

> Lorenzo: Are you still Green?

I press my palm to the counter grounding myself.

> Dorothea:Green with a yellow border.

> Lorenzo: Understood.

That word should not make me feel safe.
But when it comes from him, it does.
At three, Lea storms through the bakery door with the

force of a woman who has received partial information and intends to extract the rest.

"You're going to his house?"

I look at Derek.

He points to Baylin.

Baylin points to the bread.

"The bread told her," Derek says.

I sigh.

Lea plants herself at the counter. "Dottie."

"Yes."

"For dinner?"

"Yes."

"Private dinner?"

"Yes."

"Do you want me to call you halfway through with an emergency?"

I pause.

That's not a bad idea.

"No," I say slowly. "But I want you to be available if I text red."

Lea's expression changes immediately.

"Always."

"And yellow means I might need a check-in but not extraction."

"Got it."

"And green means don't interrupt me unless the book-store catches fire."

"What if the bookstore catches fire but romantically?"

"Lea."

"Fine."

She reaches across the counter and squeezes my uninjured hand.

"You're bringing the key."

"I'm trying."

"That counts."

After closing, I stand in my apartment wearing a towel and staring at my closet.

Again.

This is becoming a ritual I did not consent to.

Dinner only.

His house.

No alcohol.

No mushrooms.

No touching unless discussed or within terms.

Green with a yellow border.

I choose dark jeans first because they are practical. Then I reject them because practical has become suspicious. I choose the pink dress from Golden Chopsticks, then reject it because repeating outfits feels like tempting the universe. Finally, I settle on a deep green dress I bought last year for a holiday market and never wore because it felt too pretty for selling cookies in the rain.

The dress is soft, long-sleeved, and fitted enough to remind me I have a body without making that body the evening's main topic. It falls just above my knees. I pair it with boots because I'm not walking into any man's house without shoes I can confidently leave in if needed.

I leave my hair down.

Then I put half of it back.

Then I take it down again.

"Green," I tell the mirror.

My reflection looks back.

Flushed. Nervous. Hair loose around my shoulders. Lips tinted, but not too much. Mascara. A little gold at my ears because Kaytie once told me every woman should have earrings that make her feel like she has a secret.

I look soft.

Not breakable.

There is a difference.

My phone buzzes.

Lorenzo: I'm attempting sauce. Pray for me.

I can't help but laugh.

Dorothea: Don't burn your house down. I'm attached to the idea of seeing it.

Lorenzo: Noted. Fire extinguisher is visible should anything happen..

I put the phone down and breathe.
Then I pick it back up and text Lea.

Dorothea: Green. Leaving in ten.

Lea: Key in hand, babe. Go be scared and
alive.

I press my palm once more.
No glow.
No visible mark.
Still, the key is there.
When I lock the bakery behind me and step into the misty evening, Coral Cove smells like rain, salt air, wet pavement, and someone's chimney smoke. The streetlights reflect in puddles. The windows of Spellbound Stories glow warm across the street. The Arcane Room's sign hangs farther down, dark and quiet.
I don't go that way.
Tonight, I walk toward Lorenzo's house.
A real door.
A real man.
A real dinner that might go beautifully, badly, awkwardly, gently, or all of the above.
My heart beats hard enough that I feel it in my throat.
Fear walks with me.
So does want.
This time, I don't make either one leave.

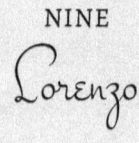

NINE

Lorenzo

There are many things I do well.

Cooking, apparently, is not one of them.

I stand in the middle of my kitchen with my sleeves rolled up, a wooden spoon in one hand, a pan of ruined garlic in front of me, and the growing suspicion that I have made a terrible mistake by inviting Dorothea Thompson into my home.

Not because I don't want her here.

That's the problem.

I want her here too much.

I want her in this house. In this kitchen. At my table. On my deck with the ocean below us and the evening light in her hair. I want her somewhere no one is watching us perform. No May. No Mrs. Talbot. No Derek pretending not to listen from behind the counter. No public strategy. No fake relationship terms doing the work of a chaperone.

Just Dorothea.

Just me.

A real dinner.

Dinner only, I remind myself.

She had said that clearly.

Dinner only.

No alcohol for her. No mushrooms. No touching unless discussed. Green with a yellow border.

I respect every part of that.

Which means I need to get the damn sauce right.

The garlic has other plans.

It goes from pale gold to bitter brown in the time it takes me to reach for basil. The kitchen fills with the acrid smell of failure.

I stare at the pan.

"You had one job," I tell it.

The garlic doesn't care.

I dump the contents into the sink, turn on the disposal, and start over.

Again.

My kitchen is beautiful, which is not the same as used.

That distinction feels more insulting tonight than usual.

The previous owner had filled the house with dark cabinets, red tile, heavy curtains, and enough decorative roosters to suggest a poultry-based curse. When I bought the place, I gutted almost everything. New floors. New windows. New paint. New light fixtures. Walls opened. Rot repaired. Deck reinforced. Bathrooms redone. The house sits above North Beach, tucked between wind-shaped pines and the long gray sweep of the Pacific, and I told myself renovation was a way to claim it.

In truth, I think renovation was a way to keep my hands busy.

Grief likes idle hands.

The kitchen was supposed to be the heart of the house.

That's what the designer said, anyway, standing right where I stand now with a clipboard and an expression of evangelical confidence. I chose marble countertops, stainless steel appliances, deep drawers, a wide farmhouse sink, and green tile for the backsplash because the sample reminded me of sea glass. I installed open shelving, then filled it with dishes I barely use. I bought good knives, good pans, cutting boards, linen napkins, a Dutch oven heavy enough to qualify as a weapon.

The room is perfect.

It has no soul.

I can argue in court. I can negotiate a hostile settlement. I can rebuild a staircase, badly at first, but eventually well enough. I can stand in front of my father and not flinch visibly.

But this kitchen has defeated me more times than I care to admit.

After Emily died, feeding myself felt absurd.

Not tragic. Not dramatic.

Absurd.

What was the point of chopping an onion for one? What was the point of washing a pan? What was the point of sitting down at a table across from an empty chair when takeout could be eaten over the sink and forgotten?

Then my mother died before she could reach me, and the idea of food became even stranger. She had cooked badly, but she had cooked constantly. Overcooked chicken. Underseasoned soup. Rice that clumped no matter what she did. She believed feeding people was love even when the food itself argued otherwise.

After she was gone, I renovated a kitchen I did not use.

Very healthy.

Very rational.

Therapy would have a field day.

The second batch of garlic starts to sizzle.

I lower the heat.

"Not today," I warn it.

The olive oil glistens. The garlic softens. I add onion, chopped unevenly because apparently knife skills require practice and humility. The tomatoes go in next. Then salt. Too much? Maybe. I stir.

It looks like sauce.

That feels promising.

I taste it.

It tastes like tomato, panic, and a man trying too hard.

I look toward the counter, where the emergency takeout menus are stacked beside two bottles of sparkling water.

Golden Chopsticks.

The Salty Gull.

That Thai place in Port Townsend that delivers only when the driver feels spiritually aligned with the distance.

I promised emergency takeout.

I may need it.

My phone lights up.

> Dorothea: Leaving now. YGY Also, no mushrooms remains legally binding.

I smile before I can stop myself and I heart 🩶 her message.

> Lorenzo:Be safe. I'll see you soon.

> Dorothea: I do what I want! ⋟(→‸←")⋟

Then she hearts 🩶 my message.
My chest loosens.
Then tightens again.
She is on her way.
I look down at myself.
Dark trousers. White shirt, sleeves rolled. No tie. I changed three times before settling on something that looked effortless, which is how I know I have lost my mind. I have never cared this much what a dinner guest thought of my forearms.

I set the table.
Not the formal dining room.
That room is too polished, too staged, too much like the kind of place my father would approve of after finding three faults. I set two places at the small table off the kitchen, near the windows that overlook the water. White plates. Blue napkins. No candles at first, then candles because apparently I'm courting ambience like a man in a commercial for olive oil.

I light them.
Then blow one out because two looks like seduction.
Then relight it because one looks like a vigil.
"Get a grip," I mutter.
The doorbell rings.
My body goes still.
The sauce bubbles behind me.
The house, usually too quiet, seems to inhale.

I wipe my hands on a towel, check the stove, then walk to the front door.

Through the glass, I see her.

Dorothea stands on my porch in a deep green dress and boots, hair loose around her shoulders, one hand gripping the strap of her bag. The porch light catches red-gold in her hair. The dress is soft, simple, and fitted enough to make me briefly forget every rule of civilized speech.

She looks nervous.

She looks like she came anyway.

That undoes me more than the dress.

I open the door.

For one dangerous second, I only look at her.

Then I remember myself.

"May I compliment you?" I ask.

Her eyes widen.

A blush moves up her throat.

"Yes."

"You look beautiful."

Her breath catches, small but audible.

She doesn't deflect.

She doesn't joke.

She stands there and receives it like it costs her something.

"Thank you," she says. "That's uncomfortable, but I like hearing it."

The sentence moves through me with unreasonable force.

"Noted."

Her mouth curves.

"Your house is very dramatic."

I glance back over my shoulder. "Thank you?"

"I mean that kindly. Mostly."

"Come in."

She steps inside.

I move back, giving her space.

The entry is too clean. I know it as soon as she looks around. Slate floor, white walls, black-framed photographs of the coastline, a bench that exists more for composition than use. The whole house carries city money trying to learn coastal restraint. Good materials. Good lines. Expensive quiet.

Dorothea is too polite to say anything immediately, which means she is definitely thinking.

I take her coat. "May I?"

She hesitates, then nods. "Yes, thank you."

I lift the coat from her shoulders carefully.

I hang her coat on the hook near the door. "I have sparkling water, tea, regular water, and coffee. The coffee is probably the safest thing I know how to make."

"The night is young."

Her gaze moves beyond me, toward the kitchen.

Her nose wrinkles.

I close my eyes.

"Say nothing."

"Did you burn something?"

"A little."

"A little can mean many things."

"In this context, it means garlic died for my ambition."

She laughs.

The sound fills the entryway and makes the house feel less expensive.

More awake.

"Show me the body," she says.

I lead her into the kitchen.

Dorothea pauses at the threshold.

Not because of the sauce.

Because of the room.

I watch her see it. The marble counters. The sea-glass tile. The wide windows. The perfect open shelves. The untouched row of copper measuring cups. The knife block still too new. The lack of clutter. The lack of history.

Her expression softens in a way I'm not prepared for.

"This kitchen is beautiful," she says.

"Yes."

"You don't use it."

I laugh once. "That obvious?"

"To me? Yes."

"Because you're a professional?"

"Because kitchens tell on people."

I lean against the counter. "What is mine saying?"

She sets her bag on a stool and looks around again, not judging. Reading.

"It says someone cared very much about making it right," she says. "But maybe not as much about living in it after."

The sauce bubbles.

The room goes quiet.

I look at the pan because it's easier than looking at her.

"That's uncomfortably accurate."

"I can stop."

"No," I say. "Don't."

Her gaze returns to mine.

There is the line again.

Truth offered gently, not softened into uselessness.

She moves toward the stove.

"May I?"

"Please."

She lifts the spoon and stirs the sauce. Her movements are immediate and sure. Not showing off. Not performing. Just hands knowing where they belong. She leans over the pot, inhales, then tastes from the spoon.

Her face doesn't inspire confidence.

"It's not terrible," she says.

"That means terrible."

"No. Terrible has a smell. This is confused."

I laugh. "Confused?"

"Yes. It wants help."

"So do I."

Her eyes flick to mine. "Do you want help, or do you want me to pretend it's fine?"

The question is gentle.

It's also sharper than any knife in my block.

I could say it's fine. I could play charming. I could save my pride with takeout and pretend the evening was always meant to be funny.

Instead, I tell the truth.

"I want help."

Her shoulders lower and she smiles. "Good."

She washes her hands at the sink, then opens the cabinets with a confidence that makes me want to hand over the entire house and see what she would do with it.

"Where are your spices?"

"Upper cabinet, right of the stove."

She opens it.

Then goes still.

"What?" I ask.

"You own twelve kinds of salt and no oregano."

"I had a consultant."

"For salt?"

"For the kitchen."

She turns slowly. "A consultant stocked your spices?"

"She made recommendations."

"Did she also recommend sadness?"

I laugh so hard I have to grip the counter.

Dorothea smiles, pleased with herself, then returns to the cabinet.

"We can work with this. Garlic powder. Red pepper flakes. Basil. A little sugar. Black pepper. Do you have butter?"

"Yes."

"Good. Butter forgives many sins."

"I have found that true of your pastries too."

"Pastry butter is holy. Sauce butter is practical."

She moves around my kitchen like she belongs to the language of it. Not to the house. Not to me. To the work. She lowers the heat, adds a little butter, a pinch of sugar, a splash of pasta water I had not known to save until she asked. She chops basil faster than I expect with the knife I barely use. She tastes again, adjusts salt, adds pepper.

I watch her.

That's all I do for several minutes.

I watch Dorothea Thompson bring life into the room I built to avoid feeling empty.

The transformation is almost embarrassing.

The kitchen doesn't look different.

It feels different.

Her bag on the stool. Her sleeves pushed slightly up. Her hair falling forward until she tucks it behind her ear with the back of her wrist. The open cabinet. The smell of garlic recovering from tragedy. The spoon tapping against the pot. Her voice telling me to stir slower.

"Slower," she says again.

I look down.

I'm stirring like I'm cross-examining the sauce.

"Sorry."

"Sauce is not a hostile witness."

"I was beginning to suspect."

She takes the spoon from me and shows me. "Like this. You're not trying to defeat it. You're checking the bottom, keeping it from sticking, helping it come together."

"Is this a cooking lesson or an accusation?"

"Yes."

I smile.

She smiles back.

The moment is too warm.

Too easy.

Then she says, "One of my foster moms used to make sauce like this."

The warmth changes.

I don't move.

She keeps stirring.

"Which one?"

"Mrs. Alvarez. Rosa." Her mouth softens around the name. "She took me in when I was thirteen. I stayed with her for eight months."

Only eight months.

The way she says it tells me it was one of the longest safe places she had.

"She taught you to cook?"

"She taught me to survive with taste."

I lean against the counter and listen.

Dorothea adds more basil.

"Rosa could stretch ten dollars into three dinners and make it feel like we were lucky. Canned tomatoes, onions, garlic, pasta, rice, beans. She said poor food didn't have to taste poor. She made me learn where every dollar went. Food, rent, bus fare, emergency cash. She had this little notebook with columns. I hated it at the time."

She smiles, but her eyes are somewhere else.

"She said, Dottie, nobody gets to call you helpless if you can feed yourself."

My chest tightens.

"What happened?"

The question is soft.

It still feels like stepping too close.

Dorothea keeps her gaze on the sauce.

"She got sick. She had cancer, but she didn't tell the agency how bad it was. I think she was afraid they'd move me sooner if they knew. When she went into the hospital, they sent me to another placement."

Her voice stays steady.

Too steady.

"I begged to stay with her sister, but there wasn't paperwork, and the sister didn't have the right approvals. So I packed my things. Black garbage bag, because that was what I had."

I close my eyes for one second.

A black garbage bag.

Thirteen years old.

Leaving the woman who taught her how to feed herself and thrive in this world.

"She died a few weeks later," Dorothea says. "No one took me to the funeral."

I don't speak.

There is nothing useful to say immediately.

She reaches for the spoon, tastes the sauce again, then nods.

"There. Better."

As if she has not just handed me something breakable. "Dorothea?"

She doesn't look up. "It's okay," she says shaking her in tiny tight movements

"No."

Her hand stills.

"That's not okay."

The kitchen goes quiet except for the bubble of sauce.

Her throat moves. "No," she says finally. "It wasn't."

The truth sits between us.

She doesn't apologize for it.

That feels important.

"Thank you for telling me," I say.

Her eyes flick up.

She nods once. "You're welcome."

Dinner is not perfect.

It's better than perfect.

The pasta is slightly overcooked because I cooked it before she arrived and forgot that timing exists. The sauce, rescued by Dorothea, is good enough that I take seconds. She makes garlic toast from the bread I nearly forgot in the oven, scraping off the too-dark edges and declaring them "rustic enough to survive." We drink sparkling water out of wine glasses because I own them and she says refusing to use pretty things is a waste.

We sit at the small table by the windows.

The ocean darkens outside, gray water turning ink-blue under the evening sky. Rain taps softly against the glass. The candles flicker between us. Not too many. Just enough.

I ask about the bakery.

She tells me about Kaytie teaching her croissants. Baylin calling rye "moody but sincere." Derek reorganizing boxes wrong every week but never making the same customer mistake twice. May buying comfort rolls for Harold while pretending they are for someone else.

Her whole face changes when she talks about the place.

Not because she becomes different.

Because she becomes more visibly herself.

I tell her about the house. The rotten deck boards. The wall I accidentally opened too far and then had to pay a contractor to fix. The kitchen designer with the salt obsession. The green tile.

"You chose that," she says.

"Yes."

"Why?"

I look toward the backsplash.

Sea-glass green. Soft, imperfect, varied from tile to tile.

"It reminded me of the water here," I say. "Not the ocean in the city. This ocean."

"Coral Cove ocean."

"Yes."

"What's different?"

"The city ocean is something you look at from a distance. Here, it feels like it knows when you're lying."

Dorothea's mouth curves.

"I hate how much sense that makes."

"I do too."

She eats another bite of pasta, then says, "You said you wanted Coral Cove to be your forever home."

I set my fork down slowly.

"I did."

"What made you leave the city?"

I knew it was coming.

I invited it, in a way. My house. My father. My mother. My grief hiding in the kitchen cabinets.

Still, the question tightens my chest.

I reach for my water. "I was married once." The words come out badly. Too abrupt. Too sharp.

Dorothea stills, but she doesn't rush to fill the space.

Her silence is not empty.

It holds.

My eyes wander to the candle flame. "Her name was Emily."

Dorothea's expression softens.

I can feel myself preparing the polished version.

Emily was sick. She died. It was difficult. My mother died the same night. I moved to Coral Cove after.

Clean.

Contained.

A tragedy with all the messy parts trimmed away.

Dorothea waits.

And because she waits instead of asking me to make it easier for her, the polished version falls apart.

"We met in law school," I say. "She hated me at first."

"Why?"

"I was insufferable."

Dorothea nods solemnly. "I believe that."

A laugh catches in my throat.

It helps.

"She was brilliant. Quiet in class until someone said something stupid, then she destroyed them with one sentence and went back to taking notes. She had this way of looking at me like she could see every act I was performing and was bored by all of them."

Dorothea's eyes stay on mine.

Something shifts.

I let it.

"We got married too young," I say. "Or maybe not. I don't know anymore. People say that when someone dies young, like time would have made the love more legitimate if we had survived longer. But we loved each other. Not perfectly. We were busy, ambitious, arrogant. But it was real."

"What happened?"

I look down at my hands.

"She got sick."

Cancer is the word.

I don't say it yet.

Sometimes grief makes ordinary words too heavy to lift.

"At first, we thought it was manageable. Then we thought it was serious but treatable. Then it became the thing every room in our life revolved around. Appointments. Lab results. Medication schedules. Insurance calls. Side effects. Hope. Bad news. Better news. Worse news."

I breathe through the tightness.

"She went into remission for a while. We planned a vacation we never took. Bought luggage. Argued about where to go. She wanted Greece. I wanted somewhere quiet with room service because I was exhausted and selfish and terrified."

"You were her husband," Dorothea says softly. "That's not the same as selfish."

The words hit.

I look away.

"She relapsed."

The room seems to tilt.

I have told this story before, but not like this. Not in my kitchen with tomato sauce on the stove and Dorothea across from me in a green dress, looking at me as if my grief is not too much for the table.

"It was fast after that. Too fast. She was home on hospice. She hated that word. Hospice. Said it sounded like a place for people with thin blankets and bad soup. She made jokes until she couldn't."

My voice roughens.

I stop.

Dorothea doesn't move.

Doesn't reach.

Doesn't fix.

She only sits with me.

That's intimacy.

Not touching.

Staying.

"I was holding her when she died," I say.

The sentence tears on the way out.

I press my thumb against the side of my glass.

"I told her I loved her. I don't know if she heard me. People say they do, but people say a lot of things when they want the living to keep breathing."

Dorothea's eyes shine.

"I think maybe love is heard differently at the end," she says.

I look at her.

"I don't mean in a pretty greeting-card way," she says quickly. "I mean, maybe hearing is not only ears by then. Maybe it's hands. Breath. Presence. Maybe the body knows who stayed."

My throat closes.

I have no answer.

Maybe That's the answer.

I look toward the window. Rain streaks the glass.

"After Emily died, the apartment felt wrong. Too quiet. Too full. I called my mother because I didn't know who else to call. I could not get the words out. I kept trying to say Emily was gone, but if I said it, then it would be true."

I stop.

My chest feels carved open.

"My mother understood anyway. She said, Stay there, mijo. I'm coming."

Dorothea's hand moves on the table.

Not toward me exactly but available.

I look at it.

Then at her.

"Green?" she asks.

The word nearly breaks me. "Yes," I say.

She reaches across the table and takes my hand.

Her fingers are warm.

Strong.

I hold on too tightly for half a second, then loosen.

She stays.

"It was raining," I say. "Hard. Hard enough that she should not have driven. I know that. She knew that. But I was crying so badly she got in the car anyway."

My voice cracks.

This time, I let it.

"She hydroplaned. Hit a truck. Dead on impact."

Dorothea's fingers tighten around mine.

"I lost them both the same night." The unpolished truth.

Not the version my father uses.

Not the version I use in therapy.

Not the version that makes me sound noble or tragic or strong.

Just the truth.

Emily died in my arms.

My mother died coming to me.

And some part of me has been standing in that night ever since, waiting for one of them to arrive.

Dorothea doesn't say it was not my fault.

I expect that. People always say it. They offer it like a blanket, but it never fits. It cannot, because guilt doesn't care about logic. Guilt is not a judge. It's a room you keep walking back into because you think if you suffer enough, the door might open.

Dorothea doesn't hand me a blanket.

She sits in the room.

"I'm sorry," she says.

Simple.

Not enough.

Enough because she knows it's not enough.

I nod.

"My father blames me."

Her face changes.

Anger.

Immediate. Hot.

I almost smile.

Not because it's funny.

Because being defended before I ask for it's a strange thing.

"He said it was your fault?"

"Yes."

"Lorenzo."

"I know."

"No," she says, and the word is sharper now. "You may know he said it. That doesn't mean you know it's wrong."

She looks almost furious.

"I called her," I say.

"She chose to come."

"I needed her."

"She loved you."

"I was the reason she was on the road."

Dorothea leans forward. "You were the reason she knew where love was needed."

The sentence hits so hard I cannot breathe for a moment.

She seems startled by it too.

Her eyes widen slightly, but she doesn't take it back.

I look down at our joined hands.

"Don't say things like that unless you mean them."

"I mean it."

The candle flickers.

Rain taps the windows.

Somewhere outside, the ocean moves in the dark.

I close my eyes.

I don't cry.

Not because I'm strong.

Because something in me is too tired to perform grief properly.

Dorothea's thumb moves once over my knuckle.

"Thank you for telling me," she says.

The words are the same ones she gave me in my original life, in some other shape of this story.

Here, they land deeper.

I open my eyes.

"I told it badly."

"You told it honestly."

A laugh breaks through my chest.

Ragged.

Real.

She smiles a little.

The food has gone cold.

Neither of us cares.

After a while, I stand to clear the plates. Dorothea rises too.

"You don't have to help."

"I know."

She picks up her plate anyway.

Choice.

Not obligation.

The two of us move around the kitchen together. It should feel awkward after what I told her. It doesn't. Or it does, but in a human way. Plates into the sink. Leftovers into containers. Sauce wiped from the counter. She shows me how to store the pasta so it doesn't become glue by morning. I listen with the seriousness of a man receiving classified intelligence.

"You really don't cook much," she says.

"No."

"Do you want to?"

I pause.

No one has asked me that.

People ask if I can cook. If I like cooking. If I eat real food. They don't ask if I want to.

"I don't know," I say.

Her eyes lift to mine.

"Good answer."

I smile faintly.

"You're stealing my word."

"I'm revising its usage."

"Very bold."

"I learned from the best."

We take tea onto the deck.

The deck is wide, cedar boards damp at the edges from the earlier rain. I turn on the outdoor heater and bring out two blankets because the coast doesn't care about romance. Below the cliff, waves break in pale lines against the dark shore. The sky has cleared enough for a few stars to appear between clouds.

Dorothea stands at the railing, blanket around her shoulders, looking out at the water.

The green dress moves softly in the wind.

My house has never looked like this with anyone in it.

I sit in one of the deck chairs.

She takes the chair beside me, not too close, not far.

"Your house has a good view," she says.

"It does."

"Does it feel like home?"

I look toward the dark water.

Another direct question.

Another door.

"Sometimes," I say. "Mostly it feels like a place I'm trying to convince to become one."

She nods.

"I understand that."

"Does the bakery feel like home?"

"Yes."

No hesitation.

Then, after a moment, she adds, "And sometimes like the only proof I exist correctly."

I turn toward her.

She keeps looking at the ocean.

"I know that sounds dramatic."

"It sounds specific."

A small smile touches her mouth.

"That's my line."

"I contain multitudes."

She laughs softly.

The silence that follows is comfortable at first.

Then not.

Because I'm aware of her beside me. The curve of her cheek. The blanket slipping slightly off one shoulder. The scent of her, sugar, rain, something floral from her hair. I'm aware that I could ask to touch her hand again and she might say yes.

I'm also aware that she is my client.

That dinner was only dinner.

That I told her one of the ugliest truths of my life, and the instinct now is to reach for warmth because grief makes men selfish if they are not careful.

So I don't reach.

I grip my mug instead.

Dorothea notices.

"Are you okay?"

"No."

Her face turns toward me.

I answer before she can worry too much.

"But I'm not alone in it. That's different."

Her expression softens. "I'm glad."

"Thank you for staying."

"You didn't ask me to fix it."

"I wouldn't."

"You might."

She is right.

I might, with someone else. I might turn pain into a seduction, a joke, a performance of vulnerability designed to earn comfort without risking real exposure.

With Dorothea, the usual games feel obscene.

"I won't," I say.

She nods, accepting the promise for what it is.

Not forever.

Tonight.

For now.

The wind moves around us.

Eventually, she checks the time and sighs.

"I should go."

I stand anyway.

"Of course."

Inside, I walk her to the door. Her coat is still on the hook. I take it down, then pause.

"May I?"

Her smile is radiant. "Yes please, thank you."

I help her into it.

My hands brush her shoulders through the fabric.

Nothing more.

Enough.

At the door, she turns to face me.

"This was a good dinner."

"The sauce was rescued."

"The sauce had potential."

"You're generous."

"I'm practical. It was cheaper than takeout."

I smile.

She does too.

Then the silence changes again.

Not demanding.

Open.

I could ask for a kiss. I did tell her I'd give full warning before any private kissing. This is private.

I keep my hands at my sides.

"Can I hug you?" she asks.

The question surprises me.

Then warms my chest and I can't hide the smile. "Yes," I say. "Green."

She steps closer and wraps her arms around me.

I hold her carefully at first.

Then she settles against me, and I let myself hold her properly. Just enough for both of us to know it's real.

Her head rests against my chest.

My chin lowers near her hair.

For a moment, my house is quiet in a new way.

Not empty.

Quiet because something is being held.

She steps back first.

I let her.

"Thank you," she says.

"For dinner?"

"For telling me. For asking. For not making me feel like I had to become someone else to be here."

My throat tightens.

"You didn't."

"I know." She smiles, small and bright. "I'm learning."

Then she opens the door and steps into the night.

I watch from the porch until she gets into her car.

She waves once before pulling away.

I stand there long after her taillights vanish down the road.

When I go back inside, the house smells like basil, tomato, garlic, tea, and Dorothea.

The kitchen is messy.

Sauce on the stove.

Two plates drying by the sink.

A spoon on the counter.

A folded napkin left slightly crooked beside her chair.

For the first time since I bought the place, I don't immediately clean everything away.

I stand in the doorway and let the room stay lived in.

Tomorrow, my father arrives.

Applegate is still moving.

The case is not won.

The fake relationship is becoming something I don't know how to name without putting both of us in danger.

But tonight, Dorothea came into my underused kitchen and helped me make something edible from what I nearly ruined.

Tonight, I told the truth badly, and she stayed.

For now, that is enough.

For now, I leave the light on.

TEN

Dorothea

Dinner with Lorenzo's father feels like a test I did not study for, in a class I never agreed to take, taught by a man who probably thinks feelings are clerical errors.

I stand in front of my mirror upstairs over the bakery and smooth both hands down my dress for the third time.

The dress is pink.

Soft pink. Not loud. Not childish. Not the shade of frosting people order for baby showers and then ask if I can make "less sweet," which is like asking the ocean to be less damp. It's a grown pink. Muted. A little warm. It's a square neckline, short sleeves, and a skirt that moves around my knees when I turn.

It looks nice.

That's the problem.

Nice feels like effort.

Effort means hope.

Hope means someone can see it and decide it was too much, or not enough, or ridiculous, or charming in a way that makes me want to peel my own skin off and hide behind the display case.

I turn sideways.

The dress still looks nice.

Terrible development.

My hair is half up again, because fully down feels too

vulnerable and fully up feels like I'm arriving prepared to discuss payroll. I have gold earrings on, the ones Kaytie gave me when I bought the bakery. Little hoops, simple, warm. She said every woman should have at least one piece of jewelry that says she survived the bad years and still has skin in the game.

She liked saying things that sounded like fortunes after two cups of coffee.

I touch one earring.

Then my palm.

Yes.

Maybe.

No.

Not visible.

Never visible.

Still there.

Tonight has too many layers.

Dinner with Lorenzo's father.

Fake girlfriend performance.

Real legal dependence.

Real feelings I'm trying not to name too loudly in case they start multiplying like sourdough starter.

Sexual tension, which is a phrase I used to think belonged in books, not in my actual body while trying to locate matching shoes.

Public scrutiny.

Coral Cove Seafood and Grill is one of the nicest restaurants in town. It's also one of the most visible. The front windows face the harbor. The bar is always full of locals pretending they did not choose their seats for maximum observation. Half the town goes there for anniversaries, business dinners, family celebrations, and strategically timed gossip.

If Lorenzo kisses me there, people will see.

If Lorenzo doesn't kiss me there, people may see that too.

If I look nervous, people will notice.

If I look too happy, May will hear about it before I make it home and Lea will text me in all capital letters.

I sit on the edge of my bed and put my head in my hands.

The bedspread is rumpled. The apartment is quiet except

for rain tapping against the window and the low hum of the bakery refrigerators below. My home feels small tonight. Not bad small. Just honest. The couch in the living room is faded blue. The walls are mostly bare because art costs money and choosing art feels like announcing permanence too loudly. The kitchen is cozy because kitchens are the one place I know how to make belonging out of very little.

I glance toward the folder on my little table.

Applegate.

The case is not gone because I have a date.

The bakery is still under threat. Lorenzo is still my lawyer. He is also my fake boyfriend. He is also the man whose kitchen I stood in last night while he told me about Emily and his mother, and I held his hand.

I still feel that hand.

Real.

Warm.

Not fantasy.

Lucian had been safe because he was made of boundaries and smoke and whatever part of me needed a guide. He could not reject me in the real way. He could not misunderstand me tomorrow because he woke up tired, or proud, or afraid. He could not decide I was too much after seeing me reach for him.

Lorenzo can.

Lorenzo is real enough to disappoint me.

That's what makes him terrifying.

That's what makes tonight matter.

My phone buzzes. I breathe once before opening the message.

> Lorenzo: Car outside in ten. How are you doing?

> Dorothea: I'm nervous. But just a little yellow around the boarder.

> Lorenzo: I've got you. We can leave at any point. Red means we go. No explanation needed.

My throat tightens.

> Dorothea: Thank you.

Then, because I'm trying to be brave and not merely polite.

> Dorothea: Also, public kiss is still a yes. You know, if it comes up. But try to warn me before.

Three dots appear.
Disappear.
Appear again.

> Lorenzo: You'll know.

I press the phone to my chest.
"Okay," I whisper to the apartment. "Okay. Real door."
The apartment doesn't answer.
Good.
If the apartment starts giving advice, I'm moving into the walk-in.
Ten minutes later, Lorenzo's car waits at the curb below the bakery.
I lock my apartment, go down the exterior stairs, and pause in the misty evening air. The bakery sign glows pink and gold behind me. Main Street shines under rain. The windows of Spellbound Stories are lit across the street, and I see Lea's silhouette near the front display.
She turns.
Somehow, from that distance, she knows.
She lifts both thumbs.
I roll my eyes.
Then I wave.
Lorenzo steps out of the car.
My breath catches.
Dark suit. Black shirt. No tie. His hair slightly damp from the mist. He looks like a man rich women describe as dangerous after one glass of wine too many, but tonight I

know what is under the polish. The grief. The old anger. The man who owns twelve kinds of salt and no oregano. The man whose kitchen still smelled like basil when I left.

His eyes move over me once.

Carefully.

Not greedily.

Still, my body warms.

"You look beautiful."

I inhale and let it reach me. "Thank you."

His expression softens. "I like saying it."

My heart does something stupid. "Dangerous," I say.

"Yes." He opens the car door for me.

"Thank you," I say getting in.

The drive to Coral Cove Seafood and Grill takes less than seven minutes, which is frankly not enough time to become an emotionally stable person. Lorenzo doesn't fill the silence with charm. He drives with one hand on the wheel, the other resting near the gearshift, not reaching for me. The quiet between us feels deliberate. A room with open doors.

"How are you?" he asks.

I look out at the harbor lights through the windshield.

"A bit nervous."

"Does it help if I tell you that you make me feel brave?" I ask.

She lets out a nervous laugh. "Is it bad if I say a little?"

"Not at all," I say chuckling.

"I'm Grateful you asked how I was instead of telling me not to be me."

His hand tightens briefly on the wheel.

"I know better."

"Because you're wise?"

"Because you have trained me."

I laugh.

It helps.

A little.

* * *

The restaurant glows ahead, warm windows against gray water. Coral Cove Seafood and Grill sits near the harbor, all dark wood, brass lights, white tablecloths, and the kind of entrance that makes a person want to check whether their shoes know how to behave.

Lorenzo parks.

Before he gets out, he turns to me.

"My father will test you."

"I assumed."

"He will be polite until he decides politeness no longer serves him."

"That sounds like a terrible superpower."

"It is."

"What does he know about me?"

"That you own the bakery. That we are dating. That I live here and he thinks this town is beneath me."

"Charming."

"He may try to make you feel small."

A sharp little laugh leaves me. "He can get in line."

Lorenzo's face changes.

Not amusement.

Understanding. "I won't let him." The words are protective. They are also a little dangerous.

I touch my palm.

"I know," I say. "But I need to not let him too."

His eyes hold mine. "Okay."

We step out of the car. The air smells like rain, salt, fried seafood, and expensive perfume drifting from the restaurant door. Lorenzo offers his arm.

I take it. His arm is solid beneath my fingers. The warmth of him through his suit travels up my hand.

Before we reach the entrance, Lorenzo slows to a stop and turns toward me. The golden light from the restaurant windows catches the sharp lines of his face.

"Dorothea," he says quietly, voice low. "Before we go in... I've been thinking. If this is going to look real, especially in front of my father, we should probably practice a first kiss. So it doesn't feel staged when people are watching."

My stomach flips hard. A practice kiss. With him.

I search his face for a moment, nerves and something warmer twisting together inside me. He's not pushing. He's offering me control.

"Okay," I whisper. "Yeah… that's actually a good idea."

Lorenzo steps closer, backing me gently against the side of the car. One hand lifts to cradle the side of my face, his thumb brushing slowly across my cheekbone. His touch is careful. Patient.

He leans in and kisses me softly at first—just a brush of warm lips, giving me time to pull away if I want to. I don't. Instead, I tilt my head up, silently asking for more.

That's when he deepens it.

His mouth moves against mine with devastating gentleness, then growing hunger. When I part my lips, he slides his tongue inside, slow and sensual, tasting me like he has all the time in the world. A low sound escapes my throat—half surprise, half need—and he answers it with a quiet groan of his own, pressing me more firmly against the car.

The kiss turns passionate. Deep. Wet. His free hand slides to my waist, pulling me closer as his tongue strokes mine in a slow, intoxicating rhythm. Heat floods through my body, pooling low in my belly. I've never been kissed like this—like I'm something precious and delicious at the same time. Every careful glide of his tongue, every soft nip of his lips, every time he pulls back just enough to let me breathe before diving back in, makes my knees weak.

For a few perfect, dizzying moments, I forget this is pretend. I forget my fears. I only feel him—his warmth, his strength, the way he's holding back just enough to keep me safe while still unraveling me completely.

A loud burst of laughter from a group of people walking toward the restaurant startles us apart.

We're both breathing hard. Lorenzo rests his forehead against mine for a second, eyes closed, jaw tight like he's trying to regain control.

"Jesus," he murmurs, almost to himself.

I can't speak. My lips feel swollen, tingling. My whole body is humming.

He pulls back slightly and looks at me, searching my face. Whatever he sees makes the corner of his mouth tilt up in a soft, almost wondering smile.

"Ready?" he asks, voice a little rough.

I nod, still dazed.

Lorenzo offers his arm again. This time when I take it, my fingers tremble slightly against his sleeve.

* * *

Inside, the restaurant hums with conversation.

Glasses clink. Silverware taps plates. Someone laughs too loudly near the bar. The hostess smiles at Lorenzo with recognition, then at me with the bright curiosity of someone adding a new chapter to a book already being read by the entire town. She seats us right away.

"Mr. Moretti," she says. "Your party is just arriving."

I look back toward the entry.

José Moretti stands near the host stand.

I know it's him before Lorenzo stiffens beside me.

José is tall, silver-haired, and severe in a dark suit that probably costs more than my espresso machine. His face is handsome in the way old money and old cruelty can be handsome, all sharp lines and controlled expression. His gaze moves over Lorenzo first, assessing. Then me.

Not assessing.

Weighing.

I know that look.

Adults in foster care had versions of it. Caseworkers. School administrators. Foster fathers who wondered whether taking in a teenage girl would be more inconvenience than virtue. It's the look of someone deciding what category to place you in so they don't have to meet you as a person.

My spine straightens as we step further inside, but Lorenzo's hand slides over mine where it rests on his arm. Not holding me in place—simply covering, steadying. Asking.

I breathe.

"Green," I whisper.

He looks down at me, his dark eyes warm, a faint smile tugging at the corner of his mouth.

"May I kiss you again?" he asks softly.

My pulse jumps, but not from fear this time. After what we just shared outside, this feels different. Safer. Like we're choosing each other again, right here in the open.

I nod, smiling before I can stop myself.

Lorenzo leans down and kisses me gently.

It's soft and slow, almost reverent. His lips are warm and sure, lingering just long enough to make my stomach flutter. There's no demand in it, only sweetness and quiet intention. The hunger we shared minutes ago is still there, banked low like embers, but right now he's giving me something gentler. Something real.

I let myself lean into him just a little. My shoulders drop. The knot of anxiety I'd been carrying unwinds, replaced by a quiet, glowing warmth. For a few beautiful seconds, I stop performing. I stop thinking about who's watching or what this is supposed to be.

I just kiss him back—softly, sincerely—and it feels surprisingly good. Natural. Like maybe I'm allowed to enjoy this, even if it's pretend.

When he pulls away, his forehead rests against mine for a brief moment, and the whole night feels different. Brighter.

Fake for show.

Not fake in me.

"My love," Lorenzo says softly, and I nearly lose the ability to stand.

Then he turns to his father.

"Papá, this is Dorothea Thompson. Dorothea, this is my father, José Moretti."

José extends his hand.

I take it.

His grip is firm.

Too firm by a fraction.

"Dorothea," he says. "A pleasure."

"Mr. Moretti."

"José is fine."

It's not fine.

Nothing about him is fine.

But I smile. "José, then."

The hostess leads us to a table near the windows. Harbor lights shimmer outside through the rain. The table is set with white linen, polished silver, and enough glasses to make hydration look ceremonial.

I had arrived almost exactly on time, but they must have held the table. The waiter appears immediately.

"Would you care to start with drinks?"

I glance at Lorenzo.

No alcohol for me tonight applied to his house. Still, I want a clear head for José. I don't need wine making me brave. Wine courage has interest rates.

"I'll have sparkling water with lime," I say.

Lorenzo's eyes flick to mine.

Approval? No. Respect.

"I'll have the same," he says.

José's brows lift.

"No wine?"

"Not tonight," Lorenzo says.

José looks at me. "Do you not drink, Dorothea?"

"I do. I also like knowing exactly what I mean when I speak. The sentence leaves me before I can soften it.

Lorenzo's mouth twitches.

José studies me.

Then smiles without warmth. "Admirable."

He orders an old fashioned.

Once the waiter leaves, silence settles in the crisp white space between us.

José takes it first.

"So. Dorothea. Lorenzo tells me you own a bakery."

"I do. Knead the Dough."

"Yes. Quaint name."

I sip my water.

Quaint can be kind from the right mouth.

From his, it's a drawer closing.

"Thank you. It does well for us."

"For us?"

"Myself and my staff. Baylin is my bread goddess. Derek works customer service. I have seasonal help during festivals."

"You employ people."

"I do."

His eyes sharpen slightly, as if he did not expect the answer to have weight.

Lorenzo leans back in his chair, but I feel him watching me. Not rescuing. Letting me speak.

"The bakery is part of the town's morning routine," he

says after a beat. "People line up around the block for her pastries when she has a new special."

José glances at him.

Something cold passes through his face at the pride in Lorenzo's voice.

"How entrepreneurial."

Another drawer.

My fingers tighten under the table.

"Thank you," I say.

The waiter returns with drinks and menus.

I use the menu like a shield.

Seafood linguine. Lobster mac and cheese. Crab cakes. Salmon. Halibut. Tuna tartare. Prices that make my bakery brain begin calculating ingredient cost and labor margins.

The waiter returns too quickly.

"I'll have the lobster mac and cheese," I say, because if I'm going to be emotionally tested, I want cheese involved. "And would you like to share the crab cakes?" I ask Lorenzo.

His eyes warm. "Absolutely."

José watches the exchange.

"Tuna tartare," he says. "And another old fashioned when you have a moment."

Lorenzo orders shrimp tacos, because he has the audacity to make seafood casual.

The waiter leaves.

José turns his gaze to Lorenzo.

"How long have you two been seeing each other?"

The question is expected.

Still, my stomach tightens.

Lorenzo reaches for his water. "Long enough to know she has strong opinions about butter, coffee, and men who underestimate her."

I almost smile.

José doesn't.

"And how did you meet?"

Lorenzo looks at me.

Not for permission exactly.

For alignment.

I nod faintly.

He turns back to his father.

"I walked into Knead the Dough on opening day," he says.

I blink.

That's not the agreed story.

Or not one we wrote down.

"I had a meeting nearby and smelled pear and cinnamon from the sidewalk. Inside, there was this woman behind the counter in a sunflower apron, trying to make a line of twenty people feel like each one had her full attention."

My heart slows.

The sunflower apron.

Rosa's apron.

I wore it opening day because it was the closest thing I had to a blessing from a mother who could not be there.

I stare at him.

"You remember that?"

Lorenzo's gaze meets mine. "I remember everything."

The words land in my chest with frightening precision.

Maybe he says them for the performance. But he remembers the apron.

No one remembers the apron.

José clears his throat. "So you were charmed by pastries and an apron."

Lorenzo doesn't look away from me. "I was impressed by competence."

My throat tightens.

I have no witty answer.

The food comes, saving me.

For a few minutes, dinner behaves like dinner.

Crab cakes are placed between us. My lobster mac and cheese arrives bubbling in a shallow dish, fragrant with butter, seafood, and toasted crumbs. Lorenzo's tacos are bright with slaw and lime. José's tuna looks sharp and expensive, which suits him.

Lorenzo offers me a bite of his shrimp taco.

Not toward my mouth.

On his fork, paused halfway, waiting.

Public.

Fake.

Maybe real.

I glance at José, who watches us with the detached interest of a man observing an exhibit.

"Green?" Lorenzo murmurs.

My face warms.

"Yes."

This time, I lean forward.

He feeds me the bite.

It's small. Publicly acceptable. Still, his eyes stay on my mouth for one fraction of a second too long, and my body notices like it's been assigned to take minutes.

The shrimp is spicy and bright.

"Good?" he asks.

"Yes."

Then he tastes a bit of my lobster mac and cheese from my fork, and I cannot decide whether feeding a man pasta in front of his emotionally abusive father counts as fake dating or entering a legally distinct second realm.

The answer is probably both.

José orders another drink.

His face changes after the second.

Not loose.

Sharper.

As if alcohol removes the polish instead of dulling the blade.

"So," he says, setting his glass down. "Has my son told you why he is here?"

Lorenzo's hand stills.

"In Coral Cove?" I ask.

"Yes."

"He loves the town."

José laughs.

Small.

Cutting.

"Does he?"

Lorenzo's expression closes.

There.

The mask.

I have seen him controlled before. In his office. At Golden Chopsticks. At his house when grief made the room too quiet. But this is different. This is not control he chooses because it serves him. This is armor snapping into place because a blow is coming and his body knows the rhythm.

My stomach tightens.

"Papá," Lorenzo says.

José ignores him.

"Did he tell you he ran here?"

Lorenzo's jaw flexes.

I set my fork down. "He told me enough."

"Oh, I doubt that." José's gaze cuts to me. "Did he tell you how he killed his mother?"

The table goes silent.

Not just our table.

Maybe I imagine it, but the whole restaurant seems to pull back.

Lorenzo goes still.

Completely still.

His face doesn't twist with anger. It empties.

His eyes are fixed on his father, but he is not here entirely. I can see it. Some part of him has been thrown backward into rain, a phone call, a night he told me about with his hand in mine and his voice breaking around the truth.

"Dad," he says.

The word is not a warning.

It's almost a plea.

José keeps going.

"Did he tell you what a fuck-up he was? How he called his mother sobbing because he could not handle losing his wife, and she died on the road because he needed her to clean up his mess?"

My body reacts before my mind does.

Heat flashes through me.

Not embarrassment.

Rage.

Clean and bright.

I know this language.

Not the specifics. Not the wealthy father, the expensive suit, the old fashioned in a crystal glass. But the shape of it. The use of a wound as a leash. The way cruelty dresses itself as truth and calls pain accountability. The way powerful adults take grief and build a cage out of it, then tell you it's your own fault you cannot breathe.

I have heard versions of this voice in foster homes.

You should be grateful.

You're difficult to place.

You make people give up.

You're resilient, aren't you?

I know emotional abuse when it sits at a white tablecloth and orders tuna tartare.

Lorenzo's hand is on the table.

I place mine over it.

His skin is cold.

That frightens me more than José.

"Lorenzo," I say softly.

His eyes flick to mine.

He looks shaken.

Not angry.

Shaken.

Like a boy has appeared under the man's suit and is waiting to be blamed again.

That decides me.

I turn to José.

"How dare you."

The words cut out of me before I can refine them.

José's eyes narrow. "Excuse me?"

"No," I say. "You don't get excused for that."

Lorenzo's hand twitches under mine.

I keep my palm there.

Not restraining.

Anchoring.

"You lost your wife," I say. "That's awful. That's grief I won't pretend to understand."

José's face darkens.

"But he lost his mother." My voice shakes, but it doesn't break. "And his wife. On the same night. He was grieving, and you turned that grief into a weapon because blaming him was easier than sitting with what you lost."

José stands halfway. "You know nothing about my family."

217

"I know what it looks like when someone uses love as punishment."

The sentence lands.

Hard.

Even Lorenzo looks at me.

I keep going because stopping would mean swallowing the truth for the sake of a man who deserves to choke on it.

"Your son did not kill his mother. He needed her. She loved him. She chose to go to him because that is what love does when someone is broken. You can be angry at the storm, the road, the truck, God, fate, whatever helps you sleep. But you don't get to put that on him because he survived."

José's mouth tightens.

I lean forward. "And if you cannot be proud of the life he has built here, fine. That's your failure. But don't come into his town, sit across from the woman he brought to meet you, and try to make him small because you cannot stand that he found a way to live without becoming you."

Silence.

Complete.

Burning.

My heart pounds so hard I feel it in my throat.

José looks at me like he wants to slap me with money, history, and every door he has ever controlled.

I look back.

No display case.

No counter.

No fantasy guide.

Just me.

Lorenzo's hand turns under mine.

His fingers close around my hand.

Not tight.

Present.

"Dorothea," he says.

His voice is rough.

I turn.

He is pale.

His eyes shine, but no tears fall.

Not here.

Not in front of José.

"We should go," he says.

I nod.

He stands slowly.

Not with immediate decisiveness.

With effort.

As if standing requires pulling himself back into his body one inch at a time.

He takes cash from his wallet and drops it on the table. Too much really, then he looks at his father.

For one second, I think he will say something.

He doesn't.

Maybe he cannot.

Maybe the silence is all he has tonight.

He keeps my hand in his as we leave.

The restaurant watches us.

I don't care.

* * *

Outside, the rain has softened into mist.

Lorenzo walks me toward the bakery, not the car.

He doesn't ask.

He knows I need my home.

For once, I don't resent being known.

The walk is quiet.

Not comfortable.

Not awful.

Full.

His hand remains around mine the whole way. When we reach Knead the Dough, the pink sign glows above the dark storefront. The bakery smells faintly of sugar and old heat even from outside. I unlock the side door that leads to the apartment stairs.

Then I pause.

Lorenzo stands beside me, face turned slightly away, jaw tight, eyes unfocused.

He is holding himself together with wire.

I know that look too.

If I let him leave like this, he will go home to that beautiful empty kitchen and clean something that doesn't need cleaning until the grief folds itself back into his bones.

I don't want that.

I also cannot make him stay.

My palm tingles.

Ask.

"I'm making tea," I say.

He looks at me.

That's not the same as an invitation.

Coward.

I breathe.

"Do you want to come up?"

His throat moves.

"You don't have to do that because you feel bad."

"I know."

"I'm serious."

"So am I."

His eyes search mine.

"Green?" he asks quietly.

My chest aches.

"Green. Dinner is over. Performance is over. This is not fake girlfriend strategy."

Something in his face breaks a little.

Then he nods. "Then yes."

I lead him upstairs.

The apartment feels smaller with Lorenzo in it.

Not because he is large, though he is. Not because he crowds it, because he does the opposite. He steps inside carefully, as if my apartment is a space he has been permitted into and doesn't want to disturb.

That hurts more than if he had judged it.

He sees the faded couch. The bare walls. The little TV. The bookshelf crammed too full. The rug with the curled corner. The kitchen with its chipped mug collection, tiny stove, and warm yellow light over the sink.

I wait for shame.

It comes, old and familiar.

Then something else comes too.

This is mine.

Not impressive.

Mine.

I close the door.

"Tea?" I ask.

"Yes."

"What kind?"

"Whatever you have."

"That's not a tea answer."

He blinks.

I open the cabinet.

"I have peppermint, chamomile, Earl Grey, and something Lea gave me called Moonlit Boundaries, which I have refused to drink because the name sounds like it will give me homework."

A small laugh leaves him.

Barely.

It's enough.

"Chamomile," he says.

"Good choice. Cowardly, but good."

"I accept the judgment."

I fill the kettle.

My hands need tasks. Water. Mugs. Tea bags. Honey. Small plates. Leftover pear danish from the bakery because tenderness without food feels unfinished to me.

Lorenzo stands near the table.

Not sitting.

Not moving.

Lost in my little kitchen like a man who has misplaced his own skin.

"Sit," I say.

He looks at me.

"Please."

He sits.

I set a plate with pastry in front of him.

"You don't have to feed me."

"I'm aware."

"Dorothea."

"I don't know what to do with tenderness unless I put it on a plate first."

The confession slips out too honestly.

His face changes.

He looks down at the pastry.

Then back at me.

"Then thank you for the plate."

My throat tightens.

I turn toward the kettle before he sees too much.

Steam rises.

Chamomile smells like grass, honey, and denial.

I bring the mugs to the table and sit across from him.

For a moment, neither of us speaks.

The apartment holds us.

Rain taps the window. The refrigerator hums. Somewhere below, the old building creaks like it's settling in to listen.

"I'm sorry," Lorenzo says.

I stare at him.

"For what?"

"For my father."

"You did not say those things."

"No. But I brought you there."

"I agreed to come."

"I should have known he would do that."

"You knew he might be cruel. You did not know which knife he would pick."

His mouth tightens.

He looks down at his tea.

"He always picks that one eventually."

The quiet way he says it makes me want to walk back to the restaurant and pour lobster mac and cheese into José's lap.

I don't, because I'm growing as a person and also because wasting lobster is immoral.

"You looked," I say carefully, "like you were somewhere else."

He closes his eyes.

"Yes."

"Back there?"

"Yes."

"With the rain?"

His fingers tighten around the mug.

"Yes."

I reach across the table, then stop before touching. "Green?"

He opens his eyes. Something raw looks back at me. "Green."

I take his hand.

His fingers close around mine. I hold them between both of my hands.

"I meant what I said," I tell him.

His jaw shifts. "I know."

"No. I need you to hear it when your father is not at the table." I lean forward. "You did not kill your mother."

His eyes shine. "Dorothea."

"You needed someone. That's not a crime."

He looks away.

"I called her."

"She came because she loved you."

"If I had not called…"

"She still would have loved you," I say. "And that love would still have existed whether she was on that road or not."

A tear slips down his face.

He turns away quickly.

I pretend not to notice, which is sometimes the kindest way to notice.

"You don't have to be fine in here," I say.

His laugh is broken. "That sounds like something I told you."

"You did. I'm revising it for household use."

A second tear falls.

He wipes it away with the heel of his hand. "I hate that he can still do that to me," he says. "I'm a grown man."

"I know, it's okay."

"I know exactly what he is doing. And still…"

"And still," I say. Because I know.

Knowing a cage exists doesn't make the bars vanish. Sometimes it only makes you more furious when you bruise against them.

He looks at our hands.

"You did not have to defend me."

"I know."

"It could complicate things."

"With your father?"

"With everything."

"I don't think that's always a bad thing."

"Why?"

The answer is too big.

I look at the little kitchen around us, because eye contact while standing at a cliff edge is poor survival strategy.

"Because I don't care if we're friends or fake dating or real dating. I would never let anyone talk to someone I love that way."

The words leave my mouth.

Love.

Lorenzo stills.

I realize what I said one second too late.

My body floods with heat.

"I mean," I say quickly, "not that I'm saying, I mean, fake relationship context, hypothetically, if I were, if this were real…"

"Dorothea." His voice is rough and vulnerable. "Was any of tonight fake for you?"

My breath catches in my chest, and my whole body flushes. Fire and ice at war for domination over this moment.

There is the door.

Plain.

White.

Ordinary.

Terrifying.

I could lie. I could say the kiss was for show. The defense was moral outrage. The tea is basic hospitality. The trembling in my hands is low blood sugar.

I'm tired of lying to stay safe.

"No," I say.

The word falls softly.

It opens everything.

"No?" he asks.

I shake my head.

"The kiss at the restaurant was supposed to be fake. It wasn't. Not for me."

His eyes search mine.

"And this?"

I look at our joined hands.

"The tea is real. The pastry is real. Me asking you upstairs was real."

His breathing changes.

I keep going because if I stop now, I might never start again. "I'm scared because you're real. Because you can say the wrong thing. Because you can want me and still hurt me. Because you can decide tomorrow that this was too much."

"I won't."

"You don't know that."

His face tightens.

I squeeze his hand.

"I'm not accusing you. I'm saying that's what makes this different. Fantasy can feel safe because it doesn't vote against you. You can."

He looks at me for a long moment.

Then he says, "I can also choose you."

Oh.

A lump forms in my throat and my eyes prick.

That's too much.

It's also exactly enough.

"Lorenzo."

"I know." His thumb brushes over my knuckles. He remembers.

"I don't know how fast this is," I whisper.

"Then we slow down."

"And if I say yellow?"

"We pause."

"If I say red?"

"Everything stops."

My breath shakes.

"And if I ask for a kiss?"

His eyes darken, heat flickering behind the gentleness.

"Then I ask how."

My whole body warms.

I stand because sitting still is impossible. He stands too, slower, careful not to crowd me. The space between us feels electric.

"Do you want me to kiss you?" he asks, voice low.

"Yes." The word comes out rougher than I expect. "Not for show. Not because of tonight. Just… because I want you."

His jaw tightens. "I want you too, Dorothea."

"Green," I say before he can ask.

The moment his mouth meets mine, something inside me cracks open.

This kiss isn't careful or polite. It's hungry. I rise onto my toes and press into him, my hands fisting in his shirt as I lick into his mouth. He groans softly, the sound vibrating against my tongue, and the restraint he's been holding finally slips. His arms wrap around me, one hand sliding up my back while the other grips my waist, pulling me flush against him.

I want more.

My fingers work at the buttons of his jacket, pushing it off his shoulders. It hits the floor with a soft thud. Lorenzo makes a surprised sound but doesn't stop me. Instead, he deepens the kiss, tongue stroking mine in slow, filthy glides that make my thighs clench. Heat pools low in my belly, shocking me with its intensity. I've never felt like this—never wanted like this.

I tug at his dress shirt, desperate to feel skin. My hands slip underneath, palms gliding over the warm, firm planes of his stomach and up his chest. He's so warm. So solid. I explore him greedily, nails grazing lightly, and he shudders under my touch.

"Dorothea," he breathes against my mouth, half warning, half plea.

I answer by kissing him harder, biting his lower lip. My body is moving on instinct now, pressing closer, hips shifting against him. I can feel how much he wants me. The evidence is hard against my stomach, and instead of fear, a thrill runs through me.

His hands roam too—under my shirt now, warm palms stroking up my ribs, thumbs brushing the underside of my breasts. The sensation makes me gasp into his mouth. I arch into his touch, silently begging for more.

He backs me against the kitchen counter, lifting me slightly so I'm sitting on the edge. My legs part and he steps between them, our bodies fitting together in a way that feels dangerously perfect. We're both breathing hard, mouths fused, hands exploring each other. I'm losing myself in the taste of him, the scent of him, the low, needy sounds he's making.

Then Lorenzo stills. His hands gently catch mine, slowing me down even as I try to pull him closer again.

"Yellow," he murmurs against my lips, voice strained with restraint. He rests his forehead against mine, eyes closed, breathing ragged. "We need to slow down, sweetheart."

I make a frustrated sound, surprising even myself. My body is aching. I want his hands back on me. I want his mouth. I want—

"I know," he says softly, as if reading my mind. One hand cups my cheek, thumb stroking tenderly. "I want you so much it's killing me right now. But this is your first time letting someone this close. I won't rush you."

My eyes sting with a sudden wave of emotion—vulnerability crashing back in after the rush of lust. The memory of him crying earlier, the way he let me see his pain with his father, floods through me again.

"I didn't expect to want this much," I admit, voice small.

"I know." He kisses me once more, soft and lingering, then pulls back with visible effort. "That's why we stop here. For tonight."

He helps me down from the counter, steadying me when my legs feel shaky. We stand there for a long moment, foreheads touching, breathing each other in. The hunger is still there, simmering under the surface, but so is the tenderness. Especially the tenderness.

"Dinner only," I whisper, echoing my earlier boundary, though we both know dinner ended long ago.

His mouth curves into a small, understanding smile. "The boundary remains."

I nod, heart doing that strange, aching thing again.

He kisses my forehead—gentle, respectful—and this time it doesn't feel like too much. It feels like safety.

At the door, he turns back one last time.

"Green?" he asks quietly.

I meet his eyes, still flushed and unsteady from everything we just shared.

"Green," I answer. And I mean it.

ELEVEN

Lorenzo

I make it halfway down the stairs before her voice stops me.
"Lorenzo?"

Quiet. Hesitant. But it hits like a hook behind my ribs.

I grip the railing, pulse already kicking up again. The taste of her mouth is still on mine. The feel of her hands sliding under my shirt, greedy and surprised by her own hunger, is burned into my skin.

I should keep walking. That would be safer for her.

But I turn anyway.

Dorothea stands in the doorway, backlit by the warm glow of her apartment. Her pink dress is wrinkled from my hands, her hair messy from my fingers. She looks flushed and uncertain, like she's fighting herself.

"Are you okay?" I ask.

She shakes her head. "No." Her throat works. "I don't want you to go."

The words land low in my gut. Want wars with caution inside me.

"I know what I said earlier," she continues, voice shaky. "About dinner being over. About the boundary. But… I don't want you to leave yet."

I take one slow step up, then stop. "Color?"

"Green," she says, then amends, "with a yellow border."

That's all I need. I climb the rest of the stairs deliberately, letting her see every movement. When I reach her, I stop just outside the threshold.

She doesn't back away. Instead, she steps aside.

I walk in. The door clicks shut behind me, and I lock it when she nods. The sound feels heavier now, more intimate.

The kitchen still smells like us—her perfume, my cologne, the faint trace of tea and the heat we left behind on the counter. My jacket is still lying on the floor where she pushed it off me.

Dorothea leans against the counter, exactly where I had her legs wrapped around me twenty minutes ago. Her eyes flick to my mouth, then drop to my chest, like she's remembering how she shoved my shirt up to touch skin.

"I don't know what to do with my hands," she admits with a nervous laugh.

"Neither do I," I say, staying near the table. Giving her space. "What do you want, Dorothea?"

Her eyes lift to mine.

"I want you to kiss me again."

My pulse kicks hard. "Green?"

"Green." She swallows. "Slow. And… ask before you touch anything new. But don't treat me like I'm breakable. I don't want to feel fragile tonight."

The quiet strength in her voice hits me deep. "Never," I promise. "If I get it wrong, tell me."

She nods, fingers pressing into the counter behind her. "There's something else you should know first."

I stay exactly where I am, giving her space.

"I'm a virgin."

The words land between us. I see the way she braces, waiting for my reaction to shift something between us. It only makes me want her more carefully—and more fiercely.

"Thank you for trusting me with that," I say softly. "It doesn't make you fragile. It doesn't make you less. It just tells me to listen even better."

Relief flickers across her face, followed by something braver. "I'm not innocent. I've felt desire. I've learned what my body likes… just not with someone real. Not with someone I have to face tomorrow."

"I'm real," I tell her. "And I'm not going anywhere just because this is new for you."

She tells me about Jammie then—how stopping felt like failure to him. My jaw tightens, but I keep my voice steady. "Stopping will never feel like failure with me. Yellow means we pause or change course. Red means everything stops. You get as much time as you need. Always."

Her shoulders ease. "Okay."

I hold out my hand. She takes it.

I kiss her knuckles slowly, then the center of her palm, watching her reaction. Her breath catches, but she doesn't pull away.

"Still green?" I murmur.

"Yes."

I step closer. She meets me halfway.

When I kiss her, it's slow like she asked—deep and unhurried. Her mouth opens under mine on a soft sigh, and this time she's the one who presses forward, sliding her hands up my chest. The memory of her earlier hunger flares between us. I keep one hand on her cheek and the other loosely twined with hers, letting her lead.

She surprises me by tugging me closer, rising onto her toes, kissing me with growing confidence. A quiet, needy sound escapes her, and it takes everything in me not to back her against the counter again.

I pull back just enough to catch my breath, but I don't stop touching her. "Color?" I whisper.

"Green," she says, voice husky. Her fingers curl into my shirt like she doesn't want me to go anywhere.

She presses her body against mine, and every careful plan I had burns away.

I keep the kiss slow like she asked, but she makes a frustrated sound against my mouth that tests every ounce of my restraint. I pull back just enough.

"Color?"

"Green," she says breathlessly. "Frustrated green."

My lips curve. "Noted."

Her eyes drop to my mouth. "Can I touch you?"

"Yes."

Her hands explore me with raw honesty—palms sliding

over my chest, tracing my shoulders, threading into my hair. She's not performing. She's discovering. It's far more intoxicating than any practiced seduction.

"You're warm," she whispers, sounding surprised.

I let out a rough laugh. "You expected ice?"

"I thought you'd feel untouchable."

I'm anything but untouchable right now. My cock is already straining against my trousers.

She pulls me back into the kiss, deeper this time. When she tilts her head, offering her neck, I ask, "Neck?"

"Yes."

I kiss her there, soft at first, then with more pressure when she grips my shoulders and whispers, "More." My tongue traces her pulse point, and she shivers hard against me. The scent of her skin—warm sugar and faint perfume—makes my head spin.

Her fingers tug at my shirt. "Can I take this off?"

We undo the buttons together. Her hands tremble, but they don't stop. When the fabric falls open, she spreads both palms across my chest, exploring the lines of muscle, the hair, the old scar near my ribs. Every touch sends heat rushing through me.

"You're real," she murmurs.

"Yes." I press her hand over my heart. "And I'm choosing to be here with you."

She looks up at me, eyes wide with fear and hunger. "I want to go to the bedroom."

The words hit me like a punch of pure want. I force myself to stay steady. "Do you want me to lead, or follow?"

"Both. Lead slowly… but keep asking."

"I can do that."

I take her hand and follow her into the bedroom. The space is softly lit, lived-in, and unmistakably hers. I stay near the door until she turns.

"Still green?"

"Green."

She turns her back to me, gathering her hair over one shoulder.

"Will you unzip my dress?"

Her voice is quiet, but steady. I step close enough that I can feel the warmth radiating from her skin.

The zipper gives a slow, deliberate rasp as I draw it down. Inch by inch, the pink fabric parts, revealing the elegant line of her spine, the soft flare of her hips, and the delicate clasp of her pale pink bra. The dress slips down her arms and pools at her waist before she lets it fall the rest of the way to the floor.

She steps out of it, then turns to face me.

For a long moment I keep my eyes locked on hers. Her pupils are blown wide, her breathing shallow. A deep flush is climbing from her chest up her throat and into her cheeks. Her arms twitch like she wants to cross them over herself, but she doesn't. She stays open. Exposed. Trusting.

Only then do I let my gaze drift lower.

The soft, full curve of her breasts rises and falls with each breath, barely contained by the simple bra. Her waist dips in gently before flaring at her hips. The pale pink panties sit low on her stomach, and I can see the faint tremble in her thighs as she stands there, letting me look.

My mouth goes dry. Heat coils low and heavy in my gut. I want to touch her so badly my hands flex at my sides, but I keep them still.

"You are so fucking beautiful to me, Dorothea," I say, voice rough.

She shifts her weight, the flush deepening. Her nipples tighten visibly beneath the thin fabric of her bra. She doesn't look away from me, even though I can see the battle in her eyes—want fighting with years of fear.

I take one careful half-step closer.

She flinches slightly at the intensity, so I soften my voice. "If that feels too big, you don't have to carry it all right now."

That seems to help. She steps forward and kisses me again, deeper and needier, her tongue sliding against mine with growing hunger. Her dress slips the rest of the way down and pools at her feet. I break the kiss only long enough to kneel in front of her.

I take my time removing her boots, pressing slow, open-mouthed kisses up the inside of her calf, then higher along her inner thigh. Her breath catches every time my lips brush her skin. By the time I reach the edge of her pale pink panties,

I can smell how aroused she is — warm, sweet, and intoxicating.

I find her eyes. "May I take these off?"

Her voice is barely above a whisper. "Yes."

I peel the soaked fabric down her legs, revealing her glistening pussy. She's dripping for me. The sight makes my cock throb painfully against my zipper. I groan low in my throat and lean in, dragging my tongue slowly through her folds, tasting her properly for the first time.

"Fuck, Dorothea," I rasp against her wet heat. "You taste so good."

She lets out a broken, needy moan that shoots straight to my cock. Her hands fly to my hair as I lick her again, firmer this time, circling her swollen clit with the flat of my tongue before sucking it gently between my lips. Her thighs tremble around my shoulders.

I slide one finger inside her tight, slick heat. She's so wet it glides in easily. When I add a second finger and curl them upward, stroking that spongy spot inside her, her hips jerk against my mouth.

"Oh god— Lorenzo—"

Hearing my name like that, desperate and wrecked, nearly makes me lose control. I suck harder on her clit, pumping my fingers faster, fucking her with them while I devour her. Her moans turn shameless, hips grinding against my face as she chases the pleasure. I can feel her walls fluttering around my fingers, getting tighter.

"More," she gasps, voice cracking. "Please, Lorenzo— don't stop—"

I growl against her pussy and give her exactly what she's begging for — relentless, wet strokes of my tongue and steady, curling thrusts of my fingers. Her thighs clamp around my head, fingers yanking my hair almost painfully as her whole body starts to shake.

When she comes, it's explosive. Her back arches hard off the bed, a raw cry tearing from her throat as her pussy pulses and floods against my tongue. I don't stop. I keep licking her through every wave, gentler but still hungry, drawing out every shudder until she taps my shoulder weakly.

I kiss my way up her trembling body — inner thigh, hip,

the soft curve of her stomach, between her breasts — until I'm stretched out beside her. She's flushed crimson, chest heaving, eyes glassy and dazed with pleasure. Her lips are parted, still trying to catch her breath.

I brush damp hair off her forehead, my own cock aching and leaking in my trousers.

"Still green?" I murmur, voice rough.

Dorothea nods, eyes still hazy with pleasure. "I want to touch you," she says, voice husky and eager.

"You don't have to."

"I want to," she repeats, more firmly this time. "I want to feel you."

She pushes my shirt the rest of the way off my shoulders. Her hands roam over my chest and down my stomach with growing hunger, nails grazing lightly. When her fingers reach my belt, she hesitates only a second before unbuckling it. I help her shove my trousers and boxer briefs down, and my cock springs free — thick, heavy, and painfully hard, the head already slick with pre-cum.

Her eyes widen as she stares at me. The flush on her cheeks deepens, but she doesn't look away. She wraps her hand around my shaft, and the first slow stroke pulls a sharp hiss from between my teeth.

"Fuck, Dorothea…"

She explores me with curious, reverent touches — sliding her palm up and down my length, thumb brushing over the sensitive head, spreading the bead of pre-cum that leaks out. Her grip tightens as she finds a rhythm that makes my hips jerk.

"Like this?" she whispers.

"Just like that," I groan. "A little tighter — yes, fuck — perfect."

I pull her into a deep, filthy kiss, tongues sliding hot and urgent while she strokes me. My hand slips between her thighs again, finding her still soaked. I circle her swollen clit with two fingers before sliding them back inside her, pumping slowly in time with her strokes.

She moans into my mouth, the sound vibrating against my tongue as she works my cock faster. Her grip is slick, warm, and getting more confident with every glide. The wet sound of her hand moving over me mixes with the obscene noises my fingers make between her legs.

I break the kiss t, breathing ragged. "You feel so good... I'm not going to last if you keep doing that."

"Good," she breathes, surprising me with the heat in her voice. She twists her wrist on the upstroke, thumb pressing right under the head exactly how I like it. My hips thrust involuntarily into her fist.

Pleasure coils tight and brutal at the base of my spine. I curl my fingers harder inside her, stroking that spot that makes her thighs shake while my thumb works her clit.

"Dorothea—" I growl in warning.

"Come for me," she whispers, almost shy but so fucking eager.

That's all it takes.

I come with a rough groan of her name, forehead pressed to hers, hips jerking as thick ropes of cum spill over her hand and onto her stomach. The pleasure is blinding. I keep fucking her with my fingers through my orgasm until she gasps and clenches around me again, riding out a smaller, trembling second release.

We stay locked together, panting, her hand still loosely wrapped around my softening cock, my fingers buried inside her. The air between us is thick with the scent of sex and sweat.

I kiss her slow and deep, tasting the new confidence on her tongue.

* * *

Afterward, we lie tangled under her quilt, half-dressed, our skin warm and damp against each other. Her head rests on my shoulder, one leg thrown over mine. The rain taps softly against the window. For a few long minutes, the quiet feels almost sacred.

Then she speaks, voice small.

"This started as an arrangement... but it's not that for me anymore."

I feel her body tense against mine. The softness in her voice shifts into fear.

"I feel too much," she whispers. "You feel like home. And homes can be taken away."

My chest tightens. Instead of pulling away, I turn toward her and gently brush my thumb across her cheek.

"Can I just hold you for a while?" I ask quietly.

She hesitates, then nods, eyes glassy. I wrap my arms around her and pull her close, tucking her against my chest. She melts into me, trembling slightly.

"Where have you been hiding?" I murmur into her hair. "This vulnerability of yours... it's so fucking beautiful, Dorothea. I want to give you mine too. I don't want to hide from you."

She lets out a shaky breath. Her fingers curl against my chest.

"This isn't fake for me either," I tell her, voice low and steady. "Not anymore. Not even a little."

Her tears spill over. "I'm scared."

"I know. And I'm not going anywhere. I'm right here."

She stays in my arms for a long time, breathing against my neck. Eventually she pulls back just enough to look at me, eyes red and uncertain.

"Is it rude to ask you to leave after... everything we just did?"

"Not at all," I say gently. "This was a lot. For both of us."

I stroke her hair, choosing my words carefully. "I'm not going to chase you from a room you've closed. This was a lot, and I'm here when you're ready. No pressure. No expectations. Just... whenever you want me here, I'll come."

She nods, biting her lip. "Thank you."

I kiss her forehead — slow, lingering — then force myself to get up and dress. She watches me from the bed, wrapped in her robe, quiet but no longer panicking. At the bedroom door, I pause.

"Goodnight, Dorothea."

"Goodnight, Lorenzo," she whispers.

The lock clicks softly behind me as I step into the rain. I stand on the landing for a moment, letting the cold water run down my face, my heart still pounding from everything we shared tonight.

As I walk down the stairs toward my car, doubt creeps in.

Did I say too much? Did I push her anyway? The fear in her eyes when she talked about homes being taken away keeps replaying in my head.

By the time I reach my car and slide behind the wheel, one thing sits heavier than all the worry.

I'm in love with Dorothea Thompson.

And if loving her means giving her space, even when it aches like hell… then that's what I'll do.

I start the engine and drive into the rain, still tasting her on my tongue, her quiet fear and quiet courage wrapped tight around my heart.

TWELVE

Dorothea

The morning of Ophelia and Lillian's wedding, I burn the first tray of almond croissants.

Not badly.

Not unsalvageably.

Just enough that Baylin takes one look at them, tilts her head, and says, "Those have seen something."

I stare at the tray.

The croissants stare back, golden at the edges, too dark at the points, still buttery and probably sellable if I call them deeply caramelized.

"They're rustic," I say.

Baylin crosses her arms.

"They are emotionally distressed."

"I'm emotionally distressed."

"I know. That's why I'm not letting you make the custard."

"I can make custard."

"Not today."

"I own this bakery."

"And today, this bakery is owned by the part of your nervous system currently trying to chew through a wall."

I point at her with the oven mitt. "That's very specific."

"You're very specific."

Derek leans around the corner with a coffee pot in hand.

"Are we all pretending not to know this is about the wedding?"

"Yes," I say.

"No," Baylin says.

I close my eyes.

The bakery is warm and loud around me. Saturday morning in Coral Cove means tourists, locals, wedding guests, regulars who claim they are avoiding wedding traffic, and at least three people who want to know whether we have anything "light" before ordering a cream-filled pastry the size of a paperback.

The ovens hum.

The display case glows.

Coffee pours. Sugar spills. The bell over the door rings and rings and rings.

Every normal sound feels too sharp this morning.

The hiss of the espresso machine. The timer beeping. The soft clatter of trays. All of it lands like static against the chaos still humming under my skin.

Because last night I let Lorenzo Moretti into my bed.

And now I have to put on another dress tonight and play his fake girlfriend at a wedding.

Fake.

The word feels absurd now. Almost offensive.

Nothing about the way he touched me felt fake.

Not his mouth between my thighs, slow and patient and devastatingly thorough. Not the way he groaned my name like it hurt him when I stroked him. Not the way he held me afterward, steady and warm, telling me my vulnerability was beautiful. Not the way he looked at me when I said he felt like home.

And definitely not the way I panicked and asked him to leave anyway.

That's the part that's destroying me.

I can handle fake. I've built an entire life on performing calm, performing capable, performing fine. I can smile through customer rushes, crying brides, broken ovens, and magical recipe books that rearrange themselves at midnight. I can fake confidence in front of his horrible father. I can even fake a first kiss in front of half the town.

But I don't know how to handle a real man who listens when I say yellow. Who holds me gently afterward instead of getting angry. Who tells me he's not going anywhere… and then actually leaves when I need space.

I don't know what to do with that kind of real.

I pull the tray of croissants from the oven, golden and flaky, and set them on the cooling rack. The warm, buttery scent fills the kitchen, but it does nothing to settle the storm in my chest.

My fingers still remember the heat of his skin. The way his heart beat hard under my palm. The way he whispered, "This isn't fake for me either," like it was simple. Like it wasn't terrifying.

I don't know if we're still pretending.

I don't know if I want us to be.

And that confusion might be the scariest thing of all.

I said yellow.

Lorenzo listened.

And I still locked the door behind him.

I did not text him after.

He did not text me either, except for case updates copied through Molly, professional and careful and brutal in their restraint.

The title insurer acknowledged the claim.

County archives located the missing exhibit.

Applegate's attorney asked for "informal discussion," which Lorenzo wrote was often code for realizing they had stepped into something with teeth.

All good news.

All terrifying.

Because legal progress makes me want to call him.

Emotional terror makes me avoid him.

I'm a woman divided by my own stupid heart and a court calendar.

* * *

By noon, Baylin kicks me out of the kitchen.

Literally.

She takes the spatula from my hand and points toward the stairs.

"Go."

"I have two hours."

"You need three."

"I don't."

"You need one hour to panic, one hour to deny you're panicking, and one hour for Lea to make you stop dressing like you want to be overlooked by even the furniture."

Derek nods from behind the register. "That math checks out."

"I hate both of you."

"No, you don't," Baylin says.

"Not effectively," Derek adds.

I leave because they are right, which is becoming a troubling pattern in my life.

Upstairs, my apartment feels too quiet.

The faded blue couch sits in the living room like it's waiting for something I'm not ready to give. The kitchen is spotless — I scrubbed every surface last night instead of sleeping, trying to erase the memory of his hands on my waist, his mouth between my thighs, the way the counter felt against my back when he had me there.

I stop in the bedroom doorway and just breathe.

The bed is made, but I can still see the indentation where he sat on the edge after I said yellow. I can still picture him buttoning his shirt wrong the first time, his fingers not quite steady, his face tight with pain he tried so hard not to put on me.

You feel like a home.

Homes can be taken.

Those words have been sitting heavy in my chest since the moment they left my mouth. Not because they were a lie.

Because they were painfully, terrifyingly true.

A real man listened when I asked him to stop. Held me while I cried. Told me my fear was beautiful. Then actually left when I needed him to — without anger, without pressure, without making me feel like I'd failed him.

And now I don't know what to do with any of it.

A soft knock sounds at the apartment door.

241

Then Lea's voice. "Open up. I come bearing fabric, eyeliner, and emotional consequences."

I laugh despite myself and go to the door.

Lea steps inside carrying a garment bag over one arm, a makeup case in the other hand, and a coffee cup tucked against her chest like a third sacred object. Her red curls are piled on top of her head. She wears black jeans, boots, and a shirt that says READ BANNED BOOKS AND MIND YOUR BUSINESS, which is rich coming from a woman who has never minded business in her life.

She looks me up and down. "Oh, babe."

"What?"

"You look like you fought a mixer and lost."

"I worked a Saturday morning."

"And had feelings during it."

"I object to the tone."

"Objection overruled."

She walks in and kicks the door shut behind her.

"Are you here as friend, stylist, or prosecutor?" I ask.

"Yes."

"Wonderful."

She hangs the garment bag on my closet door and sets the makeup case on my bed. Then she turns back to me, hands on hips. "Before mascara, we talk."

"I was afraid of that."

"You should be."

I sit on the edge of the bed because my knees have decided to be dramatic.

Lea sits beside me, close enough that our shoulders touch.

For a second, neither of us says anything.

That's how I know she is serious.

Lea's usual mode is verbal confetti. Helpful, sharp, glittering, impossible to fully clean up. Silence from her has weight.

"How are you?" she asks.

I sigh. "Don't do that."

"Do what?"

"Ask gently. It makes me suspicious."

"Fine." She shifts to face me. "Did you actually tell Lorenzo what you needed last night, or did you punish him for not magically knowing how not to scare you?"

The question hits so hard I inhale. "There she is," I say weakly.

"Answer."

I look down at my hands.

My nails are short. Flour is still caught under one despite scrubbing. The burn from the coffee is nearly healed, pink and tender on the back of my hand.

"I told him some things."

"What things?"

"That I needed slow. I also told him, he should ask before touching anything new. I didn't want to feel breakable. That if I went quiet, he should ask where I was."

Lea's face softens.

"That's good."

"It was."

"And then?"

My throat tightens.

"And then he did all of that."

"Okay."

"And then I panicked."

Lea nods slowly. "Because he ignored you?"

"No." I shake my head. He's never ignored me.

"Because he pushed?"

"No."

"Because he made you feel small?"

"Goddess no."

"Because he treated you like you were breakable?"

"No."

"Because he got it right?"

I close my eyes.

I press my palm to my thigh. "Yes."

Lea exhales. "Dottie."

"I know."

"No, I don't think you do."

"I told him he felt like a home. Then I told him homes can be taken."

Lea's expression breaks open for one second.

Then she pulls herself together because she knows pity makes me mean.

"That's honest," she says.

"It's pathetic."

"It's not pathetic. It's the wound talking."

"The wound is very chatty lately."

"Yes. Because you finally stopped shoving a croissant in its mouth."

A laugh catches in my throat.

Lea reaches for my hand.

I let her take it.

"So what did he do?" she asks.

"He stopped. He listened. He said the legal work would continue. He offered email updates, Molly copied, transfer to another attorney if I wanted one."

Lea's brows lift.

"Damn."

"I know."

"That man has been reading the assignment."

"That's the problem."

"No. That's the opportunity."

I groan and lean back on my hands. "Please don't be wise today. I'm not dressed for it."

"You're about to be."

She squeezes my hand.

"Did you ask for slow, specific, honest in bed?"

"Yes."

"Did you ask for slow, specific, honest after?"

I stare at the wall.

The apartment suddenly feels too small.

"No."

"What did you ask for?"

"I asked him not to make me responsible for his hope."

Lea is quiet. "That's not wrong," she says.

"I know."

"But did you tell him what you needed, or did you flee because real love doesn't come with a guide?"

My eyes burn.

I think of The Arcane Room, and Lucian. Of all the ways that I've learned from him.

The hallway.

The final door.

The hot spring.

I was made to show you the door, Dorothea. Not to become the room you hide in.

"I hate that you know how to say the worst sentence," I whisper.

"I'm gifted."

"Cursed."

"Both."

I wipe under my eye before tears can ruin makeup I'm not wearing yet.

"In The Arcane Room, I could ask because it was safe," I say. "I mean, safe in the way a magical sex castle can be safe, which is not a sentence I ever expected to say sober."

Lea nods with impressive solemnity.

"Lucian asked. He waited. He stopped. But he was fantasy. He was made to be a threshold."

"And Lorenzo?"

"Lorenzo is real." My voice breaks. "He can be careful and still mess up. He can choose me and still leave someday. He can love me and still die, or change, or realize I'm too much work. He can become another place I learn how to lose."

Lea's thumb moves over my knuckles.

"Yes," she says.

I look at her, startled. "Not helpful."

"It's true. He can. All of that can happen. Real love is not safe because nothing bad can happen. Real love is safe when you can tell the truth and stay in the room long enough to decide what happens next."

My chest aches. "I didn't stay in the room."

"No. You asked for a pause. You said yellow."

"That's different."

"It's different," she agrees. "Yellow is allowed. But yellow is a pause, not a disappearing act."

I close my eyes.

Yellow.

Pause.

Not ending.

Not forever.

Not run, lock door, and emotionally dig a moat.

"Did I break it?" I ask.

Lea's face softens. "I don't know."

My stomach drops.

"I'm not going to lie to you," she says. "You might have hurt him."

"I know."

"But he also sounds like he understood more than you think. He didn't chase. He didn't punish. He didn't use the case to make you behave. He paused, just like you asked. That should matter."

"It does."

"So today, maybe you don't fix everything. Maybe you start with honest. Not pretty. Not perfect. Honest."

I look toward the garment bag.

"The wedding feels like a terrible place for honesty."

"Weddings are emotionally manipulative rituals with flowers. They are perfect for honesty."

"That's horrifying."

"Yes."

A laugh slips out.

Lea stands and claps her hands once.

"Good. Now that I have lovingly kicked your internal furniture around, put on the dress."

"I have a dress."

"No, you have dresses you would choose if you wanted to disappear into a very polite wall."

"That sounds useful."

"You're not wearing a wall to a wedding."

She unzips the garment bag.

The dress inside steals the air from the room.

Green.

Not simple green.

Not one flat shade.

Deep emerald at the bodice, softening into moss and sea-glass where the skirt catches light. The fabric is satin, but not too shiny, with a faint texture that moves like water when Lea lifts it. The neckline is elegant without being severe. The sleeves are delicate, sheer enough to soften my arms. The waist is fitted, the skirt long and flowing, with a slit that is not scandalous but definitely has opinions.

It's beautiful.

It's also not practical.

Not even slightly.

You cannot haul flour in this dress.

You cannot wipe a counter.

You cannot disappear behind a display case.

This is a dress for being seen.

Absolutely not.

"Oh no," I say.

"Oh yes."

"Lea."

"Dottie."

"It's too much."

"It's exactly enough."

"It's green."

"Yes."

"His eyes are green."

"An unfortunate coincidence."

"You're lying."

"Obviously." I step closer and touch the fabric.

It's cool beneath my fingers.

Green as Lorenzo's eyes, yes.

But not only.

Green as basil in his kitchen. Green as sea-glass tile. Green as the word I say when I choose to keep going. Green as the first thing pushing through soil after a long winter. Green as growth, even when growth is rude enough to split the seed open.

"It's too pretty," I whisper.

Lea comes to stand beside me. "No. You're just used to beauty having to be useful before you trust it."

"I don't know if I can wear this."

"Yes, you do."

"I'll feel exposed."

"You will be dressed."

"That's not what I mean."

"I know."

The dress glows between us.

I think of every apron I have worn like armor. Flour on my hands, sugar in my hair, a counter between me and everyone else. The bakery makes me visible in a way I can survive because people are looking at what I make.

This dress means they will look at me.

Not Dottie the baker.

Dorothea.

A woman with a body. A heart. A voice. A claim on more than survival.

My palm tingles.

Green.

Yellow.

Red.

"I'm scared," I say.

Lea smiles softly. "I know, babe."

"I want to wear it."

"I know that too."

"Bossy oracle."

"Put on the dress."

I do.

It takes longer than expected because the zipper sticks halfway and Lea says several unholy things about formal-wear manufacturing. But then the dress settles over me, cool and heavy and soft. It fits too well, which feels suspicious. The waist hugs me. The neckline opens my collarbones. The skirt moves when I breathe.

I stand in front of the mirror.

For a moment, I don't recognize myself.

Not because I look unlike myself.

Because I look like a version of myself I have been refusing to meet.

My hair is still in its work bun. My face has no makeup. There is a faint dusting of flour near one temple. My eyes are tired from crying. Still, the dress changes the frame.

I look softer.

Stronger.

Not hidden.

My first instinct is to make a joke.

My second is to cover my stomach with my hands.

My third is to stand still and let myself be seen by my own reflection.

I choose the third.

Barely.

Lea watches me in the mirror. "Stunning, love. Just stunning," she says.

My eyes fill. "Thank you." I laugh and wipe my eyes carefully.

"Sit. Makeup," Lea says patting my shoulders.

I sit at the little vanity I bought at a thrift store and almost painted twice before giving up. Lea stands behind me and starts with my hair, taking it down fully, brushing through the waves with careful fingers.

"You always try to compromise with your hair," she says.

"My hair is a health code concern."

"You're not baking at the wedding."

"People may still expect snacks."

"They can cope. You're only job is to enjoy yourself today."

She curls the pieces around my face, not too perfect. Soft waves. Romantic, but not fragile. Then makeup. Light foundation. A touch of blush. Soft gold on my eyelids. Mascara. A deeper rose on my lips than I would choose for myself.

When she is done, I look like me after someone turned the light slightly higher.

"I look…"

"Beautiful," Lea says.

I wince.

"Receive it."

"I'm trying."

"You look beautiful."

I take a breath. "Thank you. I do look beautiful."

Her smile is immediate and devastating.

"Yes, you do."

I look in the mirror again.

The woman looking back is not practical.

Not hidden.

Not protected by flour, counters, or exhaustion.

Green dress. Gold earrings. Soft hair. Trembling mouth.

Alive.

My phone buzzes on the vanity.

Lorenzo.

My heart trips.

I pick up the phone.

> Lorenzo: Car is outside whenever you're ready. No rush. I will meet you there.

Three dots, and then nothing. I almost reply but I give him a moment. To see what he was going to say.

> Lorenzo: Are we Green?

No assumption that I will ride with him or perform before I'm ready.
He sent a car, not himself.
He gave me space.
That hurts in the tender place.
I type slowly.

> Dorothea: Green with a yellow border. Thank you for the car.

Then I delete the sentence.
No.
Not enough.
I type again.

> Dorothea: Green with a yellow border. I want to talk tonight, if you're open to that. Not at the wedding table. Somewhere quiet.

Three dots appear.
Disappear.
My heart tries to climb out of my dress.
Then his reply comes.

> Lorenzo: I'm open. Slow, specific, honest.

I press the phone to my chest.
Lea watches my face. "What?"
"He said slow, specific, honest."
Her eyes soften. "Well."
"Yeah."
"Did you tell him you wanted to talk?"

"Yes."

"Look at you, using the key."

I laugh, but it turns wet at the edges. "Barely."

"Barely counts."

I stand.

The skirt whispers around my legs.

Lea helps me into my shoes, then steps back and looks me over with the seriousness of a general preparing a queen for battle.

"Okay," she says. "Rules."

"Of course there are rules."

"Rule one: you're not there to perform gratitude for being included."

"I'm not?"

"No. You're Lorenzo's date, fake or not, and also a person invited into a joyful room. You belong in joyful rooms."

My throat tightens.

"Rule two," she continues, "you don't shrink for José Moretti. If he looks at you like you're a résumé he wants to reject, you remember that he is a miserable man in a fancy suit and you're wearing a dress that could legally start a religion."

I laugh.

"Rule three: yellow is allowed. Green is allowed. Red is allowed."

I nod.

"Rule four: if you talk to Lorenzo, tell him what you need. Don't make him guess and then fail him for guessing wrong."

"That one feels pointed."

"It's sharpened."

"Noted."

"Rule five: if the wedding cake is dry, you tell me immediately."

"That's not emotionally relevant."

"It's to me."

My smile fades. "What if I hurt him too badly?"

Lea's reaches for my hand and holds it between hers. "Then you apologize."

"What if that isn't enough?"

"Then you survive the consequence of truth. But you don't go back to lying to avoid it."

My chest aches.

The hard thing about Lea is that she loves me enough not to make all answers soft.

"I don't want to lose him," I whisper.

"I know."

"I don't know how to keep him without making him the place I put all my fear."

"Then don't keep him like a place. Meet him like a person."

A person.

Not a home to lose.

Not a fantasy to hide in.

Not a fake boyfriend to perform beside.

Lorenzo.

Real, flawed, trying.

I can meet him there.

Maybe.

The car horn gives a soft, polite beep outside.

I jump.

Lea pulls me into a hug before I can panic.

Careful, because makeup.

"You're not alone," she says against my hair.

"I know."

"Say it."

"I'm not alone."

"Again."

"I'm not alone."

"Good. Now go make emotionally brave choices in expensive fabric."

I laugh into her shoulder.

Then I pull back, grab my clutch, my phone, and the small folded copy of the fake relationship terms from my drawer.

Lea sees it. "You're bringing the agreement?"

"Yes."

"Why?"

"Because everything is revisable."

Her smile goes soft. "Damn right."

At the door, I pause and look back at the apartment.

It's still small.

Still mine.

Still full of old furniture, thrifted dishes, unfinished walls, and the life I built out of necessity.

For once, leaving doesn't feel like abandoning safety.

It feels like taking some with me.

I step outside.

The afternoon is bright after rain, the whole town washed clean and shining. The car waits at the curb below the bakery. Across the street, Spellbound Stories glows in the sun. Downstairs, I can hear the faint sounds of the bakery still moving without me.

The bakery can keep breathing when I'm not inside it.

Maybe I can too.

I lift the skirt carefully and descend the stairs.

The driver opens the door.

I slide into the back seat, green satin pooling around me like water, my heart pounding hard enough to hurt.

My phone buzzes once more.

Lorenzo: For what it's worth, I'm nervous too.

I stare at the message.

Then I smile. He told me the truth before I had to ask.

Dorothea: Good. I hate being the only one.

Lorenzo: Never.

The car pulls away from the curb.

I touch my palm.

Green.

With a yellow border.

But still very green.

THIRTEEN

Lorenzo

I arrive at Lighthouse Point thirty-seven minutes early.

That's not nerves.

That's logistical preparedness.

That's what I tell myself while standing near the stone path with a bouquet in my hand, adjusting my cuffs for the fourth time and watching the road like a man waiting for either salvation or sentencing.

The bouquet was a mistake.

Not because it's wrong. Because it's too right.

Sunflowers. Orange roses. A few stems of white ranunculus tucked between them. Warm, bright, stubborn flowers. The florist, Lillian's cousin, had tied them with a green ribbon before giving me a look that said she knew exactly who they were for and had already told three people telepathically.

Coral Cove does not need phones.

It has women with flower shears and opinions.

The bouquet feels strange in my hands. Not heavy. Significant.

I have brought women flowers before. Expensive arrangements sent to offices, hotel rooms, apartments. Roses delivered because roses are what men send when they want to be forgiven, noticed, or invited back. I have treated flowers as currency. Gesture. Signal.

These are different.

Dorothea will notice the sunflowers.

She will probably understand too much.

She has a talent for that.

I glance toward the ocean.

Lighthouse Point sits high above the water, the old white lighthouse rising against the late afternoon sky like something out of a painting people buy when they want to feel peaceful without actually doing the work. The grass is bright from the morning rain. The cliffs drop into dark rock and silver foam. The ocean moves below us, gray-blue and restless, and the air smells like salt, roses, damp earth, and the faint citrus of something being mixed at the outdoor bar.

The wedding is ridiculous.

Beautiful, yes.

But ridiculous.

There are white chairs arranged in a crescent facing the lighthouse. Garlands of orange marigolds, yellow roses, and soft pink peonies loop between the rows. Glass lanterns hang from shepherd's hooks along the aisle, each with a candle waiting for dusk. Beyond the ceremony space, a clear-topped reception tent glows with string lights, chandeliers, and more flowers than most botanical gardens would risk in one place.

Ophelia and Lillian wanted color.

They achieved it with force.

The dance floor has been laid beneath the tent, its polished wood reflecting twinkle lights like trapped stars. The cake table is draped in velvet. The guest tables carry mismatched vintage glassware, tiny gold frames with table numbers, and centerpieces that look casual only if one has no understanding of money, labor, or florists with vision.

Guests move through the space in jewel tones and linen suits, laughter rising over the low sound of waves. It should be easy to breathe here.

It's not.

My father stands near the bar.

José Moretti looks as if someone placed him into the wedding by court order. Dark suit. Silver hair. Bourbon in hand, despite the hour. Face composed into the kind of polite neutrality that makes people thank him for attending and then leave quickly.

He has not approached me despite glancing at me twice.

The bruises from dinner are not visible. That's the thing about fathers like mine. They leave no mark anyone can point to. Only weather. Only a room going cold when they enter. Only a man in a suit standing at his cousin's wedding with flowers in his hand, feeling twelve years old and furious about it.

Dorothea defended me.

I still don't know what to do with that.

She did not soothe the wound. She stood between me and the hand holding the knife and said no.

No one does that.

Not for me.

People assume I don't need defending. I built a whole life around making that assumption easy. Sharp suit. Sharper voice. A reputation for winning, charming, ruining, leaving first. I made myself into a man no one feels responsible for protecting.

Then Dorothea Thompson, in a pink dress with anger in her eyes, looked at my father and said he did not get to make me small.

I touch the green ribbon around the bouquet.

My phone buzzes.

> Dorothea: Almost there. Green a full yellow hemline.

I smile despite myself.

> Lorenzo: I'm at the entrance. We can take a minute before joining anyone.

Her reply comes almost immediately.

> Dorothea: Thank you. Also, if I trip in this dress, please let the record show I was brave and not graceful.

> Lorenzo: The record will reflect courage, not coordination.

Dorothea: Good lawyer.

My chest tightens.

Good.

The word should not still undo me.

It does.

A black sedan pulls into the circular drive.

I straighten before I can stop myself.

The driver steps out, rounds the car, and opens the back door.

Dorothea emerges in green.

For one breath, the whole cliffside goes quiet.

Not literally. The ocean still moves. Guests still laugh. Someone near the bar still says something too loudly about signature cocktails. The violinist is tuning near the ceremony arch.

But for me, everything narrows.

Dorothea steps from the car carefully, one hand gathering the skirt so it doesn't catch. The green dress falls around her like water and living leaves, emerald at the bodice, softer where the skirt catches the light. Her hair is down in waves, red-gold and soft around her shoulders. Gold earrings move at her ears. Her mouth is colored a deep rose that makes every thought in my head stumble.

She looks beautiful.

No.

That word is not enough, and piling better words on top of it will not help. Radiant, exquisite, stunning, breathtaking. All of them sound like poor evidence for an obvious fact.

She looks like herself, seen fully.

That's what steals my breath.

She spots me.

For a second, uncertainty flickers across her face. Not about the dress. about me. About last night and the door she closed and the conversation she asked for tonight.

I start toward her.

Slowly.

The bouquet feels enormous in my hand.

When I reach her, I stop at a careful distance.

"Hi," she says.

"Hi."

Her gaze drops to the flowers.

"Oh."

"I brought these for you." I glance down at them, suddenly aware that I may look like a man auditioning for sincerity with props. "They are not an expectation. Just flowers."

Her mouth curves.

"Just flowers?"

"Beautifully arranged, symbolically loaded flowers."

"That sounds more accurate."

"May I compliment you?"

Her eyes lift to mine.

The question matters. It always matters. Especially now.

"Yes."

"You look extraordinary."

Her breath catches.

I watch her take the words in. I can almost see the old instinct rise, the urge to dismiss, joke, hand the compliment back before it can settle on her skin. This time she doesn't.

"Thank you," she says. "That's still uncomfortable."

"But?"

"But I like hearing it."

I smile. "Noted."

She takes the bouquet.

Her fingers brush mine.

Small touch.

My body notices anyway.

Her gaze moves over me. "You look good too."

"Only good?"

Her eyes narrow, but her smile grows. "Don't fish at a wedding."

"I would never."

"You absolutely would."

"Yes."

A laugh leaves her, soft but real.

Something in me loosens.

Behind her, Lea stands near the car, having clearly appeared from nowhere because that woman's life is ninety percent dramatic timing. She gives me two thumbs up, then points at her own eyes and then at me.

I assume that means, Don't hurt her or I will murder you in a bookstore.

Fair.

I nod once.

Lea smiles brightly and disappears toward the parking area, leaving Dorothea and me alone at the edge of the wedding.

Alone, except for one hundred guests, a cliff, a lighthouse, and half of Coral Cove pretending not to watch us.

Dorothea looks toward the ceremony space.

"That's a lot of flowers."

"Lillian is a florist."

"That explains the expertise. Not the restraint."

"There was no restraint."

"I respect that."

A breeze lifts a strand of her hair across her mouth.

I want to tuck it back but I don't.

She catches the movement of my hand before I stop it.

"Green," she says quietly.

I look at her. "For hair," she clarifies, cheeks coloring.

I reach slowly and brush the strand away, tucking it behind her ear. My fingers barely graze her skin.

Her breath changes.

Mine does too.

"Green?" I ask.

She nods. "Green."

No yellow border. Not in that second.

I offer her my arm.

She looks at it before putting her hand in the crook of my elbow.

The first test arrives before we make it ten steps.

Ophelia's Aunt Margot, who has never met a boundary she did not consider a decorative suggestion, intercepts us near the champagne table.

"Lorenzo," she says, smiling too brightly. "And this must be Dorothea."

Dorothea's hand tightens slightly on my arm.

Not enough for anyone else to notice.

I notice.

"Aunt Margot," I say. "Dorothea Thompson."

"I know, sweetheart. We all know Knead the Dough." Margot turns to Dorothea. "Those pear pastries of yours nearly caused a fight at book club last month."

Dorothea smiles. "That sounds like book club needed a fight."

Margot laughs delightedly. "So tell me, how did this happen?"

Dorothea stills.

The first public question.

The fake relationship agreement rustles in my memory.

No charity language. No pity narrative. Dorothea controls her personal history.

I look at Dorothea.

Her choice.

She sees the question in my face.

For one second, she looks ready to retreat. To let me answer. To let the fake story carry her like a chair someone else pulls out.

Then she inhales "He came into the bakery," she says. "And kept ordering black coffee like a cry for help."

I close my eyes.

Margot laughs so hard she touches her necklace.

Dorothea continues, voice steadier now. "Then he recommended I stop calling small burns nothing, which was irritating."

"I provided basic medical guidance," I say.

"You were bossy."

"I was accurate."

"You were both."

Margot looks between us with open delight. "Oh, I like this."

Dorothea's cheeks color, but she doesn't pull away from my arm.

She leans in a fraction.

Performance?

Maybe.

Real?

Definitely.

"We are figuring it out," Dorothea says.

The exact phrase she told Derek, from what Molly reported through the surveillance network that apparently manages my life.

Not a lie.

Not a confession.

Something between.

Margot presses a hand to her chest. "Well, I hope you do. He looks at you like you hung the moon."

Dorothea's grip tightens again.

My lungs forget what they are for.

I look at her.

Her face has gone pink, but she doesn't look away from Margot.

"Does he?" she asks softly.

Margot's smile gentles. "Oh, honey. Everyone can see it."

There is a moment.

A dangerous one.

Dorothea could laugh or deflect. She could say, you should see him in court. I just hope she doesn't flee to the nearest flower arrangement and hide.

Instead, she turns her face toward me.

Just enough.

Public.

Private.

Testing the air between us.

I meet her gaze.

I don't smile the charming smile.

I don't rescue either of us with a joke.

I let her see it.

Yes.

I do.

She swallows.

"Good to know," she says.

Her voice is not quite steady.

Margot sighs like she has just been handed a romance novel with a glossy cover and excellent pacing.

"Go sit, you two. The ceremony is starting soon."

We move away.

Dorothea exhales hard once we are out of earshot.

"That was a lot."

"Just a bit."

"She said everyone can see it."

I breath her in and maintain my control.

"Can they?"

This is not a wedding question.

This is us. Yellow paused. Door half-open. Her in green. Me holding sunflowers like an idiot. The whole town gawking.

"Yes," I say. "If they know where to look."

Her throat moves. "Okay."

"Yellow?"

She thinks. "Yes, but with green stitching."

I almost smile. "That's getting specific."

"I contain multitudes."

"Yes, you do."

We take our seats near the middle, close enough to see the ceremony clearly, not so close that my father can easily reach us. José sits three rows back on the opposite side, separated by family politics, floral abundance, and what I assume is divine mercy.

He doesn't look at me.

He looks at Dorothea.

Not in the same way as dinner.

Less dismissive.

More unsettled.

I don't trust it.

The music begins.

Conversations quiet.

A hush moves over the cliffside.

The sun has started its slow descent, turning the water below into hammered gold. The lighthouse rises behind the ceremony arch, white stone touched with warm light. The air tastes like salt and petals. Glass lanterns flicker along the aisle even though dusk has not fully arrived, their little flames trembling in the wind.

Lillian comes first wearing the most bright, glowing, sunlit orange dress that moves around her like marigold petals. Her dark curls are pinned with tiny yellow flowers, and her bouquet is an explosion of color, wildflowers, roses, ranunculus, and greenery spilling over her hands. She walks down the aisle alone, smiling so widely the entire crowd seems to soften around her.

Dorothea leans closer.

"She looks so happy."

"She is."

"I love that dress."

"So does she."

Dorothea glances at me.

"You know her well?"

"Through Ophelia. Lillian's flower shop did the arrangements for a few events I helped sponsor when I was trying to make Coral Cove believe I was approachable."

"Did it work?"

"No."

She smiles. "Maybe because you described it like litigation."

"Possibly."

Then Ophelia appears.

The crowd shifts.

Ophelia wears white, but calling it traditional would be a lie. The gown is full and sweeping, the skirt catching the light with threads of silver that shimmer like moonlight over water. She twirls halfway down the aisle, because Ophelia has never in her life resisted a dramatic entrance, and silver flashes through the fabric.

The crowd laughs, applauds, and a few people actually say "ooh," because sometimes people are clichés and it's wonderful.

Lillian's face crumples at the sight of her.

Ophelia laughs and starts crying at the same time.

Dorothea presses her fingers to her mouth.

I look at her instead of the brides.

Not because the ceremony is not beautiful.

Because Dorothea watching happiness is almost more intimate than kissing her.

She watches like someone who has spent years believing joy belongs to other people and is now trying to learn its shape without touching it too hard.

Her hand rests on her lap.

I turn mine palm up between us.

No pressure.

She looks down.

Then places her hand in mine.

Green.

The officiant is Lillian's grandmother, a tiny woman with bright red glasses and a voice strong enough to command sailors, brides, and possibly weather patterns. She speaks about love as a garden, but not in the obvious way. Not all bloom and sweetness. Soil. Pruning. Patience. Rot becoming nourishment. Seasons of abundance and seasons of bare branches.

Dorothea's hand tightens.

I wonder if she hears what I hear.

Love is not a home that cannot be damaged.

Love is a living thing people tend.

Ophelia reads her vows first.

She is funny, dramatic, and surprisingly raw by the end.

"You taught me that being known did not have to mean being trapped," she says to Lillian, voice breaking. "You gave me room to become less impressive and more honest. I did not know that was love until you."

Dorothea's fingers flex in mine.

My chest tightens.

Then Lillian reads hers.

"I spent so much of my life making beautiful things for other people," she says. "Flowers for weddings, funerals, apologies, birthdays, first dates, last goodbyes. I thought love was something I arranged and delivered. But you made me understand that I'm not only the hands making the bouquet. I get to be the one holding it too."

Dorothea inhales sharply.

I turn my head.

A tear slides down her cheek.

She doesn't wipe it away.

The brides exchange rings. The crowd cheers when Ophelia nearly drops hers and Lillian catches it. Then the officiant declares them married, and Ophelia dips Lillian into a kiss so dramatic one of the groomsmen whoops and someone's grandmother shouts, "That's my girl!"

Flowers burst over the aisle as the recessional begins.

Not thrown.

Released.

Tiny petals from hidden cones and baskets, orange, pink, yellow, and white, spinning in the wind like the wedding itself has come apart beautifully.

Dorothea laughs.

The sound moves through me like sunlight.

After the ceremony, the cocktail hour begins near the tent. Guests drift toward drinks and appetizers. A jazz trio starts playing near the dance floor. The lighthouse glows behind us as the sun lowers, and the first evening star appears above the water.

Public performance resumes.

Someone asks if we are serious.

Someone else says Dorothea looks stunning and asks whether she made the wedding cake. She says no, then critiques the frosting from across the lawn with the focus of a surgeon. A man from the chamber of commerce jokes that I finally found someone sweet enough to balance me out. Dorothea says, "You have clearly never seen me during a supplier delay," and the man laughs, startled into respect.

She is nervous.

I can feel it.

But she doesn't shrink.

Not once.

She leans into my hand on the small of her back when Aunt Margot passes again. She lets me introduce her as Dorothea, not Dottie, and I watch her notice. She tells someone the bakery is not only pastries but payroll, licensing, inventory, baking science, community, and "approximately eleven hundred daily decisions about butter."

By the end of cocktail hour, three people have asked for her card.

She brought cards.

"You're networking at a wedding," I murmur as she tucks the card case back into her clutch.

"You're the one who said public strategy matters."

"I meant for us."

"I contain multitudes."

"So you've said."

Her smile fades slightly as she looks across the lawn.

I follow her gaze.

My father stands near the edge of the tent, speaking to Ophelia.

José's expression is controlled, but not cruel. Ophelia says something with her hand on his arm. He looks away from her toward the ocean. Then toward Dorothea.

I tense.

Dorothea notices.

"Color?" she asks.

The word from her mouth, directed at me, lands deeper than I expect.

I look at my father.

My body knows old weather.

"Yellow," I admit.

Her hand slides into mine.

"Then we pause."

Such a simple thing.

Pause.

Not fight. Not perform. Not prove.

Pause.

We step away from the crowd toward a stone wall overlooking the cliff. The wind is cooler here, carrying salt and the faint sound of waves below. Dorothea stands beside me, her green dress moving around her legs.

"I'm not going to ask if you're okay," she says.

"Thank you."

"I'm going to ask if you want to talk or stare dramatically at the ocean."

I laugh.

It surprises me.

"Dramatically at the ocean."

"Excellent choice."

We stare.

For several minutes, we say nothing.

That should be impossible for me.

It's not.

Then Dorothea speaks, quietly. "You're building a good life here."

I look at her.

She keeps her gaze on the water.

"I know your father doesn't see it. Or won't. But I do." Her fingers tighten around mine. "Your office. Molly. William. The way people trust you when they are scared, even if they also cross the street to avoid you because you ruined their brother-in-law in a shed dispute."

I huff out a laugh. "The shed was over the property line."

"I know. Everyone knows. It was apparently a very legally significant shed."

"It was."

She turns to me. "You're not wasting your life in Coral Cove."

My throat tightens.

She says it without drama.

Not as a grand defense.

Not as a speech thrown at my father.

Only truth, handed to me quietly where no one else is supposed to hear.

Except someone does.

Because when I look past her shoulder, my father stands near the path, close enough that I know he caught at least the last sentence.

Dorothea follows my gaze.

Her hand tightens.

José looks at her first.

Then me.

For once, he doesn't immediately speak.

The silence feels strange on him.

Then Ophelia appears behind him, saving or complicating the moment. Hard to tell with Ophelia.

"Uncle José," she says, slipping her arm through his with a bride's authority no one can refuse. "Lillian says you're not allowed to brood near the cliff. It ruins the floral energy."

Dorothea's mouth twitches.

José gives Ophelia a look. "Floral energy?"

"She is a florist and a bride. Today, floral energy is legally binding."

I almost smile.

Ophelia turns to Dorothea. "I'm so glad you came. You look incredible."

Dorothea's cheeks warm. "Thank you. The wedding is beautiful."

"All Lillian. I wanted dramatic. She wanted alive. This is both."

"It sure is."

Ophelia looks between us.

Then, softer, "Found family has a way of making places feel bigger than they are."

The sentence lands near all of us.

José looks at her.

Ophelia squeezes his arm.

"Some of us move to small towns and become more ourselves," she says. "Not less."

I go still.

My father's gaze flicks to me.

Ophelia smiles brightly as if she has not just slipped a blade between his ribs with perfect bridal grace.

"Now come on," she says. "Lillian wants a photo with the Moretti men before everyone gets too drunk to stand symmetrically."

She leads him away.

But José stops after two steps.

He looks back at Dorothea.

Then at our joined hands.

Something passes over his face.

Not softness.

Not yet.

Something less armored.

A crack in stone.

The reception begins under the clear tent as dusk settles fully.

The lighthouse beam turns slowly above us, sweeping white light over the darkening water. The full moon rises behind thin clouds. The tent glows gold, every chandelier and string light reflected in glassware and polished wood. The flowers seem brighter in the dark, orange and yellow and pink alive against white linen.

Dinner is loud, warm, and full of laughter.

Dorothea sits beside me, not across. Her knee brushes mine under the table once, and she startles. Then, after a moment, she lets it happen again.

Small thing.

Real thing.

My father sits two tables away. I feel him like weather, but not as sharply as before. Dorothea's hand appears on my thigh under the table for one brief second when someone mentions mothers in a toast.

A check-in.

Not a claim.

I cover her hand with mine.

Green.

After dinner, the brides have their first dance.

Lillian and Ophelia dance beneath the lights while the ocean moves black beyond the tent. Lillian's orange dress glows like sunset. Ophelia's white dress catches silver and turns moonlit. They laugh halfway through, then cry, then laugh again. That's love, maybe. Not elegance. Not performance. Emotion refusing choreography and being beautiful anyway.

When the floor opens, I turn to Dorothea. "Dance with me?"

Her eyes widen. "In front of everyone?"

"You don't have to do this for the fake relationship."

"I'm not asking for the fake relationship."

She looks at my hand.

Then at the dance floor.

Then at me.

"Green," she says.

I lead her onto the floor.

The song is slow, old, and soft enough to make people feel sentimental even if they have no right. I place one hand at her waist, then pause.

"Still green?"

Her mouth curves. "Yes."

Her hand settles on my shoulder.

We begin to move.

She is stiff at first.

"You can step on me," I say.

"That sounds like a dangerous invitation."

"I have excellent shoes."

"I'm worried about your feet, not the shoes."

"I will survive."

She relaxes by degrees.

Not all at once.

Dorothea never opens like a door thrown wide. She opens like dough rising, slow and warm, changing because the conditions are finally kind enough to allow it.

People watch. I feel their eyes burning into me. I feel my father's too.

But Dorothea stays.

Near the end of the song, she rests her cheek against my chest.

My hand tightens at her waist.

"Green?" I whisper.

"Green."

When the song ends, I don't want to let her go.

I do anyway.

Before we can leave the floor, José approaches.

My whole body locks.

Dorothea feels it instantly.

Her hand finds mine.

Yellow, her touch says.

Pause.

I breathe.

José stops in front of us.

For once, he doesn't look like he has rehearsed his expression.

That alone is unsettling.

"Dorothea," he says.

She straightens slightly. "José."

His mouth tightens at the sound of his name. Not because she says it wrong. Because she says it without fear.

"I owe you an apology."

The reception noise seems to dim.

I stare at him.

Dorothea doesn't.

She looks directly at him and waits.

José eyes flick to mine before he gives her his attention. As if eye contact has become a task requiring effort.

"My behavior at dinner was unacceptable," he says. "What I said about Lorenzo's mother was cruel."

My breath stops.

He has never said that.

Not once.

Cruel.

From his own mouth.

"I have told myself for years that I was speaking truth," he continues. His voice is lower now. Rougher. "But grief doesn't become truth because a man repeats it often enough."

Dorothea's fingers tighten around mine.

José looks at her.

"You were right. I blamed him because blaming him gave me somewhere to put what I could not survive feeling."

I cannot move.

Some part of me is eight years old. Sixteen. Thirty. Standing in a hospital hallway with my father's grief becoming a sentence I would serve for years.

Dorothea stays beside me.

Not speaking for me now.

Only there.

José's gaze shifts to me.

"I'm sorry, Lorenzo."

The words enter me strangely.

Not like healing.

Not even close.

More like a door I did not know was locked clicking once in the dark.

I don't know what to do with them.

My mouth opens.

Nothing comes out.

For once, my father doesn't punish the silence.

"I should not have said those things," he says. "Not then. Not ever. Your mother loved you. That's why she went. That's not your crime to carry."

The reception blurs.

I look away.

Not because I forgive him.

Not because everything is solved.

Because my body has been waiting years for those exact words, and now that they are here, I don't trust them yet.

Dorothea's thumb moves over my hand once.

I breathe. "I don't know what to say," I manage.

José nods. "You don't have to say anything."

That surprises me almost as much as the apology.

He looks at Dorothea again. "I apologize to you as well. I insulted you, your relationship with my son, and the life he has built here because I did not want to see it."

Dorothea's voice is quiet. "Do you see it now?"

José looks around.

At the tent. The flowers. Ophelia laughing with Lillian near the cake. Molly arguing with William at a table. Guests dancing. The lighthouse. The ocean. The town.

Then he looks at me.

"I'm beginning to."

Dorothea nods. "Then that's a start."

Not forgiveness handed over fully wrapped.

Not absolution.

A start.

José accepts it.

"I would like to know you better," he says. "Both of you. If you will allow it."

Dorothea looks to me. It's my choice.

I think of every cruel call. Every accusation. Every time his love arrived dressed as leverage.

I also think of Ophelia saying people become more themselves here, not less.

I think of Dorothea defending me, not because I was weak, but because I deserved defending.

That's the thing.

She did not make my father behave.

She made me believe I was worth standing beside.

That changes the weather more than José's apology ever could.

"Maybe," I say.

José nods once.

Maybe.

Not yes.

Not no.

Revisable.

His mouth moves like he almost smiles, then decides not to risk it.

"Maybe is more than I deserve."

"Yes," Dorothea says.

I cough to cover a laugh.

José looks at her.

For the first time, there is something like respect in his eyes. "Fair."

He leaves us there on the edge of the dance floor.

I stand still long after he goes.

Dorothea turns toward me.

"Color?" she asks.

The question nearly undoes me.

I look at her in the green dress under the wedding lights, flowers in her hair from the ceremony, eyes full of worry and strength and tenderness she is still learning how to let herself give.

"Yellow," I say.

"Okay."

"But not bad yellow."

"What kind?"

"Too much at once yellow."

She nods. "I understand that one."

We step away from the crowd and walk toward the lighthouse.

The path curves behind it, away from the tent and music. The moon is fully up now, silver on the water. The lighthouse beam sweeps overhead, slow and steady, touching the rocks below, the flowers along the cliff, Dorothea's face.

We stop near the railing.

For a while, we only breathe.

The wedding continues behind us. Laughter. Music. Applause as someone announces cake. The world going on beautifully without needing us to perform.

"I wanted to kiss you when he apologized," I say.

Dorothea's eyes lift. "Why didn't you?"

"Because I did not know whether it was comfort, gratitude, performance, or want."

Her face softens. "And?"

"And all of them were tangled."

She steps closer. "That's honest."

"I'm trying."

"I know you are."

The wind moves through her hair.

I touch the bouquet ribbon still wrapped around her wrist. She tied it there after setting the flowers at our table, a small green thread against her skin.

"You changed the weather tonight," I say.

Her brow furrows. "What?"

"With him. With me. Everywhere you stand, the room has to decide whether it's going to keep lying."

She looks away, overwhelmed.

"I did not do anything magical."

"No."

I tuck a loose strand of hair behind her ear, because she already gave me green for that and still leans into it now.

"You did something harder."

Her eyes shine. "Lorenzo."

"I thought I needed you beside me so my father would see I had built something respectable."

"And?"

"And tonight, watching you, I realized I wanted you beside me because you make me want to believe my life is already worth respecting."

Her mouth trembles. "That's a very large sentence."

"Yes."

"I don't know what to do with it."

"You don't have to do anything tonight."

She exhales. "Slow, specific, honest?"

"Yes."

"I'm sorry I hurt you."

The words come softly.

I still. "Last night," she says. "I asked for yellow, and I needed yellow, but I also ran. I didn't ask for what I needed after. I made you guess, then left you outside the door."

My chest tightens. "You were scared."

"Yes. And I hurt you."

I don't rescue her from that truth.

She deserves the dignity of being accountable.

"Yes," I say. "You did."

Tears gather in her eyes. "I'm sorry," she says.

"I know."

"I don't want to make you responsible for my fear."

"Good."

"But I also don't know how to stop being afraid."

"I'm not asking you to stop."

"What are you asking?"

The question hangs between us.

I could ask for everything.

"Keep telling me the truth before you run," I say.

Her breath catches.

"That's it?"

"For now."

"And what will you do?"

"I will tell you when something hurts instead of turning it into charm."

A tear slips down her cheek. "That sounds hard."

"It will be."

"Okay."

"Okay?"

She nods.

"Green," she whispers.

My chest aches.

"Green."

This time, when I lean closer, I pause. "Kiss?"

Her answer is immediate.

"Yes."

I kiss her under the lighthouse, with the moon on the water and the wedding lights glowing behind us.

It's not fake.

No one is watching closely enough for performance to matter.

It's not a promise that nothing will hurt.

It's not a solution to Applegate, my father, her fear, my grief, or the complicated ethics of loving someone whose case I'm still fighting.

It's only a kiss.

Slow.

Specific.

Honest.

Her hands slide into my jacket. Mine settle at her waist. She rises into me, and for a moment the whole world is ocean, light, and the taste of rose lipstick on my mouth.

When we pull apart, she rests her forehead against my chest.

"Forehead?" I ask, because I remember.

She laughs softly. "Green."

I kiss her forehead.

Careful.

Reverent.

Not a claim.

A thank you.

A beginning.

Behind us, someone cheers from the tent. The cake is being cut. The brides are probably laughing. My father is somewhere under the lights, beginning whatever maybe will become. Applegate is still waiting. The hearing is still ahead. Tomorrow will still demand work.

But tonight, Dorothea's hand finds mine.

This time, when guests see us walking back toward the tent together, I don't wonder whether we look convincing.

I only wonder how long it will take the rest of the world to catch up to what is already true.

FOURTEEN

Dorothea

A day off is a strange and suspicious thing.

People talk about them like they are restful. Restorative. Necessary. They say things like you deserve it and take care of yourself and the bakery will survive one day without you.

The bakery might survive.

I'm less certain about me.

By eight in the morning, I have already woken up twice, checked my phone four times, made coffee, reheated that coffee, answered one text from Baylin, opened my email, closed my email, opened it again, stared at Lorenzo's name in my inbox, and stood at the top of the stairs listening to the bakery below like a mother listening for a child breathing in the next room.

The ovens are on.

Baylin is there. Derek is there. May dropped off breakfast dumplings for them because "Dottie's day off should not mean everyone else has to eat sad toast," which is both kind and judgmental.

Everything is fine.

Fine remains a suspicious word.

I stand in my apartment wearing soft black leggings, an oversized sweater, and the expression of a woman who has been told she cannot go downstairs and touch the display cases. My backpack sits on the couch, packed with a blanket, a romance novel, a water bottle, and a notebook I may or may not use to write down every possible way my life could still collapse.

Day off.

Relax.

Be normal.

I walk to the door.

Then stop.

Then turn around.

Then walk to the kitchen and wipe an already-clean counter.

"No," I tell myself.

The counter is not impressed.

I pick up my phone.

No new messages from Lorenzo.

There are case updates from yesterday. Formal emails. Professional subject lines. Attachments. Notice of tender to the title insurer. Demand letter to Applegate's counsel. Draft stipulation. Words that should be comforting because they mean progress is happening.

They are comforting.

They are also terrifying.

Because the more real the legal work becomes, the more real everything else becomes too.

The wedding was two days ago.

Two days since the lighthouse, the flowers, the moon over the ocean, José's apology, Lorenzo's hand in mine, the kiss behind the lighthouse, and me admitting I hurt him when I ran.

Two days since he said, Keep telling me the truth before you run.

Two days since I said green and meant it.

We have texted.

Careful things.

Warm things.

No one has pushed.

Pushing gives me something to brace against. Care gives me room to choose, and choice is much more frightening.

My phone buzzes.

I nearly throw it.

> Baylin: If you come downstairs before noon,
> I'm putting you on dish duty and telling
> everyone you failed vacation school.

I stare at the message. Then type back.

> Dorothea: Vacation school sounds fake.

> Baylin: So did your legal boyfriend situation,
> and yet.

> Dorothea: Rude.

> Baylin: Accurate.

> Baylin: Go outside. Let the town see you as a
> person and not an apron with legs.

I look down at myself.

No apron.

It feels indecent.

I grab my backpack before I can change my mind and head out.

The bakery stairs lead down to the side door. I pause at the bottom because the smell hits me, butter, yeast, sugar, coffee, cinnamon, warm bread, dish soap, old wood. Home. Work. Safety. Prison, if I let it become that.

Through the little window in the side door, I can see Baylin moving behind the bread wall. Derek is at the counter, nodding too seriously while Mrs. Talbot points at something in the pastry case.

They are fine.

The bakery is breathing without me.

That should be a relief.

But it also hurts a little.

I step onto the sidewalk.

Coral Cove is awake and showing off.

The morning rain has washed everything clean. Storefronts shine under strips of pale sun. The flower boxes outside Lillian's shop overflow with late-summer color, orange, pink, yellow, purple. Spellbound Stories has a display of beach reads and haunted lighthouse novels in the window because Lea believes every season can be improved with ghosts. The harbor glints at the end of the street, boats rocking gently in their slips. The air tastes like salt and coffee and wet pavement.

I walk slowly because I have nowhere I'm supposed to be.

That's also suspicious.

A tourist couple stops in front of Knead the Dough and points at the sign. My whole body wants to turn around and tell them the almond croissants are best before ten and the pear danishes should be eaten warm.

I don't.

Derek can handle it.

Baylin can handle it.

People can choose pastries without my emotional supervision.

Probably.

I make it half a block before Cora from the flower shop calls, "Dottie, your dress at the wedding was gorgeous."

I freeze like I have been accused of theft.

Then remember compliments are not subpoenas.

"Thank you," I call back.

Cora smiles. "Green is your color."

My face warms.

I keep walking.

Green is more than a color now. It's a door. A pulse. A word in Lorenzo's mouth. A risk I keep choosing with a yellow border.

By the time I reach Golden Chopsticks, my stomach has started to remember it's a body with needs and not merely a container for legal anxiety. The restaurant is quieter during lunch prep, but the kitchen already smells like ginger, garlic, scallions, chili oil, and broth. A bell chimes when I step inside.

May looks up from behind the counter.

Her smile is immediate and dangerous.

"Dottie."

"May."

"You're not wearing an apron."

"I know."

"Should I alert the papers?"

"Please don't."

She wipes her hands on a towel and leans over the counter. "Day off?"

"Allegedly."

"That means you're here for food and emotional meddling."

"I'm here for takeout."

"Food and emotional meddling," she repeats.

I sigh and look at the menu board, even though I know it by heart.

"Sesame noodles. Cucumber salad. Scallion pancakes. And whatever dumplings you think will make me less unbearable."

"Pork and chive."

"Bold."

"Necessary."

She enters the order, then studies me.

I brace myself.

"So," she says.

"No."

"You don't even know what I was going to ask."

"Yes, I do."

"How is Lorenzo?"

"Ask Lorenzo."

"I did. He looked like someone who had been kissed by God and threatened by paperwork."

I close my eyes. "Why are you like this?"

"Community service."

"Gossip is not community service."

"Incorrect."

May's smile softens. "I saw you two at the wedding," she says.

"A lot of people did."

"Yes. But I've known Lorenzo since he arrived in town, and I've known you longer. I know the difference between show and substance."

My fingers tighten around the strap of my backpack.

"It started complicated," I say.

"I figured."

"That's all I'm saying."

"That's more than enough."

She turns to grab a container from the shelf, then pauses. "The lawsuit?"

My stomach tightens.

"Better. I think. Lorenzo found old records. The title insurer is involved. Applegate may not have what they thought they had."

"Good."

"I'm afraid to believe that."

May nods.

Not with pity.

With recognition.

"Sometimes good news is harder to hold than bad news," she says. "Bad news gives you a job. Brace. Fix. Survive. Good news asks you what you might do if the crisis ends."

I stare at her.

"Did Lea call you?"

"No. Why?"

"That sounded like her."

May laughs. "Honey, women who run businesses learn a few things without a bookstore oracle."

The kitchen bell rings. She goes to grab my order but keeps talking.

"I will not tell you everything will be fine, because I hate when people say that. They mean well, but it's lazy comfort. I will tell you this instead. Lorenzo is very good at standing between people and what tries to take from them."

"I know."

"And you're very good at standing, period."

I make a face.

"If you call me resilient, I'm leaving."

May points at me with a takeout bag.

"I would never. Resilient is what people say when they want to praise you for surviving something they did not help you through."

My throat tightens. "Exactly."

"You're not resilient," she says, pushing the bag toward me. "You're rooted. There's a difference."

The words land somewhere low in my chest.

Rooted.

Not bouncing back.

Not adapting for other people's comfort.

Rooted.

Stubborn enough to grow where I choose.

"Thank you," I say.

May's expression warms. "You're welcome."

I pay, and she doesn't let me leave without a second bag.

"What's this?"

"Extra dumplings."

"I ordered enough."

"No one ever ordered enough dumplings."

"May."

"For the park. Eat them in the gazebo. Rest like a person who understands calories."

"You and Baylin are in a conspiracy."

"Yes. We have minutes."

I leave before I cry in Golden Chopsticks, because crying in a restaurant where everyone knows your order feels like surrendering too much power.

Chetzemoka Park is bright with late afternoon sun by the time I reach it.

The grass is damp but not muddy. The wind moves through the trees, bringing ocean air up from the water. Children shout near the playground. Someone throws a tennis ball for a dog that seems deeply committed to never returning it. An older couple sits on a bench sharing fries from The Salty Gull. The whole park feels ordinary in a way that hurts.

Life, continuing.

People eating lunch. Children climbing. Dogs refusing obedience. Sun on wet leaves.

No one here knows Applegate Holdings has occupied my chest for days like a second heart.

No one here knows Lorenzo Moretti touched me like asking was sacred.

No one here knows I found a magical recipe book hidden under the bread wall of my bakery and then decided to conduct pastry ethics experiments like a deranged domestic scientist.

I spread my blanket beneath a tree first.

Then move it because the ground is too damp.

Then choose a bench.

Then reject the bench because a bench is not restful, it's waiting in public.

Finally, I head toward the gazebo.

My gazebo.

Not legally. I have learned the law is far too particular for that kind of sentiment. But in the private map of Coral Cove inside my head, the gazebo belongs to my quieter self. The self who comes here with takeout, a book, and the hope of being outside without being fully exposed.

I stop before I reach it.

The gazebo has been transformed.

Flowers climb the railings.

Not a few flowers.

A full, breathtaking spill of them. Soft cream roses. Yellow ranunculus. Orange marigolds. Pink peonies. Green vines woven around the posts. Little glass jars hang from hooks, each one holding a small candle waiting for dusk. The wooden floor is covered with layered blankets and pillows in warm shades of cream, rust, gold, and green. A low picnic table sits in the center, set with plates, cloth napkins, sparkling water, and a tiny vase of sunflowers.

For one second, I'm not in Chetzemoka Park.

I'm back in another room that was not a room.

A sanctuary of steam and flowers.

Warm water.

Soft light.

Lucian's voice saying, I was made to show you the door, Dorothea. Not to become the room you hide in.

My hand tightens around the takeout bag.

This is not that.

This is real.

The air smells like ocean, grass, flowers, and Golden Chopsticks.

The floor is old wood under blankets, not enchanted stone.

The sound is children laughing somewhere beyond the trees, not trickling water.

And standing in the middle of it all is Lorenzo.

He wears dark trousers and a white shirt with the sleeves

rolled up. No jacket. No tie. His hair moves slightly in the wind. He holds a manila envelope in one hand and looks almost nervous.

Lorenzo Moretti, feared attorney, legal attack dog, man with cheekbones that should be regulated by city ordinance, standing in a flower-filled gazebo with paperwork like a romantic menace.

"Hi," he says.

My throat closes.

"Hi."

He looks at the bags in my hand. "Golden Chopsticks?"

"Yes."

"I should have known."

"I brought enough dumplings for one emotionally responsible woman."

His mouth curves.

"I brought enough food for two emotionally complicated people."

"That sounds more realistic."

I look around again.

The flowers.

The pillows.

The little candles.

The carefulness of it.

"What is this?"

His expression turns more serious.

"You said the gazebo was where you go when you want to be outside without being exposed."

I swallow.

"I remembered."

"I can see that."

"I asked Lillian for help with flowers. Ophelia contributed the pillows and said, and I quote, 'If you're going to create a public emotional ambush, at least make it tasteful.'"

A laugh breaks through my throat, wet at the edges.

"It's tasteful."

"I was told that matters."

"It does."

He takes one step closer, then stops. "Is this too much?"

The question nearly undoes me.

Yes.

No.

Maybe.

It's too much because it's beautiful. Because it's real. Because he built me a sanctuary in the middle of a park without knowing he was echoing the place where fantasy first taught me how dangerous safety could be.

It's not too much because he asked.

I press my palm against my thigh.

"Green," I say. Then, because truth matters, "Overwhelmed green."

His face softens.

"Thank you for telling me."

I step into the gazebo.

The boards creak under my boots.

Real.

The flowers move in the breeze.

Real.

Lorenzo stands still and lets me look.

"You didn't know," I say.

His brow furrows. "Know what?"

"That it would remind me of something."

His face shifts. "The Arcane Room?"

I nod.

"I can take some of it down," he says.

"No."

"Dorothea."

"No. It's just…" I breathe in. The flowers smell clean and alive. "In The Arcane Room, there was a sanctuary. A place after everything. Warm water, flowers, quiet. It was beautiful, but it was also a goodbye. It was where I had to choose to leave fantasy."

His eyes stay on mine.

"This doesn't feel like goodbye," I say.

"What does it feel like?"

My chest aches.

"A real version."

The words settle between us.

Lorenzo's grip tightens slightly on the envelope.

"That's what I wanted," he says. "Not the Arcane Room part. I didn't know about that. But the real version."

My eyes burn.

"Why?"

"Because you deserve a place to rest that is not also the place where you work."

Rude.

Beautiful.

Rude.

"I'm bad at that."

"I know."

"Everyone knows, apparently."

"You're not subtle."

"Excuse me."

"You're many things, Dorothea. Subtle about needing rest is not one of them."

I glare at him.

It fails because my eyes are too wet.

He gestures toward the blankets.

"Sit?"

I look at the envelope.

"Is that legal or romantic?"

"Yes."

"Terrible answer."

"Accurate answer."

I sit.

He waits until I'm settled, then sits across from me, leaving space between us. I place my Golden Chopsticks bags beside his picnic basket.

"What did you bring?" I ask.

"Fruit. Cheese. Bread from your bakery, because Baylin threatened me if I purchased bread elsewhere. Sparkling water. Lemon bars."

"You brought my own lemon bars to me?"

"I was told they pair well with emotional updates."

"By whom?"

"Molly."

"Of course."

He sets the manila envelope on the low table.

My heart changes rhythm.

"Is it bad?"

"No."

"Don't lawyer me."

His eyes meet mine.

"It's good."

The word lands, but I don't trust it yet.

He slides the envelope toward me.

"This is not a gift in the romantic sense. This is a case update. I wanted you to have the documents in your hands. And I wanted you to hear it somewhere you could breathe."

I pick up the envelope.

My hands shake.

He notices.

Doesn't comment.

I open it and pull out the papers.

The top page is a letter from Applegate's counsel.

My eyes skim.

Stipulation.

Dismissal.

With prejudice.

Release of claims.

I stop understanding after that.

"Tell me," I whisper.

Lorenzo leans forward, forearms braced on his knees.

"Here is the concrete version. Applegate's claim relied on an alleged defect in the old Harbor Hearth trust transfer. They argued Kaytie's predecessor did not have full authority to sell the building because of a supposed surviving beneficial interest."

"Harlan Pruitt."

"Yes. Or, more accurately, a descendant of Harlan Pruitt who assigned whatever he thought he had to Applegate Holdings."

"Did he have anything?"

"No."

The word is clean.

My breath catches.

Lorenzo continues, steady and precise.

"County archives found the missing Exhibit C. It doesn't support Applegate's claim. It references the release Mabel mentioned in her letter. The title company also located a complete copy of the 1981 Release of Beneficial Interest signed by Harlan Pruitt, plus the recorded Trustee Correction Affidavit. That means the interest Applegate claims to have acquired was already released decades ago."

I stare at him.

"So they bought nothing."

"They bought either nothing, or a lawsuit they hoped would scare you into surrendering before anyone proved it was nothing."

My fingers tighten on the paper. Anger bubbles through me.

Not panic this time.

Anger.

"What happens now?"

"The title insurer accepted the tender. They will cover defense costs for the title portion. After I sent the archive documents and indicated we were prepared to seek fees, challenge standing, and explore sanctions, Applegate's counsel agreed to dismissal with prejudice and a recorded release of any alleged claim."

"With prejudice means…"

"They cannot refile the same claim."

I press the paper to my chest.

The gazebo blurs.

"It's over?"

"In practical terms, yes."

My breath breaks.

He keeps talking because he knows I need the full truth, not just comfort.

"The court still has to enter the dismissal order. The recorded release has to be processed. I will monitor both. If Applegate tries any other angle, we respond. But this claim, the one threatening your ownership, is done."

My mouth opens.

Nothing comes out.

My building.

My ovens.

My apartment.

The display cases.

The bread wall.

Baylin and Derek's jobs.

Kaytie's mug.

The hidden book.

The first place I got to keep.

Still mine.

A sound leaves me.

Not elegant.

Not even slightly.

I cover my mouth with one hand, but the sob comes anyway.

Lorenzo moves closer, then stops.

"Color?"

I cry harder.

"Green," I manage. "Hug. Please."

He is there immediately.

Not crushing me.

Not making the moment his.

He wraps his arms around me, and I fold into him with the papers still clutched between us. My face presses against his shirt. He smells like clean cotton, rain, and the faint trace of coffee. His hand moves slowly over my back, steady and warm.

"It's still mine," I whisper.

"Yes."

"They can't make me leave."

"No."

"I don't have to pack."

His hand stills.

Then his arms tighten one careful degree.

"No," he says, voice rougher now. "You don't have to pack."

The words break something open.

I cry for the building.

For the girl with the garbage bag.

For Rosa's kitchen.

For Kaytie's note.

For every room I left because someone else decided I was temporary.

For the bakery below my apartment, still standing, still mine, still breathing without me for one impossible day.

Lorenzo holds me through all of it.

When the first wave passes, I pull back enough to wipe my face with my sleeve.

Very elegant.

Very romantic.

He reaches into the picnic basket and hands me a napkin.

"Thank you."

"You're welcome."

I look at the papers again.

Dismissal.

Release.

With prejudice.

The words are dry and formal and possibly the most beautiful legal poetry I have ever read.

"I don't know how to be this relieved," I say.

"Start small."

I laugh through the last of the tears.

"Everyone keeps saying that."

"People are wise."

"People are repetitive."

"Also true."

He pours sparkling water into two cups.

Then opens the food.

Because he has apparently learned that tenderness also belongs on plates.

We eat slowly.

Golden Chopsticks dumplings, scallion pancakes, cheese, fruit, Baylin's bread, lemon bars. It's a ridiculous meal. An excellent one. The gazebo smells like flowers and garlic and ocean air. The cushions are soft beneath us. Children laugh somewhere across the park. A dog barks. The world continues to be ordinary while mine rearranges around relief.

I try to read the court documents again.

Lorenzo takes them gently from my hand.

"You can read them later."

"I like proof."

"I know. You have it. It will still be proof after lunch."

Fair.

Annoying, but fair.

I eat a dumpling.

It tastes like victory and pork.

After a while, the relief settles enough for the next fear to rise.

Because apparently my nervous system is a bakery with endless back stock.

"There's something I need to tell you," I say.

Lorenzo's expression changes, not alarmed, but attentive.

"Okay."

"It's strange."

"We live in Coral Cove."

"Stranger than usual."

"That's a high bar."

"I'm serious."

"So am I."

I look at the flowers around the gazebo. The green vines. The sunflowers on the little table. The water beyond the trees.

This is the moment.

If he laughs, something will close in me.

If he dismisses it, I will survive. I know that. I can survive almost anything. That's not the question.

The question is whether I can be fully believed by someone real.

I take a breath.

"In the bakery, there's a hidden compartment under the bread wall."

His brows lift.

"I found it the day before I was served. Inside, there was a wooden box. And in the box, there was a book. The Hearth Book of Knead the Dough."

I watch his face.

No mockery.

Only focus.

"Like a recipe book?"

"Yes. But not only. It has recipes with ingredients that are not normal. Heart-cinnamon. Rose sugar. Salt of honest appetite." I wince. "It sounds ridiculous out loud."

"It sounds very Coral Cove."

"That's not the same as ridiculous?"

"Sometimes there is overlap."

I laugh despite myself.

He smiles, but gently.

"Keep going."

I do.

I tell him about the note.

Magic doesn't make a thing true. It reveals what has been mixed in.

I tell him about the warning not to serve what I would fear receiving. About the cinnamon rolls for warm regard. About changing the recipe because I did not want to manipulate anyone. About making only six. About May crying because the roll tasted like her mother's kitchen. About people leaving softer but not enchanted into anything I could see.

I tell him about my fear after the papers arrived. That maybe Applegate knew. Or the man in the raincoat had been looking for the book, not records.

That maybe the building was more than a building in ways none of the legal documents could name.

Lorenzo listens.

The whole time.

No interruption except once to ask, "Who else knows?" and when I say Lea knows pieces and Baylin suspects because Baylin suspects everything, he nods like that is practical information, not evidence that I have lost my mind.

When I finish, my hands are cold.

He looks past me for a moment, toward the park, thinking.

My stomach drops.

Then he says, "I believe you."

Three words.

That simple.

That impossible.

I stare at him.

"You do?"

"Yes."

"You don't think I'm making it up?"

"No."

"Or that I'm confused?"

"I think you're careful with truth. Especially when you're scared of how it will be received."

That's unfairly perceptive.

My throat tightens.

"Also," he adds, "I have lived in Coral Cove long enough to know that dismissing magic outright is how a man ends up humiliated by a tea shop."

A laugh bursts out of me.

It feels like a door opening.

Lorenzo reaches for my hand.

Stops before touching.

"Green?"

"Green."

He takes my hand. "Thank you for trusting me with this."

"I was afraid to."

"I know."

"I thought you might not believe me."

"I believe you."

The second time hits even harder.

He glances toward the direction of Main Street.

"From a legal and practical standpoint, we need to protect the compartment."

My heart stutters.

"Legal and practical?"

"Yes. Separate from whether magic is admissible, which I hope we never have to litigate because I refuse to hear William's opinion on enchanted cinnamon in open court."

I laugh again.

He continues, serious now.

"If Applegate came in asking whether Kaytie left anything, he may have been looking for records, the book, or both. Either way, he knew there could be something hidden. We should change the locks if you have not already. Add a camera near the side entrance and one in the front. Inventory what is in the box. Photograph everything. Keep the original where you want it, but consider a fireproof safe for the book when it's not in use."

My chest warms.

He is not trying to take it.

Not trying to decide for me.

He is helping me protect it.

"Would photographing it be dangerous?" I ask. "If it's magic?"

"I don't know. That's a sentence I never expected to say in a property case."

"It's a weird day."

His thumb moves over my knuckles. "Would you feel comfortable showing it to me sometime?"

I hesitate.

Not because I don't trust him.

Because the book feels like a heart under floorboards.

"Maybe."

He nods immediately.

"Then maybe."

No pressure.

No push.

Maybe remains a door.

I look at him and feel something inside me settle.

Not because everything is safe.

Because he believes the strange thing.

He believes me in my legal terror, my emotional mess, my magical bakery confession, and the part of me that is still learning how to sit in a gazebo without waiting to be asked to leave.

"Lorenzo?"

"Yes?"

"I didn't think I would ever meet someone I could trust with all the different kinds of impossible in my life."

His face changes.

Softens. Opens.

I keep going before I lose the nerve.

"I keep waiting for you to make me feel foolish."

"I will try very hard not to."

"I know." My voice shakes. "That's the problem."

"Why?"

"Because you keep giving me reasons to believe you."

The wind moves through the flowers.

A candle jar swings lightly from the gazebo post even though it's not lit yet.

Lorenzo's hand tightens around mine.

"I don't want to be another fantasy you escape into," he says.

"You're not."

"I don't want to become another home you're terrified to lose."

My throat closes.

"I know."

"What do you want me to be?"

The question is quiet.

No demand.

Still, it opens the ground beneath me.

What do I want?

Not what do I owe?

Not what can I afford?

Not what is safest?

What do I want?

I look at the man in front of me. The flowers he arranged without knowing he was recreating a sanctuary. The legal documents proving I can keep my building. The food spread out between us. The hand holding mine. The eyes that are green like risk, like growth, like a yes with room for yellow.

"I want you to be real with me," I say.

"I can do that."

"I'm afraid of being too slow for you."

"I would a lifetime if it meant being with you."

"Honest?"

"Yes."

"I want you to tell me when I hurt you, and I want to learn how not to run just because I'm scared."

His eyes shine. "I want that too."

"I want the case to be over before we make any huge decisions."

"Agreed."

"I want to kiss you in this gazebo."

His breath catches. "Very agreed."

I laugh.

Then I lean forward into him. Lorenzo meets me halfway.

The kiss is soft at first, because everything important between us seems to begin with softness now. His hand cups my cheek. Mine slides into the front of his shirt. The flowers move around us. The ocean air cools my wet face. Somewhere in the park, a child yells for a dog named Pickles, which is not romantic but very real, and somehow that makes the kiss better.

No fantasy room could have invented this exact moment.

No magical guide.

No velvet castle.

No perfect script.

Just Lorenzo laughing against my mouth because of a dog named Pickles, and me kissing him harder because real joy is apparently absurd and poorly timed.

When we pull apart, his forehead rests against mine.

"Forehead?" he asks.

I smile.

"Green."

He kisses my forehead.

I close my eyes.

The gesture no longer feels too intimate.

Or maybe it does, and I'm simply ready to hold it.

"I think I love you," I whisper.

The words leave before I can dress them up.

They hang between us, trembling.

Not a demand.

Not a contract.

Not a promise I know how to keep perfectly.

A truth with a yellow border.

Lorenzo goes still.

I open my eyes.

His are wet. "Dorothea."

"It's all I can hold right now."

His smile breaks, soft and aching. "Then hold think."

A tear slips down my cheek.

"What about you?"

He brushes it away with his thumb. "I think I love you too."

My heart hurts.

"Think?"

His mouth curves. "I know. But I will say think because that is the size of word you can hold today."

That destroys me.

In the best way.

I laugh and cry at the same time, which is unattractive and inconvenient and apparently what my body has decided love looks like this afternoon.

Lorenzo pulls me close.

I let him.

Not because I'm not afraid.

Because I am. And for the first time, I feel like I can be afraid and still want things. The bakery is mine.

Magic is real.

Applegate lost.

And fantasy taught me the shape of a door, but this man built me a place to sit in the real world and waited for me to choose whether to enter.

The gazebo glows around us as the sun shifts toward evening.

Flowers.

Blankets.

Dumplings.

Legal documents.

A hidden spellbook under the bread wall.

A love confession careful enough not to crush what it names.

For the first time in my life, hope doesn't feel like something waiting to be taken.

It feels like something rising.

Slowly.

Stubbornly.

Mine.

FIFTEEN

Lorenzo

I don't cook this time.

That may be the clearest proof of personal growth I have achieved all week.

The first time Dorothea came to my house for dinner, I tried to make sauce and nearly committed crimes against garlic. She rescued the meal, the kitchen, and possibly my dignity, though that last part remains debatable.

Tonight, I order takeout from Sirens Bistro like a man who has learned humility and respects professional kitchens.

There are crab cakes, roasted vegetables, garlic mashed potatoes, grilled salmon, lemon butter sauce packed separately, because I know better than to let sauce travel unchecked, and a chocolate torte I did not technically need but ordered anyway because Dorothea deserves dessert that was not made by her own hands.

I set everything out on the kitchen island, then change my mind and move it to the small table by the windows.

Then I move it back to the island because the table looks too formal.

Then back to the table because the island looks like we are eating during a deposition.

By the time I'm done, I have moved dinner three times and learned nothing useful about myself except that love makes a man deeply inefficient.

I stand in the kitchen and stare at the table.

Two plates. Two napkins. Sparkling water. Tea waiting near the kettle because Dorothea likes options and I like being prepared for her. Candles, but not too many. Flowers, but not the full gazebo treatment. Tonight is not a public emotional ambush, tasteful or otherwise. Tonight is private. Softer. A place to breathe after the court papers, the wedding, the confessions, the relief.

A place to be real without the whole town watching us decide what real means.

The flowers sit in a low vase at the center of the table. Sunflowers, rosemary, and a few small white roses. Not extravagant. Warm. Kitchen flowers. The kind that look as if they belong near bread, not chandeliers.

Dorothea would approve of that distinction.

At least, I hope she would.

My house feels different now.

Not dramatically. The floors are still too clean. The entry still looks like a designer assembled restraint and called it coastal elegance. The shelves are still too organized because I remain a man with problems.

But the kitchen has changed.

I keep basil now. Oregano too, because Dorothea looked at my spice cabinet like it had personally betrayed her, and I don't like disappointing her in ways that involve dried herbs.

A cutting board sits near the stove because I use it. The green tile behind the counter has flour in one grout line I have not scrubbed away yet, left from the morning she came over to teach me how to make breakfast that did not come from a paper bag. There is a jar of wooden spoons beside the range. A cookbook on the counter. A bag of coffee from her bakery near the machine.

The kitchen is not fully alive.

But it has a pulse now.

I glance toward the small box on the counter.

Plain black velvet.

Too dramatic, maybe.

I almost bought a wooden one. Then a brass one. Then nothing at all, because the object inside doesn't need presentation. It needs care.

A key.

Not an engagement ring. Not a demand. Not a trap disguised as romance. Not the kind of grand gesture a man makes when he wants to skip the slow work and leap straight to ownership.

A key.

A door open.

An invitation with no clock attached.

Still, the box makes my stomach tighten.

Dorothea knows what it means to lose rooms. To pack. To be told a place is not hers after she started believing it might be. I won't hand her a key like a claim.

I will hand it to her like a choice.

If I get that wrong, I deserve Lea's promised bookstore murder.

My phone buzzes.

> Dorothea: Leaving the bakery now. Green. Nervous green, but green.

I can't help but smile.

> Lorenzo: Dinner is here. No mushrooms. No experimental garlic incidents. Nervous here too.

> Dorothea: Good. I hate being the only one.

> Lorenzo: Never.

I set the phone down and breathe.

Never is a large word.

Too large, maybe.

But it's true in the only way I can mean it tonight.

She won't be the only one afraid. Not with me. Not if I can help it.

The doorbell rings eight minutes later.

I move toward the entry, then stop myself from moving too fast.

Slow.

Specific.

Honest.

I open the door.

Dorothea stands on my porch in a long black trench coat, her hair loose around her shoulders, cheeks pink from the cold evening air. Rain has gathered in tiny beads along the fabric of the coat. Her lips are deep red, and her eyes look too bright.

She is holding herself very still.

That's how I know this is not simple confidence.

"Hi," she says.

"Hi."

I don't look past her face.

Not because I don't notice the coat. I notice the coat. I notice the way she grips it closed. I notice her bare legs below the hem and the black shoes that make her look taller, steadier, like she chose them for more than appearance.

But I wait.

"You look beautiful," I say.

Her mouth curves.

"You haven't even seen the outfit."

"I saw you."

Her expression changes.

Softens.

"Oh." She breathes in.

Still receiving.

Still practicing.

"Thank you."

That quiet little I know does something to my chest.

She steps inside.

When I turn back, she is watching me with an expression I cannot fully read. Nervous. Proud. Scared. Determined. All of it at once.

"Dinner smells good," she says.

"I outsourced."

"Wise."

"I'm capable of learning."

"Jury is still deliberating."

I smile. "Harsh."

"Fair."

She stands in the entry a second longer.

Then she looks down at her coat.

My heart slows.

"Lorenzo."

"Yes?"

"I wanted to surprise you."

My body goes very still at her words. "Okay."

"And I need you to know I'm still nervous." Her voice is soft, but she doesn't look away. Brave enough to bring fear with her and name it before it can run the room.

"Thank you for telling me."

Her throat moves. "I'm proud of it," she says. "The surprise. What I'm wearing. The fact that I chose it. I don't want you to treat me like I'm fragile."

"I won't."

"But I also don't want to pretend I'm suddenly not scared of being seen."

I take one slow breath. "Then we let both things be true."

She nods. "Yes."

"What do you need from me?"

She looks relieved that I ask. "Look at me."

"Do you want to open the coat, or do you want me to?"

Her cheeks flush brighter. "I do."

I keep my hands at my sides.

Dorothea unties the belt.

Slowly.

There's no performance, this is meaningful for her.

The coat opens.

For one second, every thought I have disappears.

Black lace. Soft skin. Curves. A matching bra and panties, delicate and dark against the warm flush of her body. She looks like temptation and courage and the first honest thing said after years of silence.

My body reacts immediately.

Violently.

I do not move.

Her fingers tighten on the edges of the coat.

I force myself to meet her eyes first.

"Still green?" I ask.

She exhales, almost laughing.

"Green. You can look."

So I do.

Not quickly.

Not hungrily enough to make her feel consumed, though hunger is absolutely there, burning through me with enough force to make speech difficult. I look because she asked me to. Because she chose this. Because being desired is not the same as being inspected, and I want her to feel the difference in my gaze.

Her shoulders tremble once.

"You're quiet," she whispers.

"I'm trying to remain civilized."

A laugh breaks out of her. "Is it too much?" she asks.

"No."

"Is it silly?"

"Not even a little."

"Do I look like I'm trying too hard?"

I shake my head. "No."

Her eyes search mine. "What do I look like?"

Mine, rises in me but I don't say it. Not after everything. "You look like a woman who chose herself before she came here," I say.

Her mouth trembles.

"That's much better than the thing I thought you might say."

"What did you think I might say?"

"Something about being sexy."

"You are."

Her blush deepens.

"But that is not the most important thing I see."

She looks down for one second.

Then back up.

"Okay."

"Can I come closer?"

"Yes."

I step closer.

Not touching yet.

The air between us changes.

She slips the coat from her shoulders, and I take it when she offers it to me. Her hands shake, but her chin stays lifted.

I hang the coat carefully.

When I turn back, she stands in my entryway in black lace and heels, trying not to fold in on herself.

I hold out my hand.

She places her palm in mine.

Her hand is warm.

I lift it to my mouth and kiss her knuckles. Then the center of her palm.

Her eyes flutter close.

"Still green?" I ask.

"Yes."

I kiss her wrist.

She shivers.

I smile against her skin.

She sways one fraction closer.

My control tightens.

Not because I want to hold back from her.

Because I want to be worthy of the way she came here, scared and proud and asking to be seen.

"Dinner first?" I ask.

Her eyes open.

She looks toward the kitchen.

Then back at me.

A wicked little smile touches her mouth, nervous but real.

"You're asking because you're polite."

"Yes."

"And because you bought dinner."

"Yes."

"And because you think eating first is reasonable."

"Yes."

Her fingers curl into mine. "I don't feel reasonable right now."

My breath leaves slowly.

"Dorothea."

"I want dinner." She steps closer. "After."

My entire body goes hot.

"After what?"

Her lips part.

She blushes, but she doesn't retreat.

"After you kiss me like this was a very good surprise."

I'm not made of stone.

I have never claimed to be.

I cup her face with both hands and kiss her.

She rises into me immediately, mouth warm and eager under mine. Not tentative like before. Not fearless either. This is something better, want with its hands open. Her arms slide around my neck, and the lace brushes against my shirt, heat through fabric, softness against restraint.

I keep the kiss slow at first.

She makes an impatient sound.

I pull back half an inch.

"Color?"

"Green. Less careful."

That nearly ends me.

"Less careful where?"

She gives me a look.

Even blushing, she manages it.

"My mouth. My waist. My back. You can touch me like you want to."

I slide one hand down to her waist.

"Like this?"

"Yes."

The other to her back, fingers spreading over warm skin and lace.

"And this?"

"Yes."

She pulls me down to kiss her again.

This time, I let more of my want into it.

Still listening.

Still careful.

But not distant. Not holding myself so far away that she has to wonder whether I'm afraid of her. My hand presses at the small of her back. Her body meets mine. She gasps into my mouth, then laughs softly when she feels how much I want her.

"That's not funny," I murmur.

"It is a little."

"It's painful."

Her eyes darken. "Good."

I freeze.

She freezes too.

Then she laughs, breathless and embarrassed.

"I mean, not pain good. I mean, I like knowing. I like that you want me that much."

I rest my forehead against hers. "You're going to kill me."

"Not before dinner."

"We have already postponed dinner."

"Good. Then we're making progress."

I laugh.

She smiles, and the smile is so bright, so much herself, that I almost forget the heat clawing through me.

Almost.

"Bedroom?" she asks.

I go still again.

She notices.

"I'm asking," she says. "Not being swept away."

"I know."

"I want to go there. I want to choose it."

My throat tightens.

"Then yes."

She takes my hand.

And leads me.

That might be what undoes me most.

Not the lace. Not the exposed skin. Not the wanting, though God knows the wanting is enough to wreck me.

It's the leading.

Dorothea walking through my house half-naked, nervous and proud, holding my hand like she has decided this door opens both ways.

In the bedroom, she stops near the foot of the bed and turns to face me.

The room is warm, lit only by the lamps on the night-stands and the soft glow from the hallway. Rain taps the windows. My bed is made, simple gray bedding turned down because I hoped, yes, but did not assume.

Dorothea notices that too.

"You turned the bed down."

"Yes."

"Optimistic."

"Hopeful."

Her face softens. "Better."

I step close enough to touch her, but I don't.

"What do you want tonight?"

Her breath catches.

The question lands differently now.

Before, it made her tremble. Tonight, she still trembles, but she doesn't look away.

"I want joy," she says.

The answer surprises me.

Then it fills the room.

"Joy?"

"Yes." She swallows. "The first time we were intimate, I was scared and learning and trying not to disappear inside my own panic. It was beautiful. It was. But tonight I don't want to only survive wanting you. I want to enjoy wanting you."

My chest aches. "I want that too."

"I want to laugh if something is awkward."

"Good."

"I want to say what I want without you making that face like you're about to go to war with my trauma."

I blink.

Then laugh because it's too accurate.

"I make that face?"

"Yes."

"I apologize."

"It's sweet, but exhausting."

"Noted."

"I want you to ask," she continues. "But I also want you to believe me when I answer."

That one lands hard.

I nod, realizing I've been second guessing her. "I understand."

"I want to go slow, but not because I'm fragile. Because slow feels good."

My voice lowers an octave. "Yes."

"And I want everything tonight."

My breath stops.

She sees it.

Her cheeks turn red, but her eyes stay on mine.

"Everything?" I ask.

"Yes."

"Green?"

"Green."

"Are you sure?"

She steps closer and places one finger against my mouth.

"I need you to ask me that when I say yellow. I need you to ask when I hesitate. I need you to ask if I go quiet." Her finger slips from my mouth to my chin. "But when I say yes clearly, I need you to believe me."

The whole arc of her is standing in my bedroom in black lace.

Not surrendering herself.

Choosing.

I kiss her finger. "I believe you."

Her eyes shine. "Good."

She reaches for the buttons of my shirt with surer hands this time. Her fingers work them open one by one, brushing my skin with every movement. When she gets impatient with a stubborn button, she curses under her breath.

"Men's clothing is fucking ridiculous," she mutters.

I laugh low, helping her shove the shirt off my shoulders. "Says the woman whose heels could commit murder."

"That was the point," she says, voice husky as she reaches for my belt.

We undress each other in a slow, heated tangle of hands and mouths. Every piece of clothing that hits the floor ratchets the hunger higher. When I slide her bra straps down her shoulders and bare her breasts, I groan at the sight. I cup them, thumbs brushing her tight nipples, and lean down to taste one, then the other. She arches into my mouth with a soft, needy sound that goes straight to my cock.

When she wraps her hand around my hard length, she's bolder now. She strokes me with long, firm pulls, learning exactly how much pressure makes my hips jerk and my breath catch.

"Fuck, Dorothea…" I rasp, kissing her deeply while she works me.

She sits on the edge of the bed and pulls me between her spread thighs. I settle my hands on her soft skin, stroking upward until my thumbs brush the slick heat between her legs. She's soaked.

"Here?" I ask, voice rough.

"Yes." Her legs part wider. "Kiss me."

"Where?"

Her cheeks flush a deep pink, but her eyes stay locked on mine with a boldness that makes my cock twitch. "Everywhere."

I drop to my knees in front of her like a man at prayer.

I start slow, kissing the soft skin of her inner thighs, savoring the way her muscles jump under my lips. I drag my mouth higher, teasing the crease where her thigh meets her body, breathing in the sweet, musky scent of her arousal. She's already glistening, her pussy swollen and dripping for me.

When I finally lean in and drag my tongue through her slick folds in one long, slow stroke, she lets out a broken moan that goes straight to my balls. I groan against her, the taste of her — warm, sweet, and addictive — flooding my mouth.

"Fuck, you're soaked," I rasp, before diving back in.

I lick her deeper, fucking her with my tongue, then move up to circle her swollen clit with firm, wet strokes. She gasps, her hands flying to my hair. I slide two thick fingers inside her tight heat, curling them upward as I suck her clit into my mouth. Her hips jerk hard against my face.

"Lorenzo— oh god—"

I work her relentlessly, sucking and licking and pumping my fingers in a steady rhythm. The obscene wet sounds of my mouth on her pussy fill the room, mixed with her ragged moans and breathless curses. She's grinding against my tongue now, chasing the pleasure without shame, her thighs trembling around my head.

I add a third finger, stretching her gently while I suck harder on her clit, flicking it with my tongue exactly how she likes. Her walls flutter and clench around my fingers, getting tighter, hotter, wetter.

"I'm— I'm so close—" she whimpers, voice cracking.

I don't stop. I growl against her pussy and double down, fucking her faster with my fingers while my tongue works her clit in tight, relentless circles. Her whole body starts shaking. Her grip in my hair turns almost painful as she rides my face.

When she comes, it's violent and beautiful. Her back arches sharply, a raw cry tearing from her throat as her pussy pulses hard around my fingers, flooding my mouth with her release. I keep licking her through every wave, gentler but still hungry, drawing out her orgasm until she's gasping and pushing weakly at my shoulders.

"Wait," she pants, voice wrecked. "Wait— I want to be on top."

My brain short-circuits for a second at the image.

"Yes," I manage.

I lie back on the bed. She climbs over me with focused determination, one knee planted beside my hip, her hand braced on my chest. Her hair falls forward like a curtain, brushing my skin. She's flushed, breathing hard, and so beautifully turned on it makes my cock throb.

"Don't laugh at me," she says.

"I'm not laughing." My hands slide up her thighs, gripping her hips. "I'm trying not to come just looking at you like this."

Her smile turns slow and wicked. She leans down and kisses me hard, then reaches between us to wrap her fingers around my cock again. She strokes me slowly, dragging the head through her slick folds, teasing herself with it until we're both breathing raggedly.

When she finally lines me up at her entrance, she looks down at me, eyes bright with nerves and raw desire.

"I want you inside me," she says, voice clear and hungry. "Now."

"Green?" I ask, jaw clenched with the effort of holding still.

"Green." She sinks down just a little, taking the head of my cock inside her. We both moan at the tight, wet heat. "Protection?"

She grabs a condom from the nightstand, tears it open, and rolls it down my aching cock with shaky but determined hands. Then she rises over me again, gripping my shoulders as she lines me up at her entrance.

"I want you inside me," she whispers, voice thick with need.

"Slow, baby. Take your time." My hands cradle her hips, thumbs stroking her skin. "I've got you."

She sinks down inch by inch.

The tight, scorching heat of her virgin pussy stretching around my cock is pure bliss. I groan deeply, fingers flexing hard on her hips as I fight the overwhelming urge to thrust up into her. She's impossibly tight, wet, and perfect. Every tiny movement pulls a soft, breathless sound from her throat.

"Fuck... Dorothea," I rasp, voice wrecked. "You feel like heaven."

She pauses when I'm halfway in, breathing hard, adjusting to my size. I reach between us and circle her clit with my thumb, slow and gentle, until she moans and sinks the rest of the way down, taking me to the hilt.

We both shudder.

For a moment we stay like that — joined completely, foreheads pressed together, breathing each other in. Then she starts to move, rolling her hips in tentative, delicious strokes. I let her set the pace, my hands sliding up her body to cup her breasts, thumbs brushing her nipples as I worship every inch of her with touch and praise.

"You're so beautiful riding me like this," I murmur against her throat, kissing and sucking softly. "So wet. So perfect. I could stay inside you forever."

Her rhythm grows bolder. I meet her with gentle upward thrusts, grinding deep every time she sinks down. The wet, intimate sound of her pussy taking my cock fills the room, driving me higher.

"I love you," I say suddenly, the words rising unbidden from the deepest part of me. "I love you, Dorothea."

Her eyes fill with tears even as she moans, her walls clenching hard around me.

"I love you too," she gasps, riding me faster. "I love you so much."

The words snap something inside me. I sit up, wrapping my arms around her, and flip us carefully so she's on her back beneath me. I stay deep inside her the whole time, never breaking our connection.

Now I worship her properly.

I kiss her deeply as I move inside her — slow, rolling strokes that grind against her clit with every thrust. I worship her breasts with my mouth, sucking and licking her nipples until she's writhing. My hand slides between us again, circling her clit as I fuck her with deep, steady strokes.

Every movement says the same thing. You are safe. You are wanted. You are loved.

When she starts trembling, I press my forehead to hers.

"Come for me, sweetheart. Let me feel you."

She breaks beautifully — back arching, a raw cry tearing from her throat as her pussy pulses hard around my cock. Her nails dig into my shoulders as she comes, sobbing my name, laughing and crying at the same time.

The feeling of her coming around me drags me over the edge right behind her. I bury my face in her neck and groan her name as pleasure crashes through me, spilling deep inside her with long, pulsing thrusts. I keep moving through every wave, gentle even as I lose myself, because she deserves nothing less.

Afterward, I don't collapse on her. I roll to the side and pull her with me, keeping her tucked safely against my chest. Her leg drapes over mine. Her hair is wild. We're both breathing like we've run miles.

For a long moment, the only sound is rain and our slowing heartbeats.

Then she says, voice soft and dazed, "That was not graceful."

I laugh so hard my chest shakes. She lifts her head, mock-offended.

"What?"

"Nothing," I say, grinning. "I'm just stupidly happy that the woman I love is lying naked in my arms criticizing her own grace after the best sex of my life."

Her mouth twitches. "It was joyful."

"Yes," I murmur, kissing her forehead. This time she presses into it immediately. "It was perfect."

She yawns, curling closer. "Dinner?"

"Dinner is definitely cold," I whisper, smiling against her hair. "Worth it."

"Can we eat cold crab cakes in bed?"

"Yes."

"Is that allowed in your very clean house?"

I look around the room, at the clothes on the floor, the rumpled bedding, the woman in my arms, and the life I can feel beginning to gather in corners that used to be empty.

"Yes," I say. "I think the house needs it."

We eat cold crab cakes and chocolate torte in my bed like emotionally exhausted heathens.

It's one of the best meals of my life.

Later, when she is wrapped in one of my shirts and sitting cross-legged against the pillows, I reach for the box on the nightstand.

Her eyes narrow immediately. "What's that?"

"A gift."

"Lorenzo…"

"That tone feels accusatory."

"You're holding a velvet box in bed after sex. Historically, that can escalate."

"It's not a ring."

Her shoulders drop so fast I almost laugh.

Then she glares. "I was not panicking."

"You were absolutely panicking."

"I was preparing."

"For what?"

"Emotional nonsense."

I sit facing her and set the box on the blanket between us. "It may still be emotional nonsense."

"Good to know."

"It's not a demand."

Her expression changes.

I continue before fear can take the room.

"It's not a proposal. It's not a timeline. It's not me asking you to leave your apartment, your bakery, or anything that is yours."

Her gaze drops to the box.

Her fingers tighten around the hem of my shirt.

"Okay."

"If you open it and hate it, we talk."

"I won't hate it."

"I want you to have room to hate it."

That stops her.

Her mouth softens.

"Okay," she says. "I have room to hate it."

I push the box gently toward her.

She opens it.

The key rests inside on a square of black velvet.

Not ornate. Not symbolic in an obvious way. Just a key with a small green ribbon tied through it.

Dorothea goes completely still.

I feel the whole house hold its breath.

"It's a key," she says.

"Yes."

"To your house?"

"Yes."

Her eyes lift to mine.

I speak carefully.

"This is yours for whenever you want to be here. No pressure. No timeline. No expectation that you use it tonight, tomorrow, or ever."

Her throat moves.

"I don't understand."

"Yes, you do."

Tears gather fast.

I take her hand.

"You told me homes can be taken," I say. "I cannot promise you nothing will ever change. I won't lie to you like that. But I can tell you this door is open to you because I choose it. And if you choose not to use the key, the door is still open. If you choose to use it only when you want dinner, tea, a nap, or someone to sit beside you without talking, it's still yours."

Her face crumples. "Lorenzo."

"You don't have to move in with me to belong here when you want to. You don't have to give up your apartment to have access to my house. You don't have to trade one home for another."

"I'm getting tears on your shirt." She laughs through it.

"It's survived worse."

"Did it survive garlic?"

"Nothing survived the garlic."

She laughs harder, then presses the heel of her hand to her mouth.

"I don't know how to accept this."

"Start small."

She gives me a watery glare.

"Everyone needs to stop saying that."

"No."

Her laugh turns into a sob.

I pull her into my arms when she leans toward me.

She holds the key between us.

For a while, she only cries.

Not like before, not panic, not grief exactly.

Release.

That can look like grief from the outside.

I'm learning the difference.

Finally, she pulls back enough to look at the key again.

"You tied it with green ribbon."

"Yes."

"Because of the color system?"

"And your dress. And my tile. And the gazebo. And because I'm apparently a sentimental man now, which is embarrassing for everyone."

She smiles. "I like sentimental Lorenzo."

"Don't tell Molly."

"She knows."

"Unfortunately, yes."

Dorothea runs her thumb over the key. "My apartment is still mine. The bakery is also still mine."

"Of course. I would never ask you to choose between us. I just want to see you whenever you want to be here."

I brush one tear away with my thumb. She leans into my touch.

"I love you," she says.

The words are small.

Certain.

"I love you too."

She looks down at the key, then closes the box around it.

For one terrible second, I think she is going to hand it back.

Instead, she sets it on the nightstand on her side of the bed.

Her side.

It's too soon for that.

I let myself think it anyway.

"I'll keep it," she says.

My chest tightens.

"Okay."

"I don't know how often I'll use it."

"Okay."

"I might panic about it tomorrow."

"Doesn't change how I feel about you. If anything your vulnerability makes me love you even more."

"I might call Lea and ask if I have made a terrible decision."

"That's completely reasonable. I'd expect you to call her whenever you need her."

"She may threaten you."

"She already has."

Dorothea smiles.

Then she settles back into my arms, her cheek over my heart.

"Tonight," she says, "I want to stay."

I close my eyes.

That's a small sentence.

It's also everything.

She presses a kiss to my chest.

* * *

Later, when the candles have burned low and rain moves softly against the windows, Dorothea falls asleep with one hand tucked under her cheek and the other resting near the little black box on the nightstand.

I stay awake a while longer. Because I want to remember this exact version of the room.

The cold takeout containers on the dresser.

The flowers in the kitchen.

Her coat by the door.

Her shoes tipped over beside mine.

The house is alive in a way I did not know it could be.

I kiss her hair once, carefully enough not to wake her. "Goodnight, Dorothea," I whisper.

She stirs, not fully awake, and murmurs, "Green."

I smile into the dark.

"Yes," I whisper back. "Green."

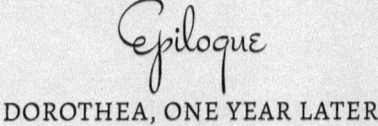

Epilogue

DOROTHEA, ONE YEAR LATER

The bakery breathes without me now.
Not all the time.
Not perfectly.

Not without a little whining from Derek, a little muttering from Baylin, and at least one text every week that says something like, the espresso machine is making a noise that sounds legally actionable.

But it breathes.

That's no small thing.

A year ago, I believed Knead the Dough would collapse if I stepped away for more than an hour. I believed the ovens needed my hands, the register needed my voice, the display case needed my eye, and the entire town would be forced to survive on dry muffins and emotional neglect if I took one full day off.

I was, as it turns out, both very important and deeply annoying.

This morning, I arrive at six-thirty instead of four.

On purpose.

The sky over Coral Cove is pale gold, the kind of early summer light that makes even wet pavement look optimistic. Main Street is still waking up. The flower shop has buckets of peonies outside. Spellbound Stories has a chalkboard sign that reads, SUMMER ROMANCE, SEA WITCHES, AND EMOTIONAL DAMAGE, ASK INSIDE. Golden Chopsticks is dark, but I know May is already in the back kitchen because the smell of ginger and broth drifts faintly down the block.

Knead the Dough glows pink and warm at the corner.

My bakery.

Still mine.

Fully mine.

Legally, publicly, unquestionably mine.

Three months after Applegate's dismissal was entered, the recorded release came through. Lorenzo framed a certified copy and gave it to me for my office with a little brass plaque that reads: THE FUCK AROUND AND FIND OUT DOCUMENT.

I told him it was not professional.

He said neither was trying to steal a bakery.

Fair.

Applegate Holdings folded faster than anyone expected once Lorenzo and William started pulling threads. The beneficial interest Applegate claimed to own had been released decades ago. The transfer defect was not a defect at all, only an old document omitted from the digital records and waiting patiently in a county basement. After that, the rest came apart. Other property owners came forward. One had been pressured into selling below market. Another had received letters almost identical to mine. The newspaper used the words pattern of aggressive acquisitions. Lorenzo used words I won't repeat near muffins.

Grant Applegate did not confess to knowing about the magic.

Men like that rarely confess to anything interesting.

But he did sign a settlement agreement, withdraw all claims, cover part of my legal costs, and agree not to pursue any additional interest in the building. More importantly, he left Coral Cove.

May said the town smelled better afterward.

I did not disagree.

I unlock the front door and step inside.

The bell above the door rings softly.

The bakery smells like butter, yeast, lemon, coffee, old wood, and new beginnings that still require mopping. The display cases are already half full. Almond croissants line one tray, glossy and perfect. Apple galettes sit beside them in careful rows. A tower of lemon bars waits near the register. Behind the bread wall, loaves cool on racks, sourdough, rye, honey oat, rosemary sea salt.

Baylin stands behind the counter with headphones around her neck and flour on her cheek.

"You're early," she says.

"It's six-thirty."

"Your shift starts at seven."

"I own the building."

"You also own a calendar."

I set my bag under the counter. "Good morning to you too."

"Good morning. You look suspiciously rested."

"I slept."

"In a bed?"

"Usually where I do it."

"For more than five hours?"

I narrow my eyes. "You're very nosy for someone entrusted with bread."

"Bread requires truth."

"Bread requires yeast."

"And truth."

Derek appears from the kitchen carrying a tray of cooling scones. He is wearing a clean apron, which feels like a miracle worthy of church bells.

"Morning, boss."

"Morning." I eye the tray. "Those look good."

"They are good. I made them."

"All by yourself?"

He straightens. "Baylin supervised emotionally, but not physically."

Baylin lifts one hand. "He only forgot the salt once."

"And then remembered before baking," Derek says.

"Growth," I say.

He beams.

Derek works full-time now. Front of house manager, though he still looks startled every time someone calls him that. He handles orders, inventory tracking, customer questions, and most of the register training for new staff. He still reorganizes the boxes wrong once a month, but now he catches himself and mutters, that's not the system, like a man haunted by cardboard.

Baylin has her own bread program, three rotating weekly loaves, a waitlist for her sourdough class, and a late-night tarot radio show on the local community station.

Tarot After Dark with Baylin.

She said the title was a joke.

Then the show got popular.

Now people come into the bakery asking if she is "the bread witch from the radio," and she pretends to hate it while keeping branded stickers in her apron pocket.

The show airs Thursday nights. She pulls one card, talks about music, myth, baking, and the kind of emotional truth people prefer to avoid until midnight. Last week, she did an episode on The Tower while discussing collapsed cakes, failed relationships, and why structure matters more when things fall apart.

Lea called it brilliant.

Derek called it "weirdly comforting."

I called it a tax write-off if she mentioned the bakery more often.

I have two newer employees now too. Mara works after-noons and has the calmest customer service voice I have ever heard. She can tell someone we are out of lemon twists and make it sound like an invitation to personal growth. Theo comes in on weekends, washes dishes, preps boxes, and makes the best iced chai in town.

Because of them, I take Tuesdays off.

Every Tuesday.

Mostly.

Fine, two Tuesdays a month without interruption and two Tuesdays with only emergency texts.

That counts.

Today is not a day off. Today is bigger.

Today is the one-year celebration of keeping the bakery.

I wanted to call it the Applegate Can Choke Festival, but Lorenzo suggested that might complicate future branding.

So officially, it's the Knead the Dough Community Thank-You Day.

Unofficially, May has been calling it the Fuck Around and Find Out Bake Sale.

I cannot control May.

No one can.

I cross into the kitchen and pause near the bread wall.

The hidden compartment is still there.

Only a few people know. Lorenzo. Lea. Baylin, because Baylin knew before I told her, which she insists is not magic but "bread-adjacent intuition." Derek knows there is a secret menu, but not the full mechanism. He says he prefers not to know because he wants plausible deniability if a scone starts speaking Latin.

The Hearth Book rests in its fireproof safe now when not in use. The safe sits in my office upstairs, bolted to the floor, protected by a security system Lorenzo picked out and a ward Lea insists she did not buy from The Arcane Room, which means she absolutely did.

The magical ingredients are cataloged, labeled, and used carefully.

Very carefully.

No reckless love-potion nonsense.

No forcing affection.

No pastries that override free will, which should not need to be said, but magical cookbooks are dramatic and sometimes ethically slippery.

The first rule of the Hearth Menu is simple:

Magic doesn't decide for anyone.

It only makes room.

Room for warmth. Room for courage. Room for honesty. Room for laughter. Room for people to remember what already lives inside them.

I open the safe upstairs before the morning rush and take out the book.

It's heavier than it should be, bound in dark leather, the title pressed into the cover in fading gold.

The Hearth Book of Knead the Dough.

For the baker who listens.

I run my fingers over the words.

The book falls open to the page that appeared the week after Applegate's release was recorded.

Not before.

After.

A folded letter had been tucked between two pages that were not there the day before. I know because I had checked. Repeatedly. With the intensity of a woman who had recently learned that magic enjoys timing.

The letter was written in Kaytie's hand.

Dottie,

If you're reading this, the bakery has decided it trusts you enough to stop pretending it's only a bakery.

I hope that makes you laugh. I know you hate when people talk in riddles let alone before coffee.

I should have told you sooner, but some doors don't open because someone else explains them. They open because you finally stand in front of them as yourself.

Knead the Dough has always had a hearth-line. That's what my grandmother called it. Not a bloodline. Not exactly. A hearthline passes through care, labor, hunger, welcome, and the stubborn kind of love that keeps feeding people even when the world gets mean.

The magic doesn't belong to the building.

It doesn't belong to me.

It belongs to the baker who understands that food is never only food.

You understood that before you believed in magic.

That's why I sold you the bakery.

Not because you were ready to use the book. Because you were already living by its first law.

Never feed someone a feeling you would be afraid to receive.

There are ingredients hidden here that can help people find what they have buried. Joy. Peace. Courage. Memory. Desire. Truth. Be careful with truth. It rises faster than yeast and spills over if you forget to give it room.

If anyone comes looking for the book, remember this: people who want power usually forget to listen. The book won't open properly for them. But people can still do damage trying to own what they cannot understand.

Protect the hearth.

Protect yourself too.

That part matters.

I know you, sweetheart. You will try to become the whole fire.

Do not.

A hearth is tended.

It's not devoured.

Let people help you carry the wood.

And when love comes, don't ask whether you're allowed to want it.

You are.

Always,
Kaytie

I cried for twenty minutes after reading it.

Then I called Lorenzo.

Then Lea.

Then Baylin, who said, "I told you bread has ancestral memory," which was not technically the point, but she brought pastries and sat with me, so I let it go.

I read the letter again this morning.

Not all of it. Just the line I still need most.

A hearth is tended. It's not devoured. Let people help you carry the wood.

Downstairs, the front bell rings.

Not opening time yet.

I close the book, return it to the safe, and head down.

Lorenzo is at the counter.

He is wearing jeans, a dark green sweater, and the black coat I told him makes him look approachable in a dangerous way. His hair is still damp from the morning mist. He has a cardboard tray of coffees in one hand and a garment bag over one arm.

My heart does the same stupid, sweet thing it always does when he walks into the bakery.

It no longer frightens me as much.

That may be the miracle.

"Good morning, counselor," Baylin says.

"Good morning, bread witch."

Derek snorts.

Baylin points at Lorenzo. "Respectful, but risky."

Lorenzo sets the coffees down. "I come bearing caffeine and legal peace offerings."

"Legal peace offerings are usually billable," I say, coming behind the counter.

His eyes find mine.

The quiet change in his face still makes every room feel warmer.

"Not this one."

He lifts the garment bag. "What's that?"

"Your apron."

"My apron is in the kitchen."

"Your old apron is in the kitchen."

I narrow my eyes.

"Lorenzo."

He smiles.

Dangerous.

Tender.

The worst combination.

He unzips the garment bag and pulls out a new apron.

It's soft green, the color of sea glass and basil and his kitchen tile. The color of yes. The Knead the Dough logo is embroidered in gold. Beneath it, in smaller letters, are the words: The Hearth Menu

I stare at it.

"Oh."

He looks suddenly nervous.

"It's not for everyday use unless you want. I thought for today, since you're introducing the new line officially."

"We are not introducing the magic officially."

"No. Only the menu."

I touch the embroidery.

The fabric is sturdy. Beautiful. Practical enough to work in, pretty enough to be seen in.

That's Lorenzo's gift language now.

Not taking over.

Making room.

"Do you like it?" he asks.

I look up.

There are customers gathering outside the front window now. May is among them, holding a covered dish. Lea stands beside her with a stack of books tied in ribbon. Mrs. Talbot is already peering through the glass, pretending she is not.

Everyone is watching. I step around the counter.

A year ago, I would have stayed behind it.

Safe. Useful. Half-hidden.

Today, I walk around.

Lorenzo notices.

His expression changes.

I take the apron from his hands and hold it against my chest.

"I love it," I say.

Then I kiss him. He smiles into the kiss.

When I pull back, his eyes are bright.

"Green?" he asks softly.

"Super green," I say.

His thumb brushes my cheek. "That's my favorite kind."

The bell rings as Derek unlocks the door.

People flood in.

Not all at once, but it feels like it. The bakery fills with voices, laughter, hugs, greetings, the clatter of chairs, and the layered smells of coffee, pastry, flowers, dumplings from May, and fresh bread cooling near the hearth wall.

The Hearth Menu sits on the chalkboard behind the counter.

Not all the magic. Not the dangerous recipes. Not the ones that require quiet rooms, careful consent, or the kind of truth better served one-on-one.

Only the gentle ones.

Heartwarming Cinnamon Rolls.

Made with cinnamon, brown sugar, orange zest, and a careful trace of hearth-warmth. For remembering why you reach for each other.

Joyful Jumble Cookies.

Chocolate chips, toasted walnuts, dried cherries, and a sparkle of laughter folded into the dough. For days that need lightness.

Serendipity Muffins.

Berry muffins with lemon crumble and a whisper of lucky sugar. For invitations, job interviews, first dates, and people who swear they are "not superstitious" while buying six.

Brave Little Scones.

Rosemary, cheddar, black pepper, and a pinch of courage salt. For hard conversations and dentist appointments.

Harmony Honey Buns.

Soft spirals of honey dough with lavender glaze. For family meetings, apology breakfasts, and anyone attending a homeowners association discussion.

Moonrise Lemon Bars.

Bright lemon, buttery crust, powdered sugar, and a little clarity. For seeing what you already know.

The descriptions are cute.

Harmless.

True enough.

The magic is lighter than before. Measured. Asked of, not demanded from. Every recipe has a note in my private book now, intention, ingredient, emotional effect, ethical boundary, observed outcome. Lorenzo says my magical pastry records are more thorough than most corporate compliance files.

I take that as a compliment.

Mrs. Talbot is first at the counter.

Naturally.

"I'll take two Brave Little Scones," she says.

I lift an eyebrow. "Big day?"

"I'm telling my sister she cannot bring her ferret to my anniversary party."

"Then you may need three."

"Make it four."

I bag them.

Mr. Jenkins buys Joyful Jumble Cookies for his grandkids and one Moonrise Lemon Bar for himself, claiming he likes the tartness. May buys Harmony Honey Buns and says nothing about who they are for, which means Harold has done something mildly irritating and will be forgiven by dinner. Lea buys one of everything for "research," then asks if the book has any recipes for making Park stop shelving romance under general fiction.

"No magic can fix that," I say.

"Tragic."

Baylin disappears briefly to call in to the radio station.

By nine, her voice crackles from the little speaker Derek set behind the counter.

"Good morning, Coral Cove. This is Baylin from Tarot After Dark, briefly appearing in daylight against my better judgment. Today's card is the Four of Wands. Celebration, community, home, the kind of joy built by people who choose to keep showing up. If you're near Main Street, stop by Knead the Dough and congratulate Dottie on one year of not letting a developer goblin steal the hearth."

The whole bakery cheers.

I cover my face with both hands.

Lorenzo laughs beside me.

"Developer goblin?" he asks.

"Legally risky?"

"Emotionally accurate."

"Good."

Around noon, when the bakery is full and the little stage outside has started hosting live music, I slip into the back kitchen for one minute to breathe.

Not hide.

Breathe.

There is a difference now.

Lorenzo finds me there, leaning against the prep table with a cup of water in one hand.

He doesn't ask if I'm okay in the old way.

He asks, "Pause?"

I smile.

"Pause."

He leans beside me, shoulder touching mine.

"Good day?" he asks.

"Very."

"Too much?"

"A little."

"Want me to clear people out?"

"No."

"Want me to distract May?"

"Can anyone distract May?"

"Not safely."

I laugh.

He takes my free hand.

The bakery noise moves around us. Voices. Music. A burst of laughter from the front. Derek calling for more lemon bars. Baylin telling someone the rye is moody because rye tells the truth.

"I read Kaytie's letter again this morning," I say.

Lorenzo's thumb moves over my knuckles. "The hearth one?"

"Yes."

"What part?"

"Let people help you carry the wood."

His expression softens. "Good line."

"She knew me too well."

"She loved you."

The words still make me ache.

But not only with grief.

"Yes," I say. "She did."

"And she was right."

"I know."

That's new too.

Knowing.

Not only hearing. Not only wanting to believe. Knowing.

I let Baylin run bread. Derek run the front. Mara and Theo handle the line. Lea organize the book giveaway table without asking permission. May boss people around near the dumplings. Lorenzo answer legal questions from Mr. Peterson and then refuse to bill him for a five-minute explanation about fence easements.

I let people help.

The world doesn't end.

In fact, the bakery runs better.

Rude, but useful information.

By late afternoon, the sun slants gold through the windows. The crowd spills onto the sidewalk and into the little courtyard beside the bakery. Children chase bubbles near the flower boxes. Couples sit at small tables with pastries and coffee. The stage outside hosts a local guitarist playing a love song badly but sincerely, which is my favorite genre of music.

I stand behind the counter, looking out at all of it.

For a moment, I'm back in every version of this place.

Eighteen years old, hired by Kaytie, afraid to touch anything too expensive.

Twenty-four, signing loan papers with hands that would not stop shaking.

Twenty-nine, finding a hidden book beneath the bread wall.

Terrified, served papers in my own doorway.

Hopeful, holding a key tied with green ribbon.

Here now.

Not hiding.

The counter is still mine.

But it's no longer a wall.

It's a place I can step around.

Lorenzo walks in from the courtyard carrying an empty tray and wearing a smear of powdered sugar on his sleeve.

I smile.

He sees me looking and stops.

"What?"

"You have sugar on your sleeve."

He looks down. "Occupational hazard of loving a baker."

"Come here."

His eyebrows lift. "In front of everyone?"

I glance around.

May is watching.

Lea is watching.

Mrs. Talbot is absolutely watching.

Derek is pretending not to watch and failing in a way that would embarrass a weaker man.

"Yes," I say. "In front of everyone."

I step around the display case.

Not fast.

Not dramatic.

Just around.

The bakery quiets by degrees.

Lorenzo sets the tray down and meets me halfway.

"This feels significant," he says softly.

He smiles.

I rise onto my toes and kiss him.

The bakery erupts.

Not into applause exactly, though Derek claps once before Baylin smacks his arm. It's more a wave of laughter, cheers, happy little sounds, the entire town doing what the entire town does best: seeing too much and deciding to love loudly.

Lorenzo's arms come around my waist.

Mine loop around his neck.

For once, being seen doesn't feel like exposure.

It feels like arrival.

When we pull apart, he rests his forehead lightly against mine.

I let him.

"Still green?" he asks.

I look around the bakery.

At the people I love.

At the shelves full of bread.

At the chalkboard menu.

At Kaytie's mug on the shelf above the register.

At the hidden hearth beneath the wall.

At the man holding me in the middle of the room, not as a rescuer, not as a fantasy, not as a lawyer with a solution, but as someone real who has chosen to keep showing up.

"Green," I say.

Then I smile.

"Always green."

Lorenzo's eyes warm.

"Always?"

I lift an eyebrow. "Don't get smug. There will still be yellow days."

"I would expect nothing less."

"And possibly red if you reorganize my spice shelf again."

"That was one time."

"It was oregano betrayal."

"I bought oregano because of you."

"And then alphabetized it."

"I stand by that."

I laugh, and he kisses me again, quick and smiling this time.

The bell above the door rings as more people come in.

The bakery fills.

The hearth holds.

Outside, Coral Cove glows in the long golden light, salt air drifting through the open door, carrying music, laughter, and the promise of evening.

I'm still afraid sometimes.

Love doesn't erase fear. Magic doesn't erase history. A key doesn't mean a door can never close.

But I'm not standing outside my life anymore.

I'm inside it.

Flour on my hands.

Sunlight on the counter.

Lorenzo beside me.

The Hearth Book waiting quietly upstairs.

A tray of Brave Little Scones cooling in the back.

And when the next customer steps up to the counter, I don't retreat behind it.

I stand there fully seen, smiling, alive, and ready to feed the world something true.

Also by Jax Wilder

Coral Cove Series

Sleighed by Love

Harvesting Love

Dawning Desire

Knead You Now

Love Rewound

Perfect Lover Spell

Haunted by Her

Red, White, and Ravished

Frosted Sugar Charms

Tarot Fantasies Series

The Devil's Temptations

Strength of the Beast

Hanged Passions

Six of Cups

Death's Embrace

Queen of Pentacles

Seven of Pentacles

Ace of Wands

Three of Swords

Lovers In The Veil

Two of Swords

Seven of Wands

Three of Cups

Coastal Cupid Series

HeartBound Souls

Witches of Coral Cove
From Hell With Love

Fae Ring Series
Alice and Her Mad Hatters
Bound By The Glass Slipper
Call of Cthulhu's Heart

Stand Alone Titles
Pride and Prejudice and Witches

Jax Wilder

Additional Books by

Rainbow Quartz Publishing

Lorelai Hamilton
Encyclopedia of Divination
Encyclopedia of Cryptids
Encyclopedia of Faeries
Encyclopedia of Supernatural Rules

Encyclopedia of Cursed Objects

Tarot Tales and Magic Spells

Teenage Tarot

Arcane In Verse

The Eclectic Witch's Grimoire

Teenage Witch's Grimoire

Find Your Bliss

Tarot Reflection Journal

Tarot Refection Journal Coloring The Tarot

Dream Journal

Fluent Tarot

Fluent Tarot Workbook

Fluent Tarot Matters of the Heart

Fluent Tarot Matters of the Heart Workbook

The Eclectic Witches Grimoire

Miranda Levi

From A Youth A Fountain Did Flow (Book 1 of The Fountain Of Youth Series)

The Sea Withdrew (Book 2 of The Fountain Of Youth Series)

What I've Tasted of Desire(Book 3 of The Fountain Of Youth Series)

A Tear In Time

Mother Nature

Restraint

In Orion's Hands

Jackson Anhalt

From The 911 Files

About the Author

Jax Wilder is a passionate romance author hailing from a charming small town nestled in the picturesque Pacific Northwest. With a heart full of love and an unyielding belief in the power of happily ever afters, Jax weaves enchanting tales of love and connection that leave readers captivated.

Jax's novels are a reflection of her commitment to celebrating the magic of love, and her characters' journeys mirror the warmth and happiness she has found in her own life. Join her on the enchanting journey of love, passion, and enduring connection through her heartfelt romance novels.

Jax Wilder